- 5

HAPPY ARE THE POOR IN SPIRIT

HAPPY ARE THE POOR IN SPIRIT

ANDREW M. GREELEY

PIATKUS

Copyright © 1994 by Andrew Greeley Enterprises, Ltd.

This edition first published in
Great Britain in 1995 by
Judy Piatkus (Publishers) Ltd of
5 Windmill Street, London W1.

**The moral right of the author
has been asserted.**

*A catalogue record for this book is available
from the British Library.*

ISBN 0-7499-0291-4

Printed and bound in Great Britain by
Bookcraft (Bath) Ltd.

CAST OF CHARACTERS

Bartholomew (Bart) Theodore Cain: Commodities tycoon
 with a liberal conscience
Julia Ross Cain: Wife to Bart
David Cain: Brother to Bart
Bartholomew Cain Junior: Son to Bart
William Cain, M.D.: Son to Bart
Jennifer Cain: Daughter to Bart
Elizabeth Marie Candace Cain (a.k.a. Candi Cain): Daughter
 to Bart
Eleanor (Leonora or Lea) Rigali Cain: Wife to David
Lourdes Hanifin Cain: Wife to Bart Junior
Vin Roberts: Editor, lover to Jennifer Cain
Timothy O'Donnell: Friend to Bart Cain
Mary Anne Haggerty: Ghost
Sean Cardinal Cronin: By the Grace of God and favor of
 the Apostolic See, Archbishop of Chicago
Most Reverend John Blackwood Ryan, Ph.D., D.D. (*Hon-
 oris Causa*): Auxiliary Bishop to Cardinal Cronin and
 Rector of the Cathedral of the Holy Name
Michael Patrick Vincent Casey (a.k.a. Mike the Cop):
 Flambeau to Bishop Ryan
Annie O'Brien Reilly Casey: Wife to Mike the Cop

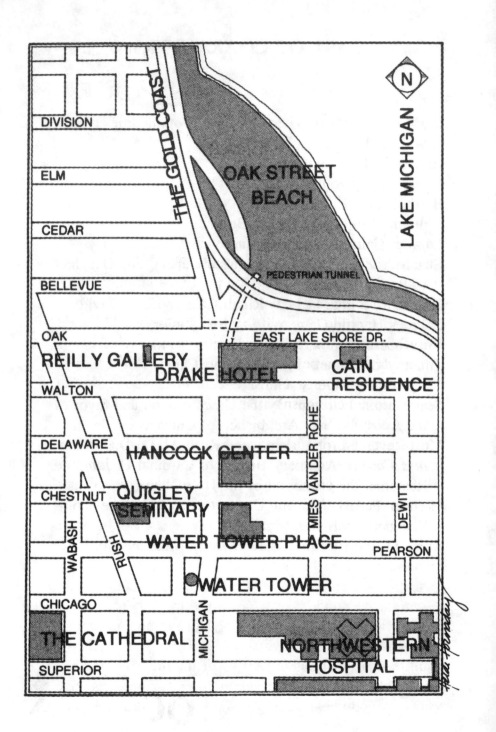

CHAPTER 1

"A GHOST IS trying to kill my dad, Father Blackie," Candi Cain insisted. "It's like totally gross."

"Indeed," I said, hoping that the sympathy in my voice drowned out my fascination.

"And I shouldn't have to love my stepmother like right away, you know? I'm like maybe in four or five years I will get around to being friends with her. But because of the ghost I go I've got to take care of her now, so that means I love her, doesn't it?"

"Arguably."

Elizabeth Marie Candace Cain, a.k.a. Candi Cain, at first glance seemed, even in maroon and gold St. Ignatius (excuse me, the proper name now is St. Ignatius College Prep) sweatshirt and black jeans, an elegant young woman of the sort you might meet at the best of Chicago's black-tie dinners. Tall, slender, and willowy with long, auburn hair, deep brown eyes, a slim, aristocratic face, clear cream complexion, and a posture of natural grace, she might be a model or a visiting English countess. Or possibly an Irish mystical poet, an illusion not harmed by solid arm muscles and substantial upper body strength, the result of conscientious exercising. This illusion passed as soon as she opened her mouth, and for two reasons: She was chewing bubble gum, and she was discoursing in that peculiar dialogue common to teenage persons of our species and culture. At once you forgot the elegance and realized that you were talking to a fifteen-year-old, going on sixteen.

"Three times," Candi Cain continued, blowing a huge pink bubble, "the ghost tried to, like, kill Daddy. I saved him once and Julia did twice. I'm like his luck is going to run out soon, you know?"

"Julia?"

"You know, my stepmother."

"Ah."

I had been hunched over my Gateway 486DX2 in my office on the first floor of the cathedral rectory working on a computer program of my design, which when perfected would enable us to enter all baptismal, confirmation, and marriage records on a single CD—along with a consolidated schedule for parish activities for the next five years. Past, present, and future on one thin slice of alloy. The only problem with the program, which is marvelously ingenious, is that it is something less than user-friendly, so much so that it works only for me. My staff is pleased to call it, with little respect but some accuracy, "Blackie's Folly."

"One Candi Cain to see you, Bish." The youngest of my associates had projected his bearded poet's face into my *sanctum sanctorum.* "Stepmother problems if you ask me."

"I did not know that such a person existed." I had sighed loudly at the interruption, my favorite West of Ireland sigh, which could also signal, though not in my case, the advent of an acute asthma attack.

My staff expresses astonishment that someone of my advanced age is able to communicate with the teenagers of our species. "After forty," one tells me, "you have to possess special gifts of nature or grace or be a little weird to endure them."

"Arguably," I respond complacently.

I had saved my work on the computer and risen to cross the corridor to one of our counseling rooms, where Ms. Cain awaited me.

"I was not aware that Bart Cain had taken to himself a new wife," I had said to the young priest.

"While you were in Ireland. The Big Boss took care of it." He had gestured towards the top floor of the rectory where dwells Sean Cardinal Cronin, by the remarkable grace of God and the strained patience of the Holy See, Archbishop of Chicago and technically the pastor of the cathedral.

He refuses even to enter the room when I am demonstrating "Blackie's Folly."

"Poor woman." I had sighed again.

"A real knockout, too. Maybe thirty years younger than he is."

"Astonishing."

"I only dragged him, you know, like away from the car." Candi Cain continued her story. "Julia saw the chandelier falling from the ceiling and screamed, and Daddy, you know, ducked and she pushed him away from the falling bucket."

"Astonishing."

"And the ghost calls after each accident and plays that song from, like, when Daddy was a kid and laughs horribly. I mean I heard her once. It was totally gross."

Our "counseling rooms" are designed to create an atmosphere of friendly relaxation, with comfortable but somewhat out-of-date and worn furniture and tasteful but low-key drapes and religious art. Perhaps like the parlor in your grandmother's house.

No popes or bishops on the wall. Not even the afore-mentioned Sean Cardinal Cronin.

"Her?" I asked Candi.

"The woman that died the day after their senior prom in 1947."

So it was not the late and long-suffering Eunice Cain who was haunting her husband. The poor woman would have had ample reason to do so.

"It's like driving me and Julia totally crazy. Dad just laughs it off as someone's idea of a joke."

"Naturally."

I was not fond of Bart Cain nor he of me, but a coward he was not.

"The song is weird too. Like 'I'll Dance at Your Wedding.' It was popular back in those days."

"Just before the Civil War?"

Candi's exquisite face knotted in a thoughtful frown. "Just after it, I think."

"Ah."

"Julia is like totally worried so she goes do you think your friend Father Blackie would like say a prayer or something to get rid of the ghost . . . she's not Catholic. Julia, I mean. Not the ghost. I guess the ghost is Catholic. And I go you should go over to the cathedral and talk to him. And she's like I never talked to a priest before. And I'm like what about the cardinal. And she goes I'm afraid of him. And I'm like no one is afraid of Father Blackie. Isn't that true, Father Blackie?"

"Possibly."

"So will you?"

"Will I what?"

"Come over to our house and like tell Julia that the ghost can't really hurt Daddy. Please!"

"She wants to talk to me?"

"Totally."

"You find her a problem, Candi Cain?"

She squirmed in her chair. "I was totally mean, Father Blackie. And when I'm mean, I'm *really* mean, you know? I'm like I guess we can't keep you out of our family, but you're totally not welcome and I'm going to hate you."

"Ah."

"Then do you know what she does, Father Blackie?"

"She begins to weep."

"Like hysterically . . . how did you know? I mean she sobs like she's going to die or something."

"And in response you . . . ?"

Candi lifted her shoulders disconsolately. "What else could I do? I threw my arms around her and told her I loved her already and that I'd take care of her and we would be great friends. I guess maybe I cried a little too."

"Astonishing."

There was clearly more to this child than bubble gum and the abolition of the archaic verb "to say." She was a nice mixture perhaps of her mother's piety and her father's harsh integrity.

"Well." She grimaced. "I'm like a Christian, you know, and the poor woman is *so* vulnerable and I have to be nice to her, don't I? And anyway Mom and Daddy didn't get along too well, but I'm sure she wouldn't mind up in heaven, would she?"

"I very much doubt it."

Eunice Cain was according to her own lights a good and generous woman, if given to many and assorted pieties. Presumably she would not resent the woman who had replaced her in her marital bed—a bed which, unless my judgment was wrong (which it rarely is in such matters), she had not occupied for many years before her untimely death in an auto accident. After she'd had too much of the drink at a Catholic Charities luncheon.

"And Bart Junior and Doctor Bill and Jennifer are like totally mean to her and Uncle Dave would like to be nice to her but Aunt Lea won't let him, so someone has to be nice to her, don't they?"

"Someone who takes Jesus seriously."

Candi ignored my praise. "Their two kids go to Ignatius— Nora and Megan . . . I mean Uncle Dave and Aunt Lea's two older kids . . . they're all right, I guess, but they're like, you know, major blondes."

"Ah."

"And," she said with a frown, "you don't have to have blond hair to be totally into being blondes, right?"

"Indisputably."

"But they're good kids," she added judiciously. "Only I have to take care of them, right?"

"Unquestionably."

Having wandered from what I considered to be the point so she could put what a teenager would consider an essential piece of information on the record, Candi continued her conversation about her father and her stepmother.

"I mean, she and Daddy are like totally unconscious, you know?"

"Ah?"

"Well"—she squirmed again—"like, you know, *obsessed* with one another. I mean they can't take their eyes off each other. They just stare."

"Yucky?"

"Hungry."

"Indeed. And what do you think of such behavior, Candi Cain?"

"Uh." A faint pink appeared on her flawless complexion. "Like I go to Brigie Devine, my best friend, it's embarrassing like you walked into their bedroom when they were fooling around, but it's also kind of neat and Daddy is happier than he's ever been. He even smiles, you know?"

"Astonishing!"

"Totally!"

So it was agreed that on the morrow at 10:00 A.M. I would call on Julia Cain at their apartment at 207 East Lake Shore Drive. I was interested in the mysterious ghost, and also in the woman who had apparently melted the austere heart of Bart Cain. From her stepdaughter's description she sounded like a most improbable agent for such a change. However, Lady Wisdom—the attractive, charming, seductive dimension of God—operates according to Her own game plan.

I ushered the candid Candi to the door of the rectory. Outside a soft and gentle mid-September afternoon burnished Wabash Avenue in a faint golden haze which made our lovely city look like it might have just emerged from a medieval French tapestry. Or a French Impressionist painting.

"You'll like her, Father Blackie," Candi insisted. "Even if she's not Catholic."

"I'm a pretty ecumenical person, Candi Cain."

"And you'll tell her that the dead can't hurt the living, won't you?" She began to lope down Wabash.

"I will."

Characteristic of women of our ethnic group, this maiden was prescribing exactly what I must do and say.

"They can't, can they?" Candi turned back toward me.

"No, Candi, the dead can't hurt the living."

"Great!" She bounded off and then turned again. "But the living can hurt the living, can't they?"

"Lamentably."

She frowned. "I know."

Then her face cleared. "But we'll stop that, won't we, Father Blackie?"

"Absolutely."

"Great!" And this time she charged off in high spirits.

Why, I wondered, was this young woman more worried about her stepmother than about her father? Perhaps because she was convinced that Bart Cain could take care of himself.

That was certainly his reputation. Bart Cain was indestructible.

Perhaps not quite, not when a vulnerable young woman crossed his path.

Well, as the prophet has written, there's no fool like an old fool.

Or perhaps Candi Cain, mostly ignored by her own mother—busy as she was with various alleged apparitions of the Mother of Jesus—had found an older woman with whom she might identify.

I should like to be able to say that I had a premonition that benign afternoon of how complicated and violent this affair would become. But possibly because of my complacency over the publication of my latest effort, *The Catholic Theology of James Joyce* (with an astonishing print run of 1500 copies), I was serenely unaware of the problems Candi's ghost and her stepmother would create for us.

CHAPTER 2

BART CAIN REMINDED me of several South Side Irish funeral directors.

He had the square handsome and flushed face, the thick, curly white hair, the broad shoulders, and the lugubrious facial expression which are almost essential for the role. Moreover, when he bore down on one after Mass in back of the Cathedral of the Holy Name, his black coat, his determined gait, and his earnest intensity reminded one (this one at any rate) of a funeral director pushing a casket down the center aisle of a church on the South Side.

I dreaded his approach on a Sunday morning even more than that of a somber and solemn funeral director. Death—like taxes and defeats of the Chicago Cubs—is inevitable and cannot be avoided. Bart Cain was another matter.

Several months before my conversation with the ineffable Candi—perhaps when he was already courting (if one could use the word) his new wife—Bart Cain and I had a fight in such a context.

"One of you should resign," he began.

It was, as I remember, a hot, very hot May morning and I was wearing my Roman collar and my Chicago Cubs windbreaker. Bart Cain's frown said that he disapproved of such garb on a priest, to say nothing of a bishop. Either wear a tie like ordinary people, he had once instructed me, or your full clericals.

"Unquestionably," I replied to his assault that morning, having no idea what he was talking about.

"There's a flagrant conflict of interest." He jabbed his finger at me.

"Deplorable."

"Either you should leave the cathedral or your brother Patrick should quit as city corporation counsel."

"Ah?" I felt the blood of a hundred generations of Irish warriors stir within me, a most infrequent feeling.

"I'm not saying that you and your brother are engaging in any inappropriate behavior," he continued implacably. "But there is an appearance of a conspiracy to violate the wall of separation of Church and State."

"Indeed?" To my astonishment I was clenching my fists.

"Cronin and Daley ought to know better than to have brothers as their top assistants. It looks terrible and offends those who are not Catholics and fear conspiracy between Irish priests and Irish politicians."

"Neither of us are what you call top assistants."

"Technically true, maybe." He did not back down. "But you know better than that. A lot of people in Chicago are offended by the way the Irish dominate Chicago politics."

"They are all elected by majority votes of the electorate."

"It still looks bad. It offends African-Americans and Hispanics and . . ."

"Lake Front Limousine Liberals."

"They have a legitimate fear of collusion between priests and pols."

"Look, Bartholomew Theodore Cain, if the gloriously reigning cardinal and the equally gloriously governing mayor want to conspire against the commonweal they can pick up the phone and talk to one another. They don't need to rely on table conversation at Ryan family Sunday dinners. Or they can converse for a minute or two at the hundreds of civil gatherings which, to escape purgatory, they are constrained to attend. They don't need Pack and me to meet in dark bars on Halsted Street."

There was in point of fact precious little about which Church and State in Chicago needed to conspire, save perhaps for having the snow shoveled away from State Street in front of the cathedral before Sunday Mass. Moreover, in the unlikely event that Packy and I did find a reason to conspire, we would do so in the plain light of day—brunch at the Beverly Country Club.

"That remark"—Bart's distinguished face turned even redder—"shows how little moral sensitivity you and your brother have."

A good priest must not lose his temper with those who hassle him, especially not after the Eucharist. Nonetheless, I did.

"Bartholomew Theodore Cain," I thundered, "you are one of the great assholes of the Western World."

One of my young associates who had been listening to elderly women with one ear and eavesdropping with the other guffawed audibly. The whole staff would know within the hour that Blackie had lost his temper.

"Maybe you're right, Bishop." Bart Cain folded his tent and slipped away, head down in dejection.

"Someday someone is going to kill that guy," the young priest said to me.

I felt sheepish because of my explosion, though not apologetic.

"Possibly," I said. "Or at least try to."

"You sure did stand up to him," the young one continued.

"The issue is whether I should have said what I did."

"Watch." He grinned. "You'll get a check for a thousand dollars for the poor of the parish before the week is out."

He was right. I accepted the check because we had enough poor to worry about, wrote Bart Cain a thank-you note, and apologized for my choice of language.

"But," Sean Cronin insisted, "your language was appropriate. The man *is* one of the great assholes of the Western World."

"Cardinals may say such things, but parish priests shouldn't."

My Lord Cronin thought that sophistry vastly amusing.

I continued to wonder why Bart Cain had backed down so quickly. As I ascended to the cardinal's room the day of my conversation with Candi Cain, I thought it possible that his romance with Julia might have even then caused a modification in his personality.

I almost said an improvement.

CHAPTER 3

"SO YOU ACTUALLY presided over a marriage for our great good friend Bartholomew Theodore Cain? Indeed, according to my sources, the bride has approximately half of his sixty-four years. Can this be true?"

I leveled this charge at Milord Cronin later that night. I had brought to his study two Waterford tumblers, both containing more than adequate amounts of Bushmill's Green Label.

A light flashed in Sean Cronin's gallowglass warrior's eyes. For a moment he looked like what he would have been in an earlier era—the head of a band of Irish wild geese, mercenary combatants taking on perfidious Albion anywhere in the world there were Brits to be found to fight against. Now the only ones this tall, haggard man with blond hair turning gray and a broad handsome face waged war with were the heads of the various curial dicasteries in Rome, most notably one Josef Cardinal Ratzinger, and those in Chicago who believed that you could turn the ecclesiastical clock back to the nineteen-fifties, and an idealized nineteen-fifties at that.

"It's not what it sounds like, Blackwood." He pushed aside a stack of Vatican documents, removed his reading glasses, and accepted the libation I offered him.

"What does it look like?" I sighed and arranged myself

in one of the Sheraton chairs with which his sister-in-law, Senator Nora Cronin, had tried to provide a touch of class to the cardinal's suite.

"Like a young woman seducing a rich man almost twice her age."

"He actually brought her over to the rectory to arrange for a marriage? On short notice, of course, and with complaints that it couldn't be on Saturday afternoon, which had been booked for a year and a half, and with a demand for an immediate dispensation because she wasn't Catholic, a refusal to attend a pre-Cana or to take any kind of premarital instructions, and the general assumption that the laws of the Church and the regulations of the parish were not designed for such as he?"

"You have it perfectly, Blackwood." The cardinal favored me with his manic grin. "And you'd be surprised how charitable I was with him."

"It will be accounted to your balance in the heavenly city. Nonetheless, the man is an asshole."

One might gather from my remarks that Bartholomew T. Cain was not one of my favorite people. He was, not to put too fine an edge on things, a stubborn, self-righteous, opinionated, contentious man. Unlike men of that sort which a priest normally encounters, however, he was an ideologue of the left and not of the right, though it was an ideology which was sui generis. Bart Cain believed in all the good liberal causes, from whales to rain forests, from abortion rights to minority set-asides, from the ordination of women to the election of bishops, from "good" government to gun-control, and believed in them with the same passion with which his ancestors had fought the Land League Wars against the aforementioned perfidious Albion. Moreover, he advanced these causes with flat assertions with which he tolerated no dialogue.

As in: "It is not right that the corporation counsel should be the brother of the rector of the cathedral."

Or: "The Church's failure to ordain women is heretical."

Or: "It is safer to live in Belfast than in Rich Daley's Chicago."

Mind you, he supported our incumbent mayor in all his campaigns, and thus felt he had won the right to criticize virtually every move the mayor made.

And he was generous to the Church (including the cathedral), which generosity, he assumed, entitled him to attack Sean Cronin as often and as vigorously as he attacked Rich Daley. Not that he was a raving fanatic. While no one would accuse him of charm, he was ordinarily perfectly civil and even respectful, even after the magazine he funded—*The Common Truth*—had attacked us, for example, because of our refusal to support tax-funded abortions. While you could not discuss his opinions with him, you could nonetheless chat amicably about such critical matters as the Bulls, the Bears, and the Sox and Cubs. A typical South Sider, he was a Sox fan, but he admitted to me that his joy over a Sox victory was not enhanced by a defeat for the Cubs, in this respect far more civilized than either the mayor or the cardinal, though not sufficiently civilized to join the ranks of us Cub fans.

Moreover, he accepted rebukes mildly enough, as when I told him in back of the cathedral after the ten o'clock Eucharist that he was one of the great assholes of the Western World after *The Common Truth* had demanded that my brother Packy resign as corporation counsel.

I am not nearly so tolerant of such folk as are the mayor and the cardinal.

Cain's reply struck me as odd. "Maybe you're right, Bishop."

His liberalism was systematic, at least by his own lights.

He supported more stringent government control of the commodity exchanges, and thus offended virtually all of his colleagues at the Chicago Board of Trade. He also endorsed the FBI when it put wired agents on the trading floor of the Mercantile Exchange to trap traders in what everyone else said were minor infractions.

Bart Cain had told the press, "There are no minor infractions when we betray a customer's trust."

Period. Paragraph. End of revelation.

No one replied that he had made his millions in the pits dishonestly, because everyone knew that he was as straight an arrow as the Chicago Irish had ever managed to produce, not that we have labored all that hard at turning out straight arrows.

Thus I respected his integrity from a distance, and even agreed with many if not most of his causes. But despite his generosity, I devoutly wished he would attend the Eucharist at some other parish, a suggestion which I have made to him on any number of occasions, most notably when he complains about such matters as the homiletic style of some of my curates.

As on one recent Sunday when he complained that our bearded poet was too "laid-back" in his delivery, an arguable position. However, his complaint assumed that a pastor, especially if he is also an auxiliary bishop, has sufficient clout to influence the way his associates preach.

I believe—and I am not proud of it—that I suggested the names of a number of parishes which would be happy to welcome him to their Sunday liturgy. Later that week I received in the mail a check for five thousand dollars to be devoted to the "poor of the parish in appreciation of all the good work you do with kids like my Elizabeth."

That being Candi's "real" name.

Being Irish, I wrote back and thanked him, and added

that the parish ought to pay him for the privilege of associating with such a wondrous child as the radiant Candi.

Thus, there are demons of guilt and virtue which torment Bart Cain, but they are, I would have thought, beyond exorcism, and I wish, like the ideologues of the right, he would go away and stop harassing us.

"There is no fool"—I repeated these wise words to My Lord Cronin as I sipped at my Bushmill's—"like an old fool."

"Bart and I are the same age." His manic grin appeared again.

"You are hardly likely to fall in love with someone like this Julia person."

"No." The cardinal pondered the dark liquid in his tumbler. "Not very likely. But it's not like you would think, Blackwood. She didn't marry him for his money."

"Ah?"

I settled down for what I came to hear: Sean Cronin's description of the fair bride. I was merely curious about the woman, not yet motivated by a sense of the dangerous urgency of the puzzle which Candi had proposed earlier in the day.

"Two things hit me when he brought her into the rectory."

"Indeed?"

"The first is that this woman had completely broken through the walls Bart has built around himself. I wouldn't say that he was giddy, but he looked at her with the adoring eyes of a twenty-year-old and he treated her like she was a goddess, respectful, tender, proud."

"This I would like to see."

"She was scared of the rectory and of me."

"I can't imagine that."

"She's a Free Methodist from a tiny place downstate, still thought the Roman Church was the Whore of Babylon."

"And she succumbed to your unquestioned charm, I presume?"

"Well"—he grinned—"she was at least smiling before they left the office. He even thanked me personally."

"No doubt with a check for the poor of the archdiocese?"

"That came later."

"Uhm. And the second thing which, to use your term, hit you?"

"The appearance of woman herself. She seemed dowdy, unattractive, shy—the kind which would be definitely out of her class with the East Lake Shore Drive set, a homely kid from rural Illinois who happened to cross Bart's path when the testosterone content of his blood was high and his superego was not functioning up to par."

"Indeed!"

"She's a chartist—you know, the kind who draw elaborate charts about the fluctuations of the commodity markets. And apparently a very good one if B.T. Cain and Sons hired her."

"A nerd?"

"Precisely—long, straight hair, thick glasses, clothes that don't fit, no makeup . . ."

"Multicolored pens in a packet?"

"In her purse, not in her jacket pocket."

"So."

"Only at the end of our first conversation down in your 'counseling room' when she finally smiled did I realize that she was a very beautiful woman hiding behind the mask of a nerd."

"Indeed!"

"She was quite a lovely bride. I could see in some sense what attracted Bart. Sumptuous, smart, and fragile. I'm sure that he was her first man."

"After her father."

The hoods pulled back from Sean Cronin's eyes and he regarded me with intense concentration, weighing, I presumed, what I had said.

"Not so long ago, Blackwood, they would have burned you at the stake as a witch."

"If your colleague in the Lord Josef Ratzinger has his way, they may still."

"You're saying she was molested by her father and that Bart is a substitute father?"

"Arguably. Incest is one of the great indoor sports of fundamentalist rural America. Bart perhaps appeals to her as a good father over a bad father."

"So it won't work?"

"Arguably not. It is possible, however, that at the present state of his life Bart Cain will not tire of a fragile and attractive daughter whom he can protect and with whom he can sleep. I suspect that is the way his first wife appeared to him before his marriage. Only afterward did he learn that in fact she was a passive-aggressive personality— very passive and very aggressive. And, if I may say so, not all that interesting or interested sexually."

"You don't miss much, do you, Blackwood?"

"It is for that," I said modestly, "that I draw my admittedly inadequate salary as a parish priest."

As we talked I pondered the curious match between Bart Cain and his Julia. Early in his first marriage he must have decided that it would not provide him much sexual satisfaction. So, firm Catholic that he was, he repressed his desires and lived according to the dictates of his conscience regardless of the price which such virtue exacted

from him. Men and women a generation younger than he
might have tried a sexual dysfunction clinic or family
counseling. But for the Bart Cains of the world that was
not an option, especially since Eunice would not accept
any such suggestion. So he channeled his desires into his
work and his political and charitable activities and his
rigid ideology. There were perhaps worse adjustments for
the Irish, especially Irish commodity traders, most notably
the Drink.

When Eunice died he was free to pursue women, but
three and a half decades of denial and repression left him
with no taste or little courage for such activities and
perhaps little confidence that the eventual payoff was
worth the effort and the risk. Then he encountered Julia
and the pent-up lusts of a lifetime exploded. All well and
good for the moment, until he discovered either that Julia
was a whiner and weeper like his first wife or that there
lurked within her the shade of a strong woman.

"Tell me more about Bart," I said to Sean Cronin.

The cardinal leaned back in the vast chair behind his
desk and savored the taste of his Bushmill's.

"He grew up in the parish next to us. Poor family, never
quite made it out of the Great Depression. Tough, hard-
working father, minor supervisor in the stockyards, union,
maybe some Communist leanings—there were influences
like that in the Amalgamated Meat Packers in those days.
Equally tough, stern mother. No time for amusement or
play. Went to work after he graduated from Leo. Night
school. Korea. DePaul after that. Made a lot of money
early and kept making it. Took care of his parents and his
brothers and sisters. One of the brothers, Dave, works with
him in the company, along with Bart Junior—neither one
very good in the pits, I'm told. Married in his early thirties.
Nice woman, but a mistake for both of them. Bart

probably didn't know what he was looking for. But a pirate like him—and he is a pirate, Blackwood, don't let the liberal ideology fool you—needed a challenging wife, sexually and every other way, and that he didn't get. Four kids, the older three jerks if you ask me . . ."

"Bart Junior, Bill, and Jennifer."

"And that cute kid."

"Candi, a.k.a. Elizabeth."

"Yeah, she seems to like the stepmother. She was the maid of honor in the wedding. Took care of Julia like her soon-to-be stepmother was her little sister. When I said how nice her stepmother looked in her bridal gown, the kid said something in that odd lingo they use which gave me the idea she had picked out the gown."

"Doubtless she did. Candi may turn out to be an appropriate daughter for a pirate."

"You remember the time that Bart brought over that wimpy little psychologist that writes for *The Common Truth*? Guy that said the two of us wanted more than anything else to do the one thing we couldn't do, sleep with a woman?"

"A.X. Robert Swipe. An inactive priest," I said, "to use the current politically correct term."

"Yeah." The cardinal drained his glass. "And you told him that he was demonstrating the same level of maturity as an eighteen-year-old bragging to a fourteen-year-old that he had just fucked a woman and there was nothing in the world like it."

"I have vague recollections that I might have said something inappropriate like that."

I considered my Waterford tumbler. Some evil spirit had doubtless been stealing from it. Otherwise how could it have become empty?

"And you said something that a moratorium ought to be

declared on the testimony of men who had violated their vows of celibacy and then attacked those of us who had kept our vows, especially if they were priest psychologists who had married nun psychologists."

"It is highly improbable that I said something that insulting." I gathered his glass and mine and prepared to return to my own rooms to refill them—being under strict orders never to leave the Bushmill's Green in his suite.

Sean Cronin was delighting in our triumph over A.X. Robert Swipe.

"He tried to tell us that we were hiding our own sexual inadequacies, and you said that he was clearly contending with his own repressed homosexual inclinations and you would ask your sister, Mary Kathleen Ryan Murphy, to recommend an appropriate analyst for him. Turns out, as you well know, that she had destroyed him at some professional meeting."

"A highly improbable account of the events in question."

I departed for my quarters, reflecting with some satisfaction that, while Swipe continued his anti-celibacy and anti-celibate crusade (complete with worthless data) in the pages of *The Common Truth*, over which Jennifer Cain presided as some sort of assistant editor, I had learned on good authority that Bart Cain had terminated his generous subsidy of the man's work.

I had a hard time finding my bottle of Green Label because, instead of returning it to its hiding place in the cabinet on the wall with the pictures of the three Johns of my youth (Kennedy, XXIII, and Unitas), I had secreted it somewhere else. In the shower, as it turned out, for reasons that escaped me then and now.

"Why all the interest in Bart Cain?" the cardinal asked when I had returned.

I told him the story recounted to me by the creamy Candi.

Thunderclouds gathered on Sean Cronin's brow. "I won't have it, Blackwood, I simply won't have it. You know that."

"I seem to recollect you have a certain aversion to such manifestations in what you are pleased to call your archdiocese."

"I will tolerate bleeding crucifixes, weeping statues, apparitions of the Madonna in which she preaches Republican propaganda, youthful miracle workers, mystical prophets with a direct line to the Almighty, but not ghosts. I have enough trouble as it is with Rome. I don't want any public exorcisms."

"It is my observation," I said, watching my tumbler to make sure that the demons did not assail it again, "that the Mother of Jesus was Jewish and hence more likely to be a liberal Democrat and a supporter of your friend Bill Clinton."

"No ghosts!" the cardinal insisted. "No way. And if anyone is haunting Bart Cain, why would it not be Eunice? Why should Mary Anne Haggerty come back after all these years?"

"Beats me," I agreed. "Mary Anne Haggerty is the girl who disappeared?"

"Yeah, a nice quiet kid. Bart's date. The Leo prom that year—to which he went against his parents' wishes—was at the Knickerbocker, where all proms used to be. Then for the day after a whole crowd of them went up to some small lake in Michigan, beyond Long Beach and Grand Beach. Mary Anne Haggerty just disappeared."

"Completely?"

"From the face of the earth. Never seen again. No body ever recovered. No trace."

"Fascinating!"

"The police up there thought that there had been an accident, maybe she was running away from an attacker, and she had drowned. Then they suspected gang rape and a cover-up. They gave all the kids a hard time, especially Bart. Then the Chicago cops worked them over. Give his parents credit, they stuck by him. Finally the cops abandoned the case. Lots of suspicions and no proof."

"No statute of limitations on murder," I said, putting my tumbler on the floor where I could keep an eye on it.

"So I'm told. It's all forgotten now, though perhaps not by Bart or by Tim O'Donnell, who was part of the crowd. Bart and Mary Anne were double-dating with Tim and they drove in Tim's car. Tim is a trader too, part of Bart's firm. As we both know, a typical shanty Irish Beverly Club drunk."

"Indeed!"

"Whatever! Ghosts, especially on East Lake Shore Drive, are simply not acceptable. I won't tolerate it." He drained his glass again, a sign that he wanted to get back to work. "I want them out of there. Immediately. See to it, Blackwood!"

Those were the words I wanted to hear. I had been assigned by a Cardinal Prince of the Church to solve a couple of mysteries—who was the "ghost" and what had happened to Mary Anne Haggerty?

There would be a couple of additional mysteries to add to the list before long.

CHAPTER 4

"YOU DON'T LOOK like a priest!" the formidable African-American woman who was the gatekeeper at the door of the Cain cooperative penthouse informed me when I had stepped out of the private elevator which had borne me to the top of the building.

It was perhaps my fault. I should have donned a black jacket over my clerical shirt instead of a Chicago Bulls windbreaker. A penthouse on East Lake Shore Drive merits at least full clerical garb and in my case ring and pectoral cross (mine a silver version of St. Brigid's cross).

East Lake Shore Drive is the most golden segment of Chicago's Gold Coast. It stretches east from the bend of drive at the Oak Street Beach and the Drake Hotel to another bend a half-mile further. Then the drive turns south again and races towards Navy Pier and Grant Park. The apartments which stretch along this brief thoroughfare do not even begin on the marketplace for less than a million and a half dollars.

The view is splendid: the beach, the parkway, the lake, Lincoln Park in the distance and the skyline of high-rise apartment buildings along the drive to the north, on this sunny morning an impressionist pastel watercolor against the blue sky.

"What parish you from?" the stern gatekeeper demanded.

25

"The cathedral," I said meekly. "I'm Father Ryan."

"You still don't look like a priest."

"I try my best."

"Do you know Father Stafford?"

"The worthy pastor of St. Egbert's."

"He's my priest. My kids go to that school. He looks like a real priest."

"Exemplary man."

"I'm gonna call him and ask about you." She closed the door in my face.

The incident would soon be a legend in the presbyterate of the archdiocese, another chapter in the Blackie mythology. The entire cathedral staff would know about it before lunch, and most of the rest of the clergy by suppertime.

I sighed, but not too heavily. The legend has its uses.

The door opened again. "Father Stafford says you are a bishop!"

"Alas, I'm afraid it's true."

"You don't look like a bishop, either." An approving smile had replaced her disapproving frown. "Father Stafford just laughed and laughed. He says you're all right."

She stood aside and permitted me to enter the apartment. The parlor was two stories high with floor-to-ceiling windows. The furnishings were, alas, not compatible with the opulence of the space. Money cannot buy good taste, not at least in the case of poor Eunice Cain.

"For a bishop?"

"Just plain all right . . . I'm Irene Jones. I sure am sorry I didn't realize you were a bishop."

"You must take good care of all who live in this house and you can't be too careful."

"You have a ring for me to kiss?"

"I'm afraid I left it at the rectory. I bet Father Stafford put you up to asking that."

She laughed enthusiastically. "He sure did. Mrs. Cain is out on the patio. You can go right on out."

The patio was a tiny roof behind the penthouse with a miniature swimming pool surrounded by deck chairs and flowerpots filled with blazing mums.

"Bishop Ryan to see you, honey," Irene Jones informed the young woman swimming a vigorous backstroke in the pool.

Julia bounced out of the pool, startled and frightened. She was wearing a black bikini which was no more modest than it had to be. I noted that Sean Cronin's eye for womanly beauty had not been deceived. Nor that of my poet associate. Julia was indeed a knockout, if now an embarrassed knockout. As my brother-in-law Joseph Murphy, M.D., had once observed (in the presence of his wife), some women look a lot better with their clothes off than on.

"I didn't know you were coming over," she said, knotting a terry-cloth robe around herself. "I'm very sorry not to be ready for you."

"Candi didn't tell you I would be here at ten o'clock?"

She smiled at the name of her stepdaughter. "She's a teenager. She told me she was going to talk to you, but she forgot to tell me when you would come or that you would come."

"Predictable behavior from one of her years."

Her face still flushed in embarrassment, Julia Cain stood across the pool from me. "She's such a dear, sweet child I don't mind that she forgets things sometimes . . . are priests permitted to talk to women in swimsuits? I'm not a Catholic and I don't know . . . ."

"Only in the mornings."

She laughed uneasily, hoping that I was joking.

"I've never talked to a priest before."

"The cardinal?"

"The cardinal is not exactly a priest, is he? I mean, he's so good-looking."

"We do ordain some attractive ones on occasion."

Julia Cain, either in a bikini or with a thick robe tied protectively if ineffectively around her body, was the sort of woman who would cause heads to turn down on Oak Street Beach, not because one might call her either beautiful or voluptuous in the ordinary sense of those words, but because she was striking, fascinating, even haunting. Not either a Venus or a Diana, much less a Juno, Julia Cain was, rather, a wood nymph. Or, given her origins, a prairie nymph. Tall, naturally graceful in her movements, and so slender that she was almost thin, with long black hair and a delicately carved face, she seemed like a statue that a skilled artist had wrought not with rich curves but with such quick and deft lines that her erotic appeal captured the observer before one noticed its ingenuity. Her gray eyes, deep-set and impassioned, perceptive and frightened, caused the observer (well, this observer anyway) to forget (mostly) her elegant breasts and held him in captive enchantment. The soul that lurked behind those eyes had wrestled with demons and had not yet lost. She seemed delicate and defenseless and yet with an inner core of strength which had not yet been tested.

Oh, yes, she'd haunt you, all right, especially if you were a rich and powerful man in your early sixties who had been celibate for four years and quasi-celibate for most of his life.

"Do sit down." She stirred as one coming out of a trance and gestured towards a patio table with two blue chairs and a blue umbrella. "Could I get you some coffee?"

"Tea?"

I noted that despite its small size and the massive John

Hancock Center looming to the south, the Cain patio would be bathed in sunlight most of the day, even during September. Naturally. Moreover, an awning rolled up on the wall could be pulled over the patio to protect it from voyeurs in the Hancock Center. Naturally.

"What kind of tea?" she asked shyly, almost as though she should have known my tastes.

"Earl Gray."

"Irene." She opened a French door. "Could you bring us two cups of Earl Gray, please?"

"Yes, ma'am."

"I find it hard to give orders to that wonderful woman," she explained, sitting across from me and releasing her hair from the braid which had contained it while she was swimming. "What do I call you? I mean, I've never had a visit from a priest before."

A faint strain of downstate accent clung to her words. I'd never heard Sean Cronin called a "cordnal" in a more charming voice.

"Call me Blackie."

"Not Ishmael?" A faint, timid smile appeared on her lips.

"Not today."

At that point Julia Cain decided that she could relax with me and be herself. I noted that she smelled faintly of chlorine.

"Can I begin, Blackie, by saying that I love my husband?" She spoke rapidly and anxiously, eager, it would seem, to convince me. "No wife has ever loved a man more than I love Bart. I didn't marry him for his money. I was earning a good living from my own work. I don't need all this luxury. I'd rather not have it. I want only him."

"You seem to have him."

She clenched her fists and her face twisted into an angry frown. "They want to take him away from me."

The more passionate her words, the richer became the prairie twang in her voice.

"They?"

"His family and his friends and his associates in the company and those terrible people at that awful magazine."

When she referred to the company she gestured at a stack of printouts piled up on a table next to a chaise lounge at poolside. They seemed sufficiently complicated, indeed, so complicated that they made "Blackie's Folly" look truly user-friendly.

"They have not succeeded," I said.

"No." She relaxed again. "Not yet, anyway. Does the cardinal work for you? I don't know much about the Catholic Church."

"There are some who say that he does, but in fact he's the big boss and I do his bidding—most of the time."

"But you're a bishop. Are cardinals higher than bishops?"

"Much higher."

"I don't belong to any church or even go to church much. I guess I'm not very religious."

"That does not follow."

Irene appeared with a tray bearing a huge teapot, two teacups, and four delicious-seeming cinnamon rolls. Julia Cain poured the tea with simple grace.

How does one sustain that grace when one has been through what I was assuming she'd been through?

"Milk or sugar?"

"Black as midnight on a moonless night."

Her eyes glinted. "You are not a character from *Twin Peaks*, Father Blackie."

"So I am told."

"A roll?"

"Thank you." I grabbed one with what I hope was not completely unbecoming haste.

"I do pray," she said. "Every day."

"Ah."

"So I guess I believe in God."

"Even if one doesn't, it may be prudent to converse with whom it may concern."

She hesitated. "Down home, I didn't trust my minister very much. He was a bad man."

"I'm sure they have no monopoly on such. We could match them."

"He did bad things to people and talked about what they had told him in confidence."

So. Had he been part of the abuse?

I remained silent while, head down, face thoughtful, she pondered her relationships with clergypersons.

"Catholics have confessors, don't they? I mean, people they can trust completely."

"With secrets, Julia Cain, not necessarily with good advice."

"Can a Protestant have a confessor?"

"At least a trusted confidant."

"Could you be my confessor?" She looked up at me with a plea in her burning eyes that no one could have resisted.

"I'm not a substitute for a psychiatrist, Julia Cain, but I'm good at keeping secrets."

"And you'd be on my side?"

"If you stand approved by the candid Candi—ah, excellent Elizabeth—would I have any choice?"

She smiled, as a proud mother would of an admired daughter. "She keeps me sane. I call her Candi when her father isn't around. I tell her that the next time she changes her name, Beth would fit her perfectly. She is a Beth." Her smile grew animated. "Don't you think so, Father Blackie?"

"Arguably. She will not be a Candi much longer."

She refilled my teacup and inched the rolls in my direction—in the nick of time or I would have reached across the table and grabbed my second. For her part Julia Cain was nibbling on a piece of one. That left a possible third for me.

"You like cinnamon buns."

"So I am told."

"Do you have a cook at the cathedral?"

"An excellent one, but she does not seem to know from cinnamon buns."

She nibbled thoughtfully on a tiny crust. "I probably should see a psychiatrist too. Could you recommend one for me?"

Now she was brisk and businesslike, systematically straightening out her life like a good mathematician would.

"Man or woman?"

She considered. "Man, I think."

"There is a certain Joseph Murphy down the street at Northwestern Hospital who is reputed to be excellent. He is, I believe, married to one of my sisters. His only failing is that he comes from Boston and talks strangely."

She nodded solemnly. "I will phone him. It's time, I think."

"Capital."

"I had no intentions of marrying anyone, Father Blackie." She had lowered her head. "When Timothy O'Donnell offered me a job drawing charts for Cain and Sons, I hesitated because everyone said that Bart Cain was a rigid and demanding brute. Their money, however, was too good to turn down."

"Indeed."

"I had seen him on the floor, of course, a big strong man who almost never smiled and reveled in the combat. Not the kind that I normally found attractive . . . well, that's not true. There was something appealing about him even then. And he seemed so lonely."

"I see."

"But I was afraid of him too."

"You thought he would hurt you?"

"No . . . the women all said that he didn't make passes. I was just afraid of him."

"Ah."

"He didn't seem to notice me when I started to work at Cain and Sons. So I relaxed. Then one day I realized that he was watching me. I'd been watched that way by men before and hated it and them, but when Bart Cain looked at me that way, like he was taking off my clothes and enjoying me, it was different. I was terrified and flattered and I suppose already captured."

I remained silent.

She hugged herself protectively. "Does that sound terrible, Father Blackie?"

"Normal, I should say."

I marveled, not for the first time in my years as a priest, at the willingness of women to share their most intimate secrets with a priest, once they had decided that he was indeed a trusted confidant. It was a delicate trust that must be protected. And cherished.

"I never thought I would be normal sexually. . . . The look in his eyes, like he had walked across the desert and I was a glass of cool, pure water, was almost unbearable. He drank me in, he absorbed me, he drained me. And I loved it. His eyes made me want to take off my clothes whenever he stared at me. It was terrible and wonderful and I could think of nothing else. I thought I would lose my mind. Our eyes would lock and we'd both look away and I'd feel all warm and soft and I'd look back at him just in time to see him looking at me. I'm afraid that I didn't do much charting on the days he was in the office."

As she described, cautiously but proudly, the blossoming of their love affair, her gestures became animated and her eyes glowed joyously. Nothing so important had happened to Julia Cain since her birth.

"The others were oblivious?"

"No one else in the firm seemed to notice. Bart Cain had a reputation for not being a womanizer. They said he was basically uninterested in women. So of course he was not interested in me. Yet there was chemistry and tension between us so thick that you could walk on it, but no one noticed. I guess we were both pretty discreet."

"Admirable."

"We never spoke to one another. Time of day, that's all. Then I realized that he was too strict in his own conscience to take the initiative. Sexual harassment of an employee." She laughed happily. "As if his presence in the office was not a sexual harassment to me."

"And vice versa?"

She blushed. "Arguably.

"It couldn't go on that way," she continued. "I saw that I would have to make a pass at him . . . something that I had never done with a man in all my life and thought I would never do . . . I'm afraid I'm blushing terribly, Father Blackie . . . yet the idea of seducing him absolutely delighted me. So I did it. I'm not very good at such things. In fact, I was pretty crude. He was ripe for the picking. As I guess I was, as far as that goes. I didn't have to be very good. Poor man was worried that he was sexually molesting me."

"On the whole it is not a bad policy to let the conquered think they are conquerors."

She threw back her head and laughed. "You know too much, Father Blackie. How can you know so much? That's a silly question, isn't it? Priests know more about love than anyone else, don't they?"

"Despite our mutual friend The Swipe."

"Despicable little beast." She dismissed him with a swipe of her hand and continued her love story. "It's still the same way, Father Blackie. The hunger is as strong as ever. Stronger. When we're in the same room we can barely keep our hands off one another. No matter how much we're together we want more. Oh, we have a lot in common. We like the same things. We laugh at the same jokes. We're good companions. But it's the hunger that brought us together and holds us together and I'm not ashamed of that."

"I should think not."

"That's not sinful?"

"Only if God made a mistake in arranging for sexual differentiation in our species."

She nodded thoughtfully. "I suppose that's true . . . money is irrelevant. It isn't even worth talking about. Age doesn't matter either. I know I won't have him forever, but one night with him is eternity . . . do I sound totally horny, Father Blackie?"

"Rather like a woman passionately in love."

"Does it make any difference that he is so much older than I am?"

"Fortunately for the human species the Holy Spirit encourages a wide variety of loves to entertain us and entrap us."

"I sure am entrapped . . . I never thought I was a sexy person. Just kind of dull and uninteresting."

"Those are the kind you gotta watch."

She laughed enthusiastically again. "I guess you're right . . . but, don't you see, I couldn't care less about his money. I want him, and nothing more. I tell him not to change his will. And he won't. In a lot of things he does exactly what I tell him to do. The others know that, but they hate me just the same because they think I'm being insidious when I say I don't want the money. Except Candi."

"Beth."

"Right!"

There was, of course, in the heads of all those who disliked her, the possibility that she would conceive a child. Or a couple of children. Bart Cain was the sort of pirate who would become proud of his virility when given an opportunity to do so. Such an eventuality would delight the creamy Candi, who would think only of the joy of a little brother or sister and not care about the presumed decline of her share of an estate. Or little brothers and sisters. But other heirs might well resent such a change in their expectations. They would be unlikely to consider that the presence of Julia at Bart Cain's bread and board might not only make his life more satisfying, but actually prolong it so that he would in fact be able to enhance their inheritances. The other heirs might even resent the longer life and the delay of their expectations.

Moreover, though she seemed unaware of the fact, Illinois law would give her a quarter of her husband's estate regardless of any will. Yet it was hard to believe that such an intelligent woman did not know about inheritance laws. If Julia was not ready to face the issue, I was not about to bring it up.

"You do believe me, Father Blackie? I mean that it's love or lust or whatever between me and Bart and nothing else?"

"Patently a mixture of the two."

"Sometimes"—she shook her head disconsolately—"I think I'm a horrible person for what I've done. I was really shameless. The way I was raised, I'm a terrible sinner."

"Consider the story of Jesus and the Samaritan woman."

"John 4:1-42," she said automatically. Our separated brothers are much better at Biblical citations than we are or likely ever will be.

"Precisely. It is a story composed by the early Church, doubtless based on its memories of Jesus's extraordinary respect for women and their attraction to him, to justify the acceptance of Samaritans into their community. It is filled with references to engagement stories in the Hebrew Scriptures, even explicitly to Jacob's well, and fertility symbols such as grain, and water. The theme, to oversimplify, is that the woman is being attracted into discipleship and that God, acting through Jesus, wooed and won the Samaritans. Thus the attraction a woman feels for a man becomes a metaphor for the way we feel for God. One could of course reverse the gender roles and the meaning would be roughly the same."

She considered me dubiously. "My minister would not have liked that interpretation."

"Indeed."

"You're saying I'm God for Bart?"

"Your sexual appeal is a hint of God's appeal—and of course vice versa."

"You Catholics are dangerous." She grinned. "Idolaters! But I'll remember that interpretation the next time I feel guilty about enjoying our love."

"I trust you don't think that way very often?"

"No." She flushed again. "Only when Bart is not around. When I'm with him, I'm having too much fun to feel guilty. And it is shameless to say that, isn't it?"

"Not in my parish, mine and your friend the cardinal's, that is. Candi mentioned something about a ghost?"

"I'm frightened about that, Father Blackie." She shuddered. "We had haunted houses down home and they terrified me. And the woman calls after each accident and says that Bart will be punished for marrying a whore— that's me, of course."

"Then the ghost does not have access to the mind of the Holy Spirit. The ghost does not purport to be Bart Cain's late wife?"

"No, poor woman. She says she's the ghost of someone who died long ago. After a senior prom. She blames Bart for her death and says he will be punished."

"Ah."

"I don't know why she would object to me and not to Eunice. It seems odd. Unless . . ."

"Unless?"

"Unless . . . well, it's all the sexual pleasure she objects to."

"Your husband does not seem troubled by the apparent accidents and the calls from the ghost?"

"Bart has a tendency to dismiss things which he doesn't want to see. The accidents are all a coincidence and the phone calls and the messages left on our line are the work of some crank."

"The combination of the two is also a coincidence?"

"He's too smart to say that. He thinks that someone who hates him—and he says that their name is legion—finds out about the accident and makes the call to scare him."

"An arguable position."

But not, it seemed to me, very likely.

"He could have been killed. That chandelier would have crushed his skull."

"Could you tell me more about each accident, Julia?"

"Well"—she composed herself and folded her hands—"the first one seemed like a real accident. We were walking by the Drake one morning and a bucket fell off a window-washing platform. The management at the Drake was apologetic. Bart laughed it off. Said it didn't come within six feet of him."

"And the call came immediately?"

"No, that evening. Candi answered the phone. The poor child was terrified."

"Indeed . . . and the second incident?"

"Candi claims to have pushed Bart out of the way of a pickup truck when he was collecting her after school at St. Ignatius. He says she has accidents on her mind and that the truck would not have hit him anyway."

"And the call?"

"It came in the evening. I answered the phone. The woman called me terrible names. She said that I had better enjoy, ah, making love—well, she used another term—with Bart because punishment would at last catch up with him for killing her. Then she played the music."

"I see."

"Both might have been real accidents, just chance, you know. But the chandelier could have killed him. It was brand-new, Waterford crystal, he had given it to me as a present—I told him that he'd spent far too much money on me—and it had been installed only the week before."

"Defective installation?"

"It looked to me like the wires had been cut."

"But it could have hit you or anyone else who happened to be standing beneath it. Or it could have fallen when no one was in the apartment."

"But it didn't. It fell when he was right under it."

"Indeed. Does your husband say anything about the disappearance and presumed death of his prom date?"

"Was she his date? I didn't even know that . . . no, he refuses to talk about it. He says there are no such things as ghosts and that's that."

"So."

"I know more about Bart Cain, Father Blackie, than anyone else in the world, more than I think he ever wanted to reveal about himself till he met me. But there are enormous parts of himself that he still hides. He's a very private man."

"A challenge that remains?"

"I tell him that I want to know all about him and he just laughs." She sighed. "But I'm determined to strip away everything . . . more tea?"

"A final half-cup. Yes, it would be sinful to let that final cinnamon roll go to waste."

In her search for the total Bart Cain she ran the risk of finding out much that she would rather have not discovered. So it is with the hunger of lovers to possess the other totally.

"I don't know why anyone who is not a ghost would want to kill him." She lowered her eyes again. "He thinks he has lots of enemies, and I suppose he does. But murder?"

"Is it conceivable that those who resent you might be trying to frighten him?"

"Sure." She looked up, her eyes unreadable. "But if they know him at all, they know that he does not frighten easily. Besides, while they may hate me, why try to kill him?"

"Before he changes the will?"

"I can't believe anyone wants the money that badly. And

there are a lot easier ways to kill a person, even to make it look like an accident."

So there were. But Julia Cain underestimated both the power of greed and the clumsiness of most killers, even, in recent years, of professional hit men.

"I think it really is the ghost," she said, shivering despite the warm September air. "Do you believe in ghosts, Father Blackie?"

"A tough question, Julia. There are phenomena of evil for which we humans have yet no adequate explanations. There is a malignancy in the cosmos beyond mere human evil which we cannot comprehend."

She nodded. "I read Lord Bullock's book about Hitler and Stalin this summer. They were terrible men but together they did awful evil—forty million dead. Can two men by themselves be that evil?"

"Precisely. Yet I very much doubt that the ghost of the late Mary Anne Haggerty is haunting your husband after all these years."

"I think I do believe it, Father Blackie," she said firmly. "I do believe in ghosts, you see. No, that's not right. I *know* that there are ghosts. Down home there are a lot of them."

I did not think it appropriate to pursue that conviction.

"You do not mind if I do a little snooping around?" I asked.

"Oh, no! Candi says you are like a totally outstanding detective. But don't tell anyone about what I've said. Bart thinks the whole affair will go away if we ignore it."

"Perhaps it will. In any event you may rely on my discretion."

She smiled ruefully. "I already have."

"Indeed." I swallowed my last bit of cinnamon bun and stood up, clumsily, as is my wont. "I must return to the cathedral and reassure myself that my staff has not moved it across the street into the empty parking lot."

"And I"—she rose with me and reached for her computer output—"must get back to my charts. I work at home now most of the time because it's a little tense around the office."

In reaching for her charts, she briefly exposed a generous vision of womanly bosom, as women are wont to do, whether consciously or not I leave to God to judge.

"What kind of computer do you use?" I asked to cover my confusion—and my delight.

The rules of the game are that a man may notice such epiphanies—why else do they happen—but must not appear to notice them.

"Gateway 486SX Nomad."

"Ah. A laptop."

"I have a docking station here and at the exchange so I can carry it back and forth. It weighs less than six pounds."

We had reentered the apartment through the French doors.

"I use their 486DX2."

"Power computing! Do you want to see my system?"

I did indeed, though I was more interested in the layout of their apartment than I was in her computer equipment.

We ascended to the second floor on the broad, curving staircase, which one would hardly have expected in an apartment, even a penthouse on East Lake Shore Drive. Beth, as she would have become by then, would create quite a scene coming down those stairs in a prom dress. Eventually in a wedding dress.

"My office, Father Blackie, is at the end of the corridor, with a window overlooking the lake. We had six bedrooms and we converted two of them to offices. Bart's is at the other end. With computerized trading, investors don't even have to leave their own homes."

"I see."

Her setup was impressive. In addition to the twenty-one-inch monitor and two printers, one for color printing, which in sum must have cost between twenty and thirty thousand dollars, her docking station was linked to a CD-Rom player, a Bernoulli box, and a Windows accelerator board.

"We have an HP paint jet at the cathedral rectory," I said with genuine humility.

"That's all anyone really needs." She laughed. "But Bart says that anyone who is in front of one of these things all day has no self-respect unless he uses state-of-the-art, top-of-the-line. Here, let me print out this chart."

She pushed a macro key and the color printer promptly produced a work which could have hung in the Art Institute. It was too good for mine enemies at the Museum of Contemporary Art.

"And what does this delightful *object d'art* tell me?"

"It says that if you think Bill Clinton is going to win in November you should sell short." She laughed. "I really don't believe it."

We strolled back towards the stairs.

"An exercise room." She pushed open a door. "One of the advantages of being married to Bart is that I don't have to go to a club to work out."

"Medieval torture devices," I said as I inspected the machinery. "You and your husband work out together?"

"Sometimes." She laughed uneasily. "Is it wrong, I wonder, for a woman to wear the kind of exercise clothes that will arouse her husband if he happens to be in the room with her?"

It was a serious question.

"What do you think, Julia Cain?"

"One part of me says it's shameless and another part says it's all right, maybe even wonderful."

"What part wins?"

"The latter—unfailingly."

"You want my reassurance?"

"It would help," she said shyly. "I must sound like an awful creep."

"I doubt that is possible, and I make the case if you were a Catholic and I was your confessor that I would refuse you absolution if you didn't promise to continue in your present custom."

She nodded solemnly. "I will remember those words the next time I lose my nerve."

"It is convenient, then, that you both are able to work at home?"

She blushed deeply. "Convenient for some things. I'm afraid that we often don't get much work done. When Candi is in school and Irene not around—and she's very careful not to be around when we're home together—we hardly do any work at all."

Whatever had been her worst experiences, however deep her sexual traumas, however much help she would eventually need to exorcise the worst of her demons, the woman was proud of her sexual conquest. Moreover, once she had admitted you into her personal world and decided that she could trust you as a confidant, she was not ashamed of her pride.

"Globex, the new network," she went on, "enables us to trade twenty-four hours a day. Bart even keeps a work-station at our bedside. An investor or a trader can wake up in the middle of the night and take a position."

I let the unintentional pun pass without notice, more or less. "Much to a spouse's dismay?"

"Depends on the spouse, doesn't it?" She blushed again. "There is the workstation, right next to the bed. At least it doesn't try to come into the bed with us. Not yet anyway."

She waved at the master bedroom as we passed it. I would have thought that it was big enough for the Chicago Bears to hold practice on a rainy day. Perhaps on the bed.

It was at the head of the stairs, I noted. Right above the dining room from which presumably the Waterford chandelier had fallen.

Interesting.

Clutching my multicolored chart, I permitted myself to be conducted to the door.

"Do you know anything about this place, Father Blackie?" She picked up a brochure on the table by the door to the apartment. "Candi insists that it is like totally awesome. She's taking me out there on the weekend."

"Great America? A delight for children of every age. My own generation and older will insist that it is nothing like Riverview used to be, even though they claim to have re-created the legendary Bobs roller coaster."

"Did you really ride on that?"

"No, but I watched people ride on it, which was a thrill in itself. Nothing can match it."

"That's what Bart says, but I think he'll come along with us anyway . . . Riverview was right in town, wasn't it?"

"At Western Avenue and the Chicago River. It's a shopping plaza now, a great loss to the city."

"I was raised to believe that such places were sinful. Now I don't care. As well damned for a goat as for a sheep."

"Indeed . . ." I searched in my pocket for one of my calling cards, and astonishingly found one in my Chicago Bears windbreaker, though it was somewhat tarnished by a chocolate stain. "Though I believe that God's love is so clever and so insidious that one makes it into the ranks of the goats only by dint of superhuman effort."

"I hope you're right." Her gray eyes were troubled again. "I surely hope you're right."

I gave her my battered card. "The number on here rings in my rooms at the cathedral, should you need me on an emergency basis."

"Do you expect that, Father Blackie?" She looked at me levelly.

"Not particularly."

"And the doctor's name is Murphy."

"Murphy, Joseph."

"And he talks funny but a different funny than you Chicagoans talk?"

"Precisely."

"Thank you very much, Father Blackie." She shook hands firmly. "Candi was right when she said I ought to talk to you."

"Arguably."

CHAPTER 5

I STROLLED DOWN East Lake Shore Drive and through the underpass beneath Michigan Avenue to Oak Street. Underpasses fascinate me, even when they are dank, covered with graffiti, and smell of urine.

Back in the warmth of the September sun and on Oak Street, I was able to find my way to the Reilly Gallery, where my relative, Mike Casey the Cop, held forth along with his wife, Anne Marie O'Brien Reilly Casey. She presides over the gallery and he, for some years retired as police superintendent, paints his mystical Chicago neighborhood scenes.

I should note for the sake of clarity that in our clan he is always referred to as "Mike Casey the Cop," as if there is another Mike Casey in the family. Perhaps a "Mike Casey the Priest," or "Mike Casey the Pol." In fact, however, there is but one Mike Casey in our large, noisy, and pushy extended family.

Annie Casey hugged me, polished my glasses, and provided me with the traditional refreshment offered me at the gallery—apple cinnamon tea (without caffeine, of course) and four (and don't ask for more!) chocolate-chip cookies.

Her husband turned away from a wondrous painting of an old Polish church lurking above the Kennedy Expressway, disapproving of what he saw, I thought, and smiled at me.

"You have your look of the bloodhound on your face, Cousin Blackie."

Some will insist that Mike Casey, who looks a bit like Jeremy Brett playing Sherlock Holmes, is my Flambeau, as if, *per impossible*, I was Father Brown. In fact, Father Brown doesn't even seem to have a parish, and it is patent I almost never leave the boundaries of my parish. There is more than enough virtue and vice, sin and redemption within its limits to keep a dozen of Chesterton's charming if faintly Edwardian priest-detectives occupied.

"Possibly." I sighed in reply.

"Who are you asking about today?" His wife, like all the women of our ethnic group, assumed as a matter of indisputable fact that she knew more about the art and science of detection than either of us would ever learn.

While we chatted, a television against one wall of Mike's studio revealed that my old friend The Swipe was performing on one of many Winfrey/Donahue imitations. I gathered that the program was an interview with four ex-priests who had married, divorced, and then remarried— with the first and second wives and in one case the third wife present for the fun. The Swipe was there as an expert on the sexuality of priests, and was assigning precise numbers to the proportions of the priests who were sexually active, gay, and pedophiliac. Based on his "twenty-five-year" study—clinical interviews, workshop discussions, and conversations with people who knew priests. Real science. Better that I concentrate on *l'affaire Cain* than permit myself to be angered by The Swipe.

"What does one know," I asked, "about a certain Bart Cain?"

Mike made a face. "I don't like ideologues, Blackie, and

particularly those kind who think that there is never an excuse for a cop to draw a gun, even when someone is pointing one at him. Every time a cop shoots in self-defense and the parents insist that their kid is not a gang member—even if he did happen to be carrying a Walther or an Uzi or a MAC-10—Bart Cain lectures the city about police brutality and that rag of his does another phony exposé of the police force."

"Indeed."

"There are some neighborhoods in this city," he continued, "where a cop is in more danger than a UN soldier would be in Sarajevo or a member of the RUC would be in Derry."

"Doubtless."

"Sure, there's police brutality, though probably less than ever before in this city. When you shout brutality every time a cop is trying to save his life, you detract from the importance of the real brutality. I hear on the street that Bart is angry at Rich Daley because the mayor won't set up a civilian review board for the police and make him chairman."

"He also supports legalization of drugs, does he not?"

"I'm not so sure he's wrong about that, damn it," Mike grumbled. "Having said all those things, he's as honest and as generous a man as this city knows."

"His self-proclaimed integrity does not bother you?"

"If you ask me," Mike said grimly, "the Chicago Irish, particularly the lawyers, could stand a little more of it."

"Not too much more." Annie laughed, refilling my teacup.

"We'll worry about that," her husband replied, "when the day comes. Hell, if Bart would smile a little more, I might half like him."

"He's had a hard life," Annie insisted.

"Marriage to Eunice Slattery was not an easy life, heaven knows."

"Michael!" Annie protested. "The poor woman is dead. And anyway, he's married now to a very sweet and pretty woman."

"Poor kid." Mike sighed. "With Eunice the Lord made them and the divil matched them. Anyway, what do you have on Bart Cain?"

"The illustrious impresario of this gallery"—I began work on the third cookie—"noted that Cain's life was very difficult when he was growing up. Indeed, what is surprising is not that he is a hard man, but a hard man on the left instead of the right. There is one aspect of his youth about which I would know more—the death of his prom date in 1947."

"That long ago?" Mike seemed genuinely surprised. "I seem to remember something about it. Some older guys talked about it when I came on the force. Girl simply disappeared. Typical cops, they thought *he* did it, but said there was no proof and no body. I'd have to think that nothing much happened or it would have come up long before this with all the publicity he gets for himself."

"Nineteen forty-seven was only forty-five years ago," his wife observed.

"There is no statute of limitations on murder," I remarked.

"Too true," Mike agreed. "Do you have any reason to think he did kill her?"

"None at all. I think it unlikely though not impossible. My reasons for interest in the subject are more current than remote."

"And you won't, or better, can't tell me anything else. Well, fair enough. I'll see if there's anything still around, though I would imagine that the files are buried if not destroyed."

"And what is to be said of his family and associates?"

Mike began to tick off information on the fingers of his right hand.

"He had a fight with his brother Dave a couple of years ago. Dave left the family firm and is working on pension portfolios for Dreyfus. I hear he is having a hard time making ends meet. His wife Eleanor, if I remember correctly, has gone back to work as someone's administrative assistant at First Chicago. Tim O'Donnell, who has been with him in that gambling business they have down at the foot of Lasalle Street since he first got into it, is no more honest than he has to be. In a lot of ways he's the exact opposite of Bart, charming, witty, drinks too much, screws around some, not untypical of a certain kind of trader. Would have made a good precinct captain in the old days. Barely escaped indictment once or twice, and has been fined by the Board a couple of times. If it wasn't for his relationship with Bart Cain, they might have tossed him. Lives in Beverly."

"Nothing wrong with that," I insisted. Most of my own clan also lives there.

"If you say so." Mike grinned. "Then there's Bart Junior, as everyone calls him. Worthless punk. Early thirties. Republican. Lives somewhere on the North Shore. Made his money by being part of his father's deals. Works for the company but spends most of his time on the boards of the Art Institute, the Lyric, and the Symphony "

"Museum of Contemporary Art," Annie corrected him. "The Art Institute wouldn't have him."

"Can't blame them. The word is that Bart Junior has no more weight than the sound of his voice. A snooty wife who forgets she was born in Visitation on Garfield

Boulevard and thinks she's high quality because she has a home in Kenilworth."

"Insufferable," Annie, normally the soul of charity, agreed.

"Not as insufferable as Jennifer, the second child." Mike ticked her off on his third finger.

"I agree completely," Anne observed. "A real bitch."

"Not married, doesn't want to marry, sleeps around, thinks she's a radical feminist when she's only a spoiled brat, pretends to work at that rag Bart publishes. Is said to sleep with Vin Roberts, the creep who edits it, even though he's married and has two kids."

"In New York," I added for the record.

"Yeah. I guess I don't have to tell you what a jerk he is." Mike moved from his fourth finger to his thumb. "Bill, or Doctor Bill as they call him—not married yet but a young playboy doctor about town, I hear—is on the faculty of Northwestern and specializes in, let me see, skin diseases, Annie?"

"Dermatology?"

"Something like that. He's supposed to be a pleasant enough fellow, a little lazy maybe, but kind of bright. That's about it, not much of a picture, is it?"

"Indeed."

I might have walked into the Reilly Gallery that late morning and asked about any prominent Chicago family and heard a similar candid account of their strengths and weaknesses. On the subject of the movers and shakers in the city, Mike was both a reference librarian and an encyclopedia.

"Poor man," Annie interjected, "should have spent more time with his children and less on making money."

"Wait a minute." Mike switched to the little finger of his left hand. "There's one more. That tall kid who hangs

around with your teen choir. Seems to give the orders.
Plays basketball at St. Ignatius. They say she could get a
scholarship to college, she's so good. Cute too. What's her
name . . ."

"Elizabeth Marie Candace Cain, a.k.a. Candi Cain."

"Wasn't that the name of a stripper twenty years ago?"

"God forbid you should tell her that."

"She's OK, isn't she?"

"So it is said."

"She's a doll," Annie insisted. "A wonderful young
woman."

"Such is my observation," I agreed, though with such an
infallible judgment from an Irish wife and mother no
assent of the faithful was necessary.

Mike went on. "So one of them made it? Not bad for
these days, is it? I'm sorry, Blackie, if I sound negative.
Try as I might, I get that way with do-gooders, especially
if they're Irish."

"Turncoats?"

"You bet."

"And just a few moments ago, Mike Casey," his wife
said, nailing him, "you wanted more integrity."

She had violated her own rules this time by granting me
two more chocolate-chip cookies. Homemade, of course.

"Hoisted on my own petard." Mike extended his arm
around his wife's waist. "But seriously, integrity is not
bleeding-heart liberalism."

"Bart Cain lives like a man with many guilts for which
to atone," Annie observed.

"The worse of which," I said, nibbling with some
restraint on a cookie, "may well be his own success in the
traders' world and the next greatest his failure as a husband
and a father."

"You can never atone for those failures," Annie said firmly.

"God might, however"—and I went for the second extra cookie—"have given him a second chance."

"He doesn't deserve it," Annie insisted, her position apparently changing during the course of our conversation.

"Which of us does?"

"You're right, Blackie," she agreed. "Mike and I had second chances we didn't deserve either."

"God does not hold with deserve," I said. "Otherwise our species would have disappeared long ago . . . but Mike, do you or your associates know of any acute financial problems for any of these good persons?"

"O'Donnell always has financial problems, but as far as I know he's not into any deeper doo-doo than usual. I hear nothing about the others, but I'll check."

"Excellent. Now I fear must take my leave lest I miss lunch at the cathedral. It has been a long time since breakfast."

I departed among complaints that I was a bottomless pit.

CHAPTER 6

TWO SMALL CHILDREN, a big sister of about four and a little brother of about two and a half, stared at me as I sat on a bench in the shadow of the Water Tower—not the giant building which houses the shopping mall and the hotel, but the actual tower after which, despite the ignorance of this fact of most college-age young people, the mall is named.

Survivor of the Chicago Fire, I tell them. They want to know what fire, and are not impressed with the legend of Mrs. O'Leary's cow.

The children and I were having a wonderful time exchanging funny faces until their mother told them that they should stop bothering that cute little priest because he was trying to rest.

Rest comes after lunch. Sometimes.

Before lunch, in the Water Tower Park, the rector of the cathedral *thinks*, not always an easy task, especially at the end of a warm, hazy, sleepy September morning.

I had exaggerated both my hunger and my need to return to the cathedral. Under ordinary circumstances I am only moderately hungry—until food is placed before me. I should also note that, despite the complaints raised to God against the fundamental injustice of the phenomenon, I don't seem to put on weight no matter how many cinnamon buns and chocolate-chip cookies I eat. I contend the reason is that I burn up all the calories by the expenditure of mental energy.

There did not seem all that much to think about. After all, was there any evidence of crime?

Nonetheless, I was striving to burn up mental energy in the small and attractive little swath of grass, trees, and bushes that hides among the canyons of the Magnificent Mile at Chicago Avenue, not exactly an oasis of peace and quiet—there are few such in Chicago—but a pleasant site from which to watch the passing parade of wall-to-wall humanity. The cacophony of noise, human and automotive, becomes a background buzz for concentration. Across the avenue, behind the firehouse, was yet another small park. Indeed, if the gloriously reigning mayor had his way, parkland would stretch all the way to the lake and beyond to Navy Pier. Unfortunately, the governor had turned the land occupied by a long-since-useless armory over to the Museum of Contemporary Art, an institution I abominated, not because I am opposed to abstract art but because I wanted more park in my parish.

What else could I expect from a Republican governor?

The children having departed, I banished these thoughts and returned to the problem at hand.

All I had was a confused and troubled family, a lovely if haunted second wife, a rigid and presumably guilt-ridden father, a possible murder almost a half century ago, and three accidents which could be construed as attempted murder.

Oh, yes, and a ghost.

Who called on the telephone, shouted obscenities at the frightened wife, threatened the husband, and played an old record of "I'll Dance at Your Wedding."

Not much to go on.

Or rather, too much to go on. The long-forgotten disappearance of Mary Anne Haggerty was probably a red herring. The alleged accidents might well have been merely accidents. The "ghost" might just as well be a crank. The first two calls had come some time after the event. The third call occurred soon after the Waterford chandelier plunged to its expensive doom—from a ceiling underneath the master bedroom—but that might have been merely a happy coincidence. Indeed, the intended victim of the first accident could just as well have been Julia. And the falling chandelier could have hit Julia or Candi or Irene. Or anyone who happened to be in the apartment. Was not Julia a more likely target for someone who feared that she or her possible children would diminish the inheritance?

The Cain family was, excepting the colorful Candi, not all that much. So it often was with the offspring of great men. The sons feel unable to compete with him and give up, hating him for the implicit demand that they be as good as he was at what he did. The daughters, unable to sleep with their adored father, sleep with almost any male who happens along. Such outcomes were not inevitable. But if families like the Cains were to avoid them, it required a special kind of wife and mother. Or special luck, as in the case of Candi, a.k.a. Beth.

So almost any one of them could be driven round the bend by resentment of the new, young, and attractive bride, especially since she was the object of an affection from Bart Cain that they had never experienced. But granting for the sake of the argument that they or Tim O'Donnell or Vin Roberts wanted to dispose of Bart Cain and/or his new wife, why would they go about it in such an improbable fashion? And why try to resurrect poor Mary Anne Haggerty?

Because they had learned that Julia was superstitious? Were he/she/they trying to drive her back to her hamlet somewhere south of I-80?

And what about Julia Cain herself? Despite her troubled background she'd made a successful sexual conquest of an important and admired man and was quite satisfied with herself. Moreover, despite her verbal rejection of wealth, she had seemed to fit quite comfortably in her affluent East Lake Shore Drive setting. Should one credit her insistence that there be no change in her new husband's will, especially since she could easily outlive him by four decades? If one were a child threatened by such a rival, should one believe her protests of generosity?

What would become of the marriage? The passion in it might moderate or even disappear. Julia might overcome her diffidence and shyness and prove a tough and determined companion for her husband. Could he live with such a rival within his own house and his own bedroom? Would not the workstation be ultimately more soothing if not quite so consoling? Indeed, as I had insisted to her, God does not set age limits or age constraints on love, but your typical May and December, or June and September, marriage labors under more problems than does the ordinary attempt at permanent union between man and woman—and the latter is never particularly easy, either.

The Cain story was a problematic one. Most likely there was nothing in it other than your usual family tragedy, induced by a man who had established once again that there was no fool like an old fool. Most likely it would work itself out according to the ineluctable human dynamics that shape such follies. The deck seemed stacked against all of them, with the possible exception of Candibeth, a leprechaunish nickname I would be well advised to keep to myself. The most a priest can expect in such ménages is that he can nudge one or the other person in a direction away from tragedy.

But there was always a possibility that in addition to the ordinary tragedies which impinge on the human condition, there was some extraordinary tragedy that threatened the Cains. I would have to assume that such was the possibility. Even likelihood. I sighed loudly for no one's benefit but God's, and trudged back to Wabash Avenue and the cathedral rectory.

In the minute or two which remained before lunch, I phoned my eldest sibling.

"Doctor Murphy."

"Bishop Ryan."

"I don't know no Bishop Ryan," she insisted crisply.

"I'm not sure I do either. There are those who will tell you that he doesn't exist."

"Or is a figment of Sean Cronin's imagination," she said with a chuckle.

"Possibly . . . I recommended your husband to another potential patient this morning."

"A beautiful woman, I suppose."

"One could make the case. He has had some experience in dealing with them."

"Punk, you're on a roll, keep it up!"

Punk is (usually) an affectionate diminutive which my siblings use when addressing me.

"I must go to lunch," I said.

"God forbid anything interfere with that."

"Tell me about dermatologists."

"You need one?"

"Hardly."

"You want general information?"

"If there be such."

"Can't beat it, punk. Ten to four every day, no night

calls, no emergencies, steady supply of patients which is not affected by Republican recessions, you mostly write prescriptions and tell them come back. If you read the professional journals, you can keep up with latest wonder salves and do a reasonably good job. Not as lucrative as urology but as good a life as you can find in our profession. Time to enjoy the money."

"So I thought. My best to your family."

"We'll see you on Sunday?"

"Sunday?"

"Your birthday is September seventeenth. We're going to celebrate it on Sunday."

"My birthday?"

"You'll be forty-seven, remember?"

"Remarkable."

"You *will* be there?"

"Surely."

If I could remember to call up my calendar program on the 486 on Sunday morning.

CHAPTER 7

DUE TO THE intervention of a number of specially gifted members of the angelic cohort, I did remember to turn on my calendar program before the Sunday Eucharists, and hence did appear, among universal and enthusiastic rejoicing, at my birthday dinner at the Murphys' house on Longwood Drive. Actually it was a mid-afternoon buffet birthday party which coincided with the halftime of a match between the forces of light and the forces of darkness, the latter inappropriately claiming to be Saints and the former, of course, represented by our beloved if often inept Chicago Bears. Darkness won, alas, in a walk.

A bitter rain had begun as I was leaving the family feast. The world was turning unacceptably dark as the autumn equinox approached. It was of no avail to question the Almighty's arrangement of the tilt of the earth which produced our seasons. If I didn't like winter, I could always move to the tropics. I have always held that if the clergy are to be dispensed from their commitment to celibacy but only for a limited period of time, the best choice would be Sunday afternoons and evenings when rectories, even the normally O'Hare-like cathedral rectory, became as quiet and as hopeful as mausoleums.

I was not eager on this gloomy September Sunday to wrestle with faded microfiche printouts from the *Chicago*

Sun, The Chicago Times, The Chicago Daily News, The Chicago Herald Examiner, The Chicago Tribune, and *The Chicago American* for the spring and summer of 1947, most of which papers, some of them of great merit, are long since defunct. Nonetheless, allies of mine, sworn to secrecy, at the two surviving papers had combed their archives for accounts of the Mary Anne Haggerty case. I owed it to them, if not to Ms. Haggerty's purported shade, to find what I could about her mysterious disappearance. There was too much death this dark and dismal Sunday afternoon. Who needed more death? Maybe Mary Anne Haggerty was the lucky one. She'd escaped life while she was still young and hopeful.

The Cain women cornered me before evening Mass, admired my new Chicago Bulls jacket, autographed personally "For Father Blackie" by His Airness, and enthused about Great America.

"The Bobs was totally awesome, Father Blackie," Julia informed me.

"Candi is corrupting your speech," I noted.

"Daddy had a good time too," Candi chimed in. "He said the Bobs was nowhere near as good as the original. But I don't believe him."

"After a certain age in life," I said with a sigh, "nothing is as good as the original. But I would not have thought your father ever went to Riverview Amusement Park."

"Twice!" Candi held up her fingers. "Isn't that gross? Like totally?"

"Was Great America a den of sin as you were lead to believe such places were when you were a child?" I asked Julia.

"Expensive"—she smiled—"but fun. Of course I was raised to think anything that was fun was also sinful."

"Bart is not feeling well as a result?"

"He had a tummyache because he ate so much cotton candy!" Candi, though hardly of the cotton variety, trumpeted. "Wasn't that gross!"

"He went to Mass at another parish," Julia explained. "He said he felt much more at ease in church with poor people like those with whom he grew up and that I could represent him here at his proper parish."

Only he wasn't poor anymore and was slumming instead of bearing witness to the past, but I let that ride. I was prepared to forgive the man much because of his two lovely women. And the cotton candy: He must truly be in love.

"Will this substitution continue?" I asked Julia.

"Oh, I think he'll be back next Sunday. Anyway, I intend to keep coming."

"Should that happen for a reasonable period of time, I will see that you receive supplies of the only things the Catholic Church gives away free—holy water and collection envelopes."

The two of them giggled and bounced into the church.

I prayed to Herself that their happiness be protected from harm.

Bart Cain at Great America? Riding the Bobs? Eating cotton candy? Perhaps the omega point was closer than I had thought.

Not very likely.

And he had actually gone to Riverview twice. I had not suspected he'd lived such a frivolous youth.

On the way out of church after Mass, Julia whispered to me, "I've made an appointment to see Doctor Murphy. I want to smooth down the roller coaster of my life."

"Admirable."

I was, as one might note, not in the best of spirits. That always happens in late September and ought not to be taken seriously. But it was not a good time to explore a springtime disappearance forty-five years ago, in the springtime of the year and the springtime of young lives.

So with little of the proper dedication I climbed the steps of the gloomy cathedral rectory (there is an elevator, but on principle I refuse to use it), poured myself a modest glass of Bailey's Irish Cream, and began to explore the assumed end of the very short life of Mary Anne Haggerty of 7725 South Dobson.

LORETTO GIRL DISAPPEARS
AFTER PROM

Mary Anne Haggerty, 15, a sophomore at Loretto High School (Woodlawn), disappeared over the weekend after the St. Leo High School senior prom. Mary Anne's father, Hubert Haggerty of 7725 South Dobson, said that county and state police in Dowagic, Michigan, were searching for the girl and had begun to fear foul play. Haggerty blamed Mary Anne's date, Bartholomew Cain of 94th and Loomis, for the girl's disappearance. "If he couldn't protect our little girl, he shouldn't have invited her to the dance," Haggerty said.

Only a single paragraph at the bottom of one of the inside pages of the *Chicago Daily News*. Not much notice for the end of a life in which at one time there had been so much hope. God grant that she has found peace and happiness, I prayed.

Mary Anne Haggerty had, courtesy of the much more sensationalist Hearst *American,* not the mere fifteen minutes of fame allegedly allotted to us in the present time, but at least a day of fame.

Banner headlines, her grammar school graduation photo, blurred pictures of the Michigan State Police in hip boots dragging a small lake, a shot of her parents huddled in each other's arms, interviews with girls who knew her, a comment from the principal of Loretto Academy, even some quotes from other young men and women (there were no teenagers in those days) who had attended the prom.

DRAG LAKE FOR PROM
VICTIM'S BODY

Dowagic, Michigan. June 13.

Michigan State Police are dragging the bottom of LaGrange Lake near here for the body of Mary Anne Haggerty, a sophomore at Loretto Academy who disappeared on a prom date here last week. Mary Anne's grieving parents, Mr. and Mrs. Hubert Haggerty, are present at the side of the lake waiting for the recovery of their daughter's body.

Police in Dowagic and Chicago continue to question five young people who were with Mary Anne on the excursion: Bartholomew Cain, who was her date, and two other couples, Timothy O'Donnell, Jane Clark, Roger Collins, and Patricia Hurley, all from Chicago. According to the young people, Mary Anne went for a walk along the side of the lake about 8:00 last Saturday morning and was never seen again. She was, they say, in good spirits and had no reason to do harm to herself.

Patricia, at whose family cottage the young people were enjoying a picnic, told reporters that Mary Anne felt "just wonderful because the prom had been such fun. She wouldn't kill herself. I know she wouldn't. And Bart Cain was with us in the cottage all the time."

In a dramatic confrontation Mary Anne's mother pleaded with Bartholomew Cain to reveal where they had hidden Mary Anne's body. "You took her soul away from us," she said. "At least give us back her body."

Television would have made much more of Mary Anne Haggerty's disappearance than even the Hearst Empire could in those days. There would have been followups every night for a week and strong pressure on the police to arrest Bart Cain. As it was, the *American* lost interest in the alleged crime. Three days later a small story reported the end of the search:

POLICE ABANDON SEARCH
FOR MISSING GIRL
MEMORIAL SERVICE SET

As Michigan State Police abandoned efforts to recover the body of Mary Anne Haggerty, a missing high school sophomore, from LaGrange Lake near Dowagic, Michigan, plans were announced for a memorial service at St. Francis DePaula Church, 78th and South Dobson, tomorrow morning at 10:30. While Bart Cain, Mary Anne's date at the St. Leo High School prom the night before her disappearance, remains the prime suspect in her disappearance, police do not plan an immediate arrest. "Unless we find her body," Lt. Carl Klein of the Michigan State Police said, "we can't be sure there was a crime."

Two years later there was a brief note in the religion section of the *Daily News* which reported:

> The graduating class from Loretto Academy (Wood-lawn) will attend a Mass in remembrance of Mary Anne Haggerty, a classmate who disappeared in Michigan two years ago. Her body was never found and no one was ever arrested.

From 1949 to the present there was never another mention of Mary Anne Haggerty in the pages of any of the Chicago papers, save in the death notices of her parents, Hubert and Regina Haggerty. She was referred to in both obituaries as "the late Mary Anne." Their only child, presumably. In the many feature articles about Bart Cain, especially after his rise to prominence as a "Board of Trade activist liberal," there was no mention of her. And nothing in the papers to indicate that her body was ever found.

I pushed aside the stack of clips. Not much. I hadn't expected there would be much.

The bodies of many murder victims are never found, especially those of women who disappear after chance encounters with men. Mary Anne Haggerty could have encountered a group of deer hunters who raped and killed her and dumped her body into Lake Michigan or burned it in an incinerator. For women the world was and still is a jungle dense with rapists, molesters, batterers, torturers, incestuous relatives, and killers.

Did they hunt deer in the Dowagic area in those days? Was it the hunting season? Those were undoubtedly questions that the Michigan State Police had asked in 1947. By now the clues were all gone. Except for the young people. Were they covering up a crime? Kids that age are usually not very good at deceiving cops. I would try to get what I could out of Tim O'Donnell, though it was not evident whether he ever knew the difference between truth and falsehood. After some sort of crisis at the

Beverly Country Club, my sister Mary Kate had remarked, "Tim doesn't lie because it is in his interest to lie but because it is in his nature to lie."

1947—I was two years old then and could not remember the era at all. My parents, God be good to them (and given my mother's disposition She'd *better* be good to them), always said it was the time of a big change in America, from the Great Depression to the "Postwar World."

I picked up the front-page story in the *American*. Mary Anne Haggerty in her eighth-grade picture seemed a quiet, serious, wanly pretty little girl, hardly the kind who would appeal to Bart Cain. Eunice was at least lively, if empty-headed. Mary Anne's parents appeared short, diffident, confused, and very angry, he a clerk at Swift and Company, she a teacher in the Chicago public schools. The girl's classmates and teachers uttered the usual sort of pieties about a young person who has died prematurely.

"Everyone liked her."

"She was kind of quiet but fun to be with."

"A very able student, serious about her studies and her religion. Quite determined in her own way."

"Very close to her parents and a very loyal member of St. Francis DePaula."

As I remembered archdiocesan history, that was the parish that had lost five hundred families on May 1 back in the late fifties. The neighborhood was mostly apartments and two-flats. As soon as blacks began moving in, the whites deserted the neighborhood. Too much danger. Black crime.

There was, it turned out, crime in Dowagic, Michigan, too.

I reached for the current Archdiocese Directory. The parish no longer existed. Its records were in the Archdiocesan Archive Center. I could check them if I wanted to, and perhaps eventually I would have to.

I studied Bart Cain and Tim O'Donnell in the *American* picture of them. Bart had not changed all that much. He was tall, strong, and grim, his bushy hair still black instead of white as it was now. He did not look like the kind of young man who would break down and confess during the police third degree. Tim had, on the other hand, aged considerably. He had lost much of his hair since the picture and put on weight. His face was bloated from almost a half century of drinking and partying. Yet the same sly charm danced in the smile he had turned on the *American*'s photographer. A persuasive liar even then, no doubt. But did he have the strength to stand up to police beatings, routine in those days long before the *Miranda* decision?

Perhaps the cops had postponed the rubber-hose stuff until they had found a body.

I sighed and wondered how the demons had managed to sneak into my room and consume most of my Bailey's.

There was no reason to think that I could solve a mystery which had gone unsolved for almost a half century. Probably someone in the prom picnic group had killed Mary Anne Haggerty, perhaps by misadventure rather than intent. The young people had disposed of her body and then deceived the police. What other explanation was there?

But that didn't seem possible. A handful of kids carry off a well-nigh perfect crime? Not likely.

So she had been attacked and killed by a passing stranger or strangers. That seemed more likely. The "ghost" was a trick being played by someone who remembered the incident and was perhaps trying to blackmail Bart Cain. His indifference to the threat was based on a certainty of his own innocence. And Blackie Ryan, bishop-detective, was down a dark and blind alley.

My phone rang.

"Father Ryan."

"Flambeau here, though I doubt that Father Brown ever sounded so discouraged."

"He lived in a more innocent age, perhaps."

"I managed to talk to a retired cop today, a man who knew the Chicago cops who worked on the Mary Anne Haggerty case."

"Ah."

"He says that they were convinced Bart or Tim did it, maybe in some kind of accident. Fooling around with her and got too rough. But they could never prove a thing. No body and couldn't break the kids' story."

"Does not that seem on the face of it highly improbable? Would girls conspire to cover up the killing of another girl? Could relatively unsophisticated young people really deceive experienced cops?"

"I raised those questions with my friend. He said that Bart Cain was a tricky fellow even then. The cops who knew about the case were cynical about his rise to wealth and power and virtue."

"I see . . . what do you think?"

"Usually cops know what they're talking about when they say they have the criminal but lack the evidence to prosecute."

"Indeed."

"Sometimes they're kidding themselves because they can't crack a case."

"I understand."

"If you want my gut feeling, the Mary Anne Haggerty story falls into the latter category."

As I said my prayers that night, endeavoring to persuade

Herself that She should orient Her plans so that they would be congruent with my judgment of how the world should work, I prayed for the repose of the souls of Mary Anne Haggerty and her parents and all the kids who died while it was still the springtime of their hope. And for Julia and Elizabeth (one rarely uses nicknames when discoursing with the Almighty, though I doubt that She would mind) Cain, both of whom were now my pastoral responsibilities.

And because I try to be as good a Christian as the aforementioned Candi Cain, I even prayed for her father.

As I was falling asleep I saw a solution to the disappearance of Mary Anne Haggerty, an improbable but brilliant solution. It fit all the data.

Then, much later, while I was doubtless in rapid-eye-movement sleep, the phone rang again.

"Father Ryan."

"Candi Cain, Father Blackie." A tense and tearful voice. "Daddy is in intensive care here at Northwestern Hospital. He fell down the stairs and broke his arm and his leg and his head."

I tried to decide whether it was a dream or a conscious reality.

"How is he?"

It was real, all right.

"They say he might have a concussion. Uncle Bill— he's a doctor, you know—says he'll be all right but he took a nasty spill."

Candibeth was fighting back her tears.

"I understand."

"They're gonna keep him for a few days to make sure he doesn't have any serious internal injuries. Is that bad, Father Blackie?"

"Normal medical practice."

"Mom kind of lost it, you know. So I gotta be sensible. Right?"

"Is he still in the emergency room?"

"Like kind of. They put him in a room of his own down the hall. Mom's with him, but he's out of it too, like, babbling and moaning."

"I'll be right over, Candi Cain."

I sat on the edge of my bed and strove to organize my thoughts.

What was the solution to the Mary Anne Haggerty mystery that I had perceived in my hypnogogic state?

I had lost it.

Mary Anne Haggerty was probably the same age when she disappeared as Candi was today.

How was that relevant?

Then I punched in the Casey number.

"Reilly Gallery." Annie was distracted but not sleepy.

"Blackie. Is Mike there?"

"Where else would he be?" She sighed languidly.

"May I talk to him?"

"I suppose so," she said with a giggle.

I glanced at my alarm clock. Three A.M. and making love? Well, to each his own, in a manner of speaking.

"Yes, Blackie." My Flambeau tried to sound casual and failed.

"Sorry to wake you up."

"I was not exactly asleep."

"Patently. Would you contact your colleague the inestimable John Culhane . . ."

"The commander of Area Six Detective Division?"

"The very same. Tell him there was an attempted murder tonight in the apartment of Bart Cain at 207 East Lake Shore Drive. The intended victim is none other than Bart Cain himself. He is presently in the emergency room at Northwestern Hospital, I gather under observation for possible internal injuries. It is imperative that Commander Culhane not know the source of this information."

"Got it."

"Sorry to have interrupted."

"Nothing that can't be resumed."

"Patently."

CHAPTER 8

"REALLY, BILL," BART Cain Junior whined, "I'm most upset that you bothered us. You know how sensitive Lourdes is to crisis calls at night. This incident is not so serious that it could not have waited till morning."

"Look, Junior," Bill Cain, M.D., responded patiently, "our father took a terrible spill. Everyone else in the family is here. You'd have been furious if I didn't call you."

"As I say, it could have waited till morning. I assume he'll still be in the hospital then."

Perhaps the only trait I truly have in common with Chesterton's priest is that I easily escape notice. Particularly when I put my mind to it. I am so undistinguished and ineffectual-looking that I am often virtually invisible. The little man who wasn't there. You could enter an elevator on which I was riding and barely notice me.

So I was the little priest who wasn't there during the quarrel between the Cain brothers in the corridor outside Bart Cain's hospital room.

Bart Junior and Bill in physical appearance resembled their mother more than their father. Both were relatively short and slight with lean, almost pinched faces and thin sandy hair and high foreheads. But there the resemblance ended. Though he was only a couple of years older than Bill, Bart Junior looked at least a decade older than his brother, mostly because a petulant frown had imprinted its line on his face and his stomach had already begun to protrude. Doctor Bill, on the other hand, smiled easily, spoke lightly, and was in excellent physical condition. He was wearing a tuxedo, which suggested that he had been somewhere with someone when he had learned of his father's accident, most likely from my good friend Candibeth.

I must stop imagining that foolish name.

At any rate, I made myself invisible and listened to the brothers Cain argue. Bill was sitting on a metal hospital chair, relaxed, indifferent, amused. Junior was striding back and forth, fretful, irate, troubled, anxious.

"What happened?" Junior demanded.

Bill shrugged lightly. "They were in bed, presumably engaged in you-know-what. The bell rang, he went down the steps to answer it, still tumescent I would imagine. He fell and broke his right forearm, his left ankle, and banged up his head. Perhaps a light brain concussion."

"He could have been killed!"

"Don't seem so eager, brother dear."

"Did she push him down the stairs?"

"Possibly. If she did, he's not likely to remember it."

"He's besotted with her!"

"Obviously. I suppose I can see why, though she's certainly not to my taste. However, the bump on the head will effectively blank out his memory."

"Who else was in the house?"

Bill lived his hands negligently. "The brat, of course."

Careful, buster. That's my Candibeth you're talking about!

It might be argued that I was blatantly eavesdropping on a highly personal and confidential conversation. I deny that flatly. First of all, I was not hiding under any eave. I was in fact standing by an elevator bank. Secondly, if one proposes to have a confidential family conversation in a hospital corridor, one ought to be alert to the ineffectual little priest standing nearby waiting for an elevator.

"Who rang the doorbell?" Junior turned fiercely on his brother.

Bill raised his hands again. "Apparently no one. The brat says that she looked in the elevator and there was no one there. The doorman said that he had not rung."

"Our ghost again, huh?"

Bill nodded. "According to the brat, there was a call from that rather peculiar spirit."

"Crazy!"

"Obviously."

"She did it!"

"The brat? Come now, brother, let's be realistic."

"The woman!"

"The fair Julia?" Bill raised an eyebrow. "What does she have to gain by doing that? He has not changed his will yet. Later on, maybe. Not now."

"Maybe he *has* changed the will."

"Not likely. Dad is not that impulsive."

"Except when he married her."

"The hormones finally caught up with him." Bill smiled pleasantly. "Not too strange after a life of repression, is it?"

"We can't let the police or the press find out," Junior insisted.

"Come on, brother, be real. Even if my colleagues here could be persuaded not to report a dubious accident, which is improbable, the police and the press will certainly find out. Dad is too prominent to keep it a secret."

"Lourdes will be frantic."

"Then you must reassure her."

"Will we have to talk about that terrible dinner party?"

"How can we conspire not to? Even if you and I agree to try to cover it up, do you think Jenny could keep her mouth shut? Or those two in there?" Bill nodded towards the door of a room about five yards down the corridor. "Not on your life!"

"Speaking of Jenny, where is she?"

"Who knows? I called her apartment. Naturally she wasn't there. Which of her bed partners was she with tonight? Who cares!"

"The stupid magazine isn't worth worrying about!"

"I think Dad-o agrees. One nice result of the new wife. Only Jenny and Vin Roberts give a damn about it."

"I do too," Junior shouted. "It humiliates me every week. That last editorial that Catholic grammar schools should hand out condoms to seventh- and eighth-graders was a disgrace! It put Lourdes in bed for two days. We can't face our friends as long as that rag humiliates us!"

"Easy, bro." Bill raised a hand to indicate the need for restraint. "There's no need to tell the whole hospital about our family fights."

Junior glanced around nervously. But despite his ardent if conservative, not to say reactionary, Catholicism (he was a member of the Opus Dei group), he did not see the humble auxiliary bishop who stood, a picture of dull stupidity, by the elevator bank.

"You weren't very strong in your arguments against it," Junior grumbled.

"Why should I be? In my circle of friends no one reads it, no one even knows about it. What's its circulation? Twenty-five thousand at the most? Why should it trouble me?"

"It's eating away at *our* money, that's why!"

"In trivial amounts . . . as I said, Dad-o seems embarrassed by it too. Humping a woman every night seems to have weakened his ideology, which can't be all bad. But he doesn't want to disappoint Jenny and he feels that he has made a commitment. Maybe the woman can change that."

"Do you think he's really banging her *every night?*"

"I think you could bank on it, bro."

"No fool like an old fool . . . is he conscious?"

"In and out."

"So I'd better go in?"

"It might be wise. I warn you, Julia and the brat are with him."

"Well." Junior hesitated. "I suppose I should. He is my father, after all."

"I'm glad you remembered."

"By the way." Junior checked himself as he was about to end the conversation. "Did you call Uncle Dave?"

"Why bother? That little bitch he's married to wouldn't let him come to the hospital anyway."

"He *is* a poor excuse for a man."

Junior walked hesitantly down the corridor. Behind his back, Doctor Bill shook his head and chuckled. It was time for the nearly invisible priest to become totally invisible. I boarded the open elevator and rode up to the top. When I came down again, Junior had returned from the hospital room.

"He looks like hell!"

"No need to worry about him, bro," Bill said ironically. "He's going to make it this time."

"Could he have had a stroke?"

"Maybe. They'll do an EEG and a brain scan tomorrow, but I wouldn't count on it. The old fool was probably so eager to get his thing back into that woman's pussy that he ran down the stairs in the dark."

"I gotta get back to Lourdes."

"One word of caution, bro." Doctor Bill raised a

warning hand. "It would be best when the police come to ask questions if you tell the truth to the best of your ability about the dinner party. You and I have nothing to lose by doing so."

"Lourdes will die if they pull up to our house in a squad car!"

"I doubt it. Presumably they'll be discreet in Kenilworth . . . and, oh, one more thing. Be prepared for the story about the Haggerty ghost to come out."

"Dear God, no!"

"Console yourself with the thought that the story will embarrass both Dad-o and the woman."

"Do you really think there's a ghost?" Junior sounded incredulous—and frightened.

"Certainly not," Doctor Bill responded easily. "Someone with a grudge against Dad-o is having a little fun. Why don't you ask your Opus Dei priests about ghosts?"

"They tell us that there are really demons at work in the world!"

"I'm sure they do."

After Junior entered an elevator, I walked up to Doctor Bill. "Is it all right to go into your father's room?" I asked meekly.

"Sure, Father." He smiled indifferently. "Despite his appearance, he'll be all right."

"I'm glad to hear that."

"Nice of you to come by at this hour of the night."

Like I say, I am virtually invisible on certain occasions. Perhaps, dare I say it, like Father Brown's mailman.

"Father Blackie!" The two women of the family, both in jeans and sweaters, embraced me enthusiastically when I, no longer nearly invisible, entered the room.

"He looks like totally awful," Candibeth informed me. "But the doctors say he'll be OK."

"He's in and out of consciousness." Julia Cain's voice was strained with worry. "Maybe he'll recognize you."

"Doubtless."

At the side of the bed, I donned my tiny stole, put the sacred oils on the bedside table, and prepared for my ritual.

Bart Cain was a mess—left arm in a sling, right leg suspended in traction, and a bandage covering most of his head. Some fall.

"Bart Cain," I announced in my best Judgment Day voice, "Bishop Ryan here. You are not going to die, but I've brought the oils along for the Sacrament of the Sick. OK?"

Naturally he opened his eyes.

I held up the oils.

He nodded his head. He might even have smiled. Obviously the blow to his head had deprived him of some of his character.

So we went through the ritual, Julia holding one hand and Candibeth the other. The latter answered all the prayers efficiently, and the former joined in where she could, though Protestant that she was, she created some confusion with the doxology at the end of the Lord's Prayer. Bart Cain answered some of the prayers, and then seemed to fall peacefully asleep.

Strange man, I thought. Traditionalist on rituals and the sacraments and still contributing to Free Choice campaigns. It would be interesting to know how he reconciled these positions. And how he'd gotten that way.

Candibeth hugged me again. "I'm so glad you came, Father Blackie. He feels better and so do I."

"That's what priests are for."

Even if it is arguable that they ought not to listen to conversations outside of a sick room.

"Bishops too?" Julia asked.

"On occasion."

"Bishops are priests too," Candibeth insisted.

The leprechaun in me took over. "I have a totally excellent new nickname for you, young woman. A transition between the present and the future one."

"What is it?" she demanded, eyes bulging with curiosity.

"I don't think I will tell you just yet."

"You totally have to tell me!"

"Well . . . it's Candibeth!"

"Ohhhh! That's totally awesome! I mean it's really excellent! Bodacious! You're the only one that can use it, Father Blackie. And you too, of course, Mom. And maybe Brigie Devine. But *no* one else!"

Except the whole student body at St. Ignatius High School.

"Candibeth," Julia said gently, "your father seems to be sleeping peacefully now. Will you watch him for a few moments while I talk to Bishop Ryan out in the corridor?"

"Sure, Mom. Except he's still Father Blackie."

"I stand corrected." She hugged the fifteen-year-old.

"That was a beautiful ceremony, Father Blackie," Julia said when we were in the corridor. "He was so troubled and now he's so calm."

"On rituals, Julia Cain, we're pretty hard to beat. In some other areas at the present we are somewhat deficient."

"And that new name—outrageous as it is—was just what the kid needed."

"I note that Candibeth now calls you Mom."

"It changed on the way over here. I hope I don't destroy that relationship." She was the shy, uncertain woman who had emerged from the swimming pool a couple of days earlier.

"The sun will set over Lake Michigan first."

"Do you believe me now, Father Blackie?"

"About the ghost? I remain skeptical."

The vision I had seen as I went to sleep of a solution to the Mary Anne Haggerty mystery teased my brain and slipped away.

"Who else could have pushed Bart down the stairs? I didn't. Candi certainly didn't. There was no one else in the house."

"He fell."

"I'm sure he didn't. He turned on the light. He'd had only one glass of wine at supper. Bart is not a clumsy man."

"Even the unclumsy trip occasionally."

"And *she* called again."

"She?"

"Mary Anne Haggerty."

"At the apartment?"

"Here at the hospital. As soon as we were in the emergency room. Even before Candi could phone the family."

"I see."

"I'm scared, Father Blackie." She shivered as she had done at poolside. "There's something very evil going on."

"Possibly."

"There was no one at the elevator door to the penthouse, and the doorman told Candi no one had come in downstairs. Yet the bell rang."

Aha, yet another locked-room mystery. Only this was a locked-penthouse mystery.

"How many times?"

"Three times, Father Blackie. Three short rings, like

someone in a hurry. You remember how the master bedroom is at the head of the stairs? I saw Bart go down the stairs, and just as the stairway curved out of sight, I saw him fall. I raced down and he was all in a heap at the foot of the stairs and blood was oozing out of a big cut on his head. I thought he was dead. Then Candi, bleary-eyed from sleep, came running down and felt his pulse. She called an ambulance. I guess I was hysterical."

"Not without reason . . . there had been a family dinner party?"

"They're terrible events, Father. Everyone for some obnoxious reason in formal dress. Bart likes to think of them as family policy meetings. He introduced me to them at a family dinner. It was like walking into a deep freeze."

"Ah . . . was there any matter of family policy subject to discussion last night?"

"That stupid magazine *Common Sense* or whatever it's called."

"*Common Truth.*"

"Whatever. Only poor, disturbed Jenny wants him to continue the subsidy. Bill and Junior are against it. So is Tim O'Donnell. Candi doesn't much care. I kept my mouth shut."

"I see. Was Vin Roberts there?"

"That terrible man? No way. He's not family. Jenny wanted to bring him, but Bart absolutely forbade it."

"Was there any resolution to the discussion?"

"Bart said he'd take the matter under advisement."

"Did he ask you your opinion, after the others left?"

"Naturally. I told him it was a silly magazine and there were a lot better ways he could help the poor."

"And he said?"

"He seemed to agree. But he feels he made a commitment to bring 'intelligent Catholic discussion' to Chicago.

The truth is that he feels he's failed Jenny and he doesn't want to disappoint her."

It was now of considerable importance that I make my way rapidly to the Cain penthouse.

"I'll be back tomorrow afternoon, Julia." I removed my stole, something I do not usually remember to do. "Don't worry, all will be well."

"Will the police come?"

"Probably."

"What should I tell them?"

"Only the truth, Julia. You have nothing to fear from the truth."

"Even about the ghost?"

"Only if the issue arises."

The police would suspect her, of course. It wouldn't help if she seemed a crazy woman who babbled about evil spirits.

I was now convinced that there would be hard times ahead for all the Cains, Julia more than the others.

I did not realize then just how hard the times would be for her.

CHAPTER 9

I PARKED IN a no-parking zone on East Lake Shore Drive. My 1955 blue Chevy Impala has never once been ticketed within the boundaries of the cathedral parish, conceivably because the vanity license plate informs the world that the driver is "BLACKI."

I defend this form of clerical privilege on the grounds that a) I have never asked for it, and b) I'm perfectly prepared to pay such fines as the city might impose.

To which my sister Eileen (the federal judge) snorts, "Chicago cops ticket the legendary Bishop Blackie! Punk, you gotta be kidding!"

Dawn was only a couple of hours off but its arrival would not be noticed. Rain continued to drench the city and a bitter northeast wind whipped in off the lake. Surf was pounding the retaining wall of the drive, across the street from the Cains' apartment building, a dirty silver foam against the dismal sky of quickly scudding low clouds.

"They're over at the hospital, Father," the doorman told me. "The police are upstairs. They had a warrant."

"Ah. I think I'll go up anyway."

There was no Irene to block my way this time. Only John Culhane, Commander of District Six.

"I thought you might show up, Bishop." He greeted me at the door.

"Indeed."

My Irish indirect communication with him had not deceived him. Nor was it intended to do so.

John Culhane is a tough and honest cop maybe about fifty, in excellent physical condition, medium height, with glasses and neatly combed brown hair. Smart as they come. A half-dozen of his detectives were poking around taking pictures with Polaroid cameras and dusting for fingerprints. As I had intended they should.

"It could be one of your locked-room mysteries," he said as he followed me to the staircase.

I peered at the supports about halfway up. Sure enough. Even my myopic eyes, aided only to some extent by glasses which my siblings' offspring have been known to compare to Coke bottles, could see the small indentations in the elaborately carved and varnished pillars on either side of the staircase caused by a thin wire.

"You have found the wire?"

"Nope."

"No!"

"We've hunted all over, Father," said a very bright young sergeant who seemed assigned to trail the commander.

"Fascinating."

"We haven't talked to the family yet. I suppose Bart Cain will raise hell that we got in so quickly."

"Doubtless. And you will respond that you obtained a warrant even at this late hour of night because you had heard a rumor of attempted murder and wanted to inspect the crime scene while the evidence was still fresh."

"How did you know we'd argue that way?" Commander Culhane grinned.

"And you found?"

"Not a lot, I'm afraid, Bishop. The doorman on duty

now came on at twelve. His predecessor told him everyone had left the penthouse at eleven-thirty after a dinner. We'll check that, of course. First thing he knew was when the ambulance pulled up to the door about twelve-fifteen. He gathered that Mr. Bart Cain fell down the stairs sometime before he came on. Answering a doorbell. Which he says was not from downstairs. There is another one, as you may have noticed, at the door from which one enters into the apartment from the private elevator."

"Between eleven-thirty and twelve-fifteen?"

"Right. He said that Mrs. Julia Cain and Miss Elizabeth Cain left with the ambulance in a state of shock approaching hysteria."

"Both of them?"

"The wife anyway . . . since then no one has entered or left the penthouse. No one was here, needless to say, when we arrived."

"Indeed."

"So at first blush, it looks like the wife or the daughter, or the two of them together, waited till everyone had gone home from their family dinner, laid the trap, rang the doorbell, which caused Bart Cain down to answer the door, heard him fall, removed the thin wire, and called the ambulance."

"I see. And where did the wire go?"

"Presumably they took it with them. Maybe dropped it in a trash can at the hospital."

"And you believe this scenario?"

"Not for a minute, not without a lot more evidence."

"Ah. And what are the grounds for your skepticism?"

"How do they fool Bart Cain while they are tying the wire? They have to do it after the guests have left and after he is in bed. Why do a daughter and a stepmother conspire to kill or maim a father? And why this technique? Are there not easier ways of disposing of an unwanted man? There's every reason based on the evidence of their rooms that all three were in bed before the accident, though we can't be certain of that. How could they be sure that Bart Cain would not tell his wife to answer the bell? He must have heard the bell himself or he would not have left his bed. If his wife was in bed with him, who rang the bell? The girl? Maybe, but she couldn't be certain which one would come down the stairs."

"If it were the stepmother and she knew about it, would she not be able to avoid the wire?"

"Sure, but all of this presupposes a conspiracy between the two. It would take both of them, working in close and delicate cooperation, to carry this off. It might be the kind of thing that two women would cook up. But why? We need a very big motive. Does the wife inherit anything? She's new, isn't she?"

"Yes."

"We'll have to find out what the arrangements are—if we get that far. It's a pretty thin case, as thin as the wire must have been."

"Is it likely that Bart Cain will remember what happened?"

"He got hit on the head, didn't he? Not very likely. I'm not sure we could prove anything to a jury. One way or another."

"But what are the alternatives?"

The young sergeant took over. "Someone else was in the apartment, stretched the wire across the staircase, rang the bell, and then, well, disappeared."

"Fascinating."

"So unless we think the stepmother and daughter did it together, and I will believe that only when I see a motive, we have one of your locked-room mysteries. Or in this case a locked-penthouse mystery."

"Indeed." I could see even then a solution to the locked-room puzzle. What I could not see then was which one of the various men and women with motives might have plotted it.

Or who the would-be killer wanted to kill.

Or whether there was in fact a serious intent to kill anyone.

"We'll see what we can dig up tomorrow. Cain didn't die and if he refuses to admit there was an attempt on his life, we can hardly go ahead with nothing more than two fresh wire marks on a staircase."

"Indeed . . . the patio?"

"The door was locked when we arrived, which doesn't prove anything, does it?"

"Not in the least . . . there must be a second elevator."

"Sure, a service elevator from the kitchen. It is locked here in the apartment and there is an alarm on the bottom. Which was operational."

"The doormen must be questioned carefully."

"Yeah. I'm not sure that the kind of man they hire for a building like this could be corrupted. Maybe, but I kind of doubt it."

"In the case of another family would you consider arresting the two women?"

"Maybe. If someone was actually killed. Especially if we could find a motive. And could explain to a jury's satisfaction exactly how they pulled it off. As it is, all we have are two new marks on the staircase."

"And a puzzle," the young sergeant added, "about what happened to the wire."

"Precisely."

"I suppose we'll go over to the hospital and ask some questions of the two women," Culhane said.

"That would be prudent," I agreed.

"You sound like you think they did it, Bishop."

I smiled benignly. "I wouldn't want to prejudice you either way, Commander."

I was quite certain that they had not. But by forcing Commander Culhane to lay out his case against them I had learned that, while he was by training and experience inclined always to suspect the closest relatives in a crime, he knew just how weak the case against Julia and Candi would appear to the media and eventually to a jury. Especially since, as I knew and he didn't yet, either one of them might have a motive but not the two of them together.

The question remained as to which one of the possible criminals had the imagination and the agility to execute such a locked-room caper.

And why bother? As the commander had said, it was a highly problematic way to dispose of an unwanted husband or father or benefactor. It might have worked, and then again it might not have worked. In fact, it did not work. Why would a killer, even a clever one, want to choose so uncertain a means of murder?

There was an obvious answer to that question too. But it took me a long time to see it.

So there were three puzzles: a) why such an odd method of mayhem? b) how did the mayhem maker escape from the locked room? and c) how did the ghost of poor Mary Anne Haggerty fit into the story—if it really did?

CHAPTER 10

"I APPRECIATE ALL you do for the kids, Bishop Ryan."
Bart Cain tried to shift in his bed and winced with pain.
"Elizabeth in particular. I never did trust those Jesuits over
at St. Ignatius. I'm glad she's close to the Church and to a
priest who respects women."

"Given my family, I don't have much choice," I said.

He tried to grin, and winced again.

Bart Cain was a young sixty-three—tall, broad, and as
hard of body as I thought him to be of mind and soul,
though today I was no longer sure of the latter two
dimensions of his selfhood. His face was square and solid
and gently marked, his eyes the deepest albeit a frigid
blue, his lips wide and supple, the kind of lips which in a
more perfect world would have been usually shaped in a
radiant smile. Dye his thick white hair black and you
might take fifteen years off his age.

Would women find him attractive? Beyond a doubt,
especially because his seeming immunity to their charms
made him an even more appealing prize. He radiated raw
physical energy and power, strong hints of powerful sexual
energies and needs. He would be a dominating and
demanding lover, yet also a sensitive one. What would he
be like in bed, a woman might well wonder, perhaps very
well aware that curiosity was a weak link in her armor.

That his marriage had been less than happy was not unknown and would have made him to many women an especially interesting prize; and that he had lived in monk-like celibacy since his wife's death added to the spice of potential conquest. So too would his reputation and his fortune. What would one have to lose by attempting to seduce him? So some had certainly tried and failed. Not only had not gotten to first base, but had not even gotten out of the batter's box.

So he would fall victim to a most improbable woman, in his head and loins, before any response from her—a shy and fragile nerd from downstate who had tried to shut off all her sexual appeal. Until she found him devouring her with those Arctic blue eyes.

God is surely a comedian. Or, if you will, a comedienne.

It had been a fruitful morning. I had visited the school, arranged for a marriage, presided over a staff meeting, instructed four couples whose children would be baptized on Sunday, signed checks, and preached at a funeral. I had also brought Communion to Bart Cain and he had begged me to come back after lunch.

Just before lunch I had received two important phone calls relating to *l'affaire Cain*.

The first had been from Mike the Cop.

"Like you said, I've checked into the background of Julia Ross Cain."

"Indeed!"

"She's a real hayseed. From a small farm at the end of the road thirty miles from Centralia."

"That, I believe, is south of I-80."

"Way south of I-80. Even south of I-70. She belonged to a rabble-rousing conservative wing of the Methodists. Went to the local high school and then on to Eastern Illinois at Charleston, a notable center of student rest."

"Almost a Hoosier."

"Hey, you do know a little geography . . . she majored in math with minors in finance and graphics design. Came to Chicago after graduation, shared an apartment with some friends from Eastern, got a job as a typist at the CBOT, and went on for a masters in math at Chicago Circle."

"University of Illinois at Chicago."

"Right. Played around with some charts in her lunch hour and one of the traders noticed. Signed her on. Even if it is witchcraft, she's very good at it and earned impressive money. Went to work at B.T. Cain and Sons for a cool hundred and fifty big ones."

"Remarkable. Twice as much as the mayor earns and almost as much as the superintendent of the public schools."

Bart Cain did not give money away foolishly. Small wonder he noticed the dowdy chartist when she came to work for him.

"Made some smart investments, as you might expect, and can live comfortably for the rest of her life. Had a small apartment in Lincoln Park. Shy. Timid. Almost reclusive. Lived quietly. Read books and went to concerts by herself. Occasional date. Nothing ever serious. Has all the courses for a doctorate in math. Working on a dissertation. As clean as a snowstorm on her native farm."

"Truly remarkable."

"I've passed all this on to John Culhane."

"Prudent."

"Annie says you are not even to think that the sweet little thing might be a criminal."

"That makes it official."

"More about David Cain. He's doing pretty well at Dreyfus, but they took an enormous cut in family income

when he left Cain and Sons and he lost all his pension
rights and benefits. His wife, Eleanor—née Leonora
Rigali—had to give up her life as a River Forest woman
of leisure and go back to work so they would be able to put
their four kids through college. He's a quiet man, hardly
belongs on the floor anyway. She's the fiery one in the
family. Two of the kids are at St. Ignatius, the other two at
St. Luke's. Good kids, apparently."

"Are they in the will?"

"Bart is supposed to have cut Dave out when they had
their fight. But the nieces and nephews apparently would
still inherit something."

"Ah."

The second call had been from an active as opposed to
a retired cop. Perhaps a future commissioner instead of a
past one.

"I never saw two more improbable suspects, Bishop,"
John Culhane had told me.

"Indeed."

"The stepmother and daughter both say that the stepmother normally answers the doorbell. According to Julia
Ross Cain, she and her husband chatted for a few minutes
after their guests had left, then went up to bed. They
peeked into Elizabeth Cain's room to make sure she had
not been upset by a family argument. She was sound
asleep. Then Julia and Bart Cain went to bed. The bell
rang. Bart Cain said one of the guests had probably forgot
something. He'd answer the door because Julia was so
sleepy. Probably pretty far gone in heat if you ask me."

"Nothing wrong with that."

"I sure as hell hope not. Anyway, he left the bedroom
door open and she saw him fall and ran after him. The kid
was right after her."

"Neither of them fell?"

"No. Maybe Bart Cain broke the wire. The cuts indicate it was very thin."

"A reasonable story."

"I checked it out with Bart Cain this morning. He doesn't remember the fall, but he does remember everything up to the doorbell and his decision to answer it. Doctors say he was pretty incoherent till just before I saw him, so he couldn't have cooked up the story with his wife and daughter, not that they showed any awareness that they might be suspects. So they're in the clear and I think she may have been the target instead of her husband."

"Arguably."

"What's this about a ghost?"

"That came up?"

"I asked about any previous attempts. Three accidents, in two of which the wife could have been the intended victim. The kid spilled the beans about the ghost. Bishop, that's plain crazy. Who was this Mary Anne Haggerty anyway?"

"I believe our mutual friend Superintendent Casey has some information. I will fax up to you some news clippings I have gathered."

"You've been into it already, huh?"

"Milord Cronin does not like ghosts."

"I shouldn't wonder. Well, I don't think much will come of it, but I'll see if I can dig up anything."

Lots of luck, I had thought as I gathered the clippings to bring to our fax in the office downstairs.

After lunch I had ventured back to Northwestern University Hospital for my third encounter in twenty-four hours with Bart Cain. I must confess that my respect for him had risen considerably since I had heard the details of his romance with Julia. He had had to discard a vast number of inhibitions and powerful walls of defense to permit the romance to begin and continue. Hence I was much more interested in him as a human person than I had ever been before.

Perhaps a little more hopeful about his salvation. Not his eternal salvation, which, I assumed, was in the hands of God's love, a love that is even more irresistible than that of Julia, but his final success as a human being.

"Julia"—he spoke slowly, choosing his words as he went—"says you've been very good to her too. I truly appreciate that."

If he had reached for his checkbook at that moment, I would have torn up whatever he gave me. He gave us or tried to give us checks like older women of a generation or two ago would jam five-dollar bills into our hands.

"She's had a very hard life. I don't know the details and I don't want to know them unless she wants to tell me. But she needs help—not for me, God knows. I couldn't ask for any more from a wife. But for herself."

"Possibly."

"I'm not sure that I'm all that good for her either." He closed his eyes as if infinitely weary. "I'm too old, too rigid, too set in my ways. If I had better control of my emotions I wouldn't . . . well, I wouldn't have pursued her."

"You gotta be out of your mind," I said flatly.

"Pardon?" He opened his eyes in surprise.

"If you were anything but a stubborn, guilt-ridden, self-hating, South Side shanty Irish fool, you'd see that you're her savior."

"I don't know what you're talking about," he said crossly. "She was an employee whom I sexually harassed and seduced and forced to marry me. She's terrified of me. She was the first day I saw her at the office and has been ever since."

"Are you turned on by women's fears of you?"

He closed his eyes. "I don't know, Bishop. I don't know. I didn't think I was that kind of man . . . but she, well, I suppose the only word to use is enchanted me from the very beginning. I wanted her and I took her even though I knew better . . . I've wanted women before, been seriously tempted to take them. I knew I had the power and prestige to do so. Terrible temptations. But this made all the others seem mild."

"Ah."

"I hardly noticed her when she came to work for us. Not a woman worth noticing, it seemed. Then one day I saw her walk by my office. God knows she wasn't being a temptress. Doesn't know how. It was like someone had kicked me in the gut. I was bowled over. I couldn't think of anything else but getting my hands on her. It wasn't just a temptation. It was an obsession. I had to have her. I knew I could have her. I would stop at nothing, absolutely nothing to take her . . ."

His voice trailed off in weary dismay as he recounted his, as he saw it, fall from grace.

And as I saw it, his fall into grace.

"She didn't respond in kind?"

"I didn't give her much choice."

"And you feel proud of your conquest and guilty that you don't feel guilty."

"You know too goddamned much," he snarled.

He winced again, his sudden anger stirring up the pain in his cracked ribs.

"I'm sorry, Bishop," he said more calmly. "That was out of line. You're right. I'm intoxicated by everything about her, drunk on lust for her. I can't get enough of her. I'm not sure that it's right for a man to want a woman that way, even if it's his wife, especially a man my age."

"Do I hear the great Catholic liberal saying that?"

"I'm a mess, Bishop. If I weren't on all these painkillers I wouldn't be spilling my guts this way."

"Indeed."

"All right, damn it," he said softly. "I am proud that I saw what a prize she was. I'm proud that I bedded her. I'm proud every time we make love. I laugh with joy that she's mine. I've never done anything so manly in my whole life. I'm out of control and I don't care. My whole life is a shambles. I don't know what I believe in anymore. I've lost my principles. I feel like I'm a hypocrite and a sham. Yet I'm gloriously vain about my conquest. I'm a terrible sinner."

Oh, yes, he'd become very interesting, had this Bart Cain.

"Nonsense."

"Would you believe me if I told you that I raped her the first time?"

"Nope."

"What!"

"You didn't rape her."

"I took her by force," he groaned.

"She resisted?"

"No."

"She fought back?"

"No."

"She was unresponsive."

"God damn it, no!"

"She protested afterwards that you had forced sex upon her?"

"No," he murmured. "No, no, no."

"Bartholomew Theodore Cain, you are quite incapable of rape. Until now you have also been incapable of abandoned passion. That seems to have changed. For which you should thank God."

He was silent for several minutes.

"I'm too old to change."

"You have it wrong. The whole point of this discussion is that you changed because of Julia's thoroughly benign influence on you and you want to change back and you can't."

"Why is she afraid of me?"

"I don't know that she is."

"Whenever I see her looking at me, there is terror in her eyes."

"Of what?"

"Of me, what else?" He stiffened with a sudden jab of pain.

"Of pleasure, of abandon, of salvation?"

"I'm not her savior."

"Yes, you are."

"For example"—he tried to calm down—"I wake up in the middle of the night with an idea for a position on the Singapore exchange. I access Globex with my computer and make the trade. I know she's watching me. She probably figures that when I'm through with the trade I'm going to want her. I turn around. She's watching me, all right, for all practical purposes naked, and there's terror in her eyes."

"And that turns you on even more?"

"I already said it did."

"It is not remotely possibly that what she sees in you which creates the appearance of terror also turns her on?"

"I don't know."

"The fact that she watches you, as you say, for all practical purposes naked, does not suggest that this might be the case?"

He sighed and closed his eyes again. "I'm not so stupid as not to have thought of that."

"Indeed."

"Now I suppose you will try to tell me that she seduced me?"

"And if she had, how does that thought affect you, one that you are also not so stupid as not to have had?"

He began to speak, and then shut up.

"We're playing truth here?" he asked.

"So I would assume."

"It would flatter the hell out of me."

"So the issue, always phony, of who ravished whom is now revealed to be phony?"

"I'm too old to be ravishing women, Father Blackie, even if they want to be ravished."

So I had come to be Father Blackie and he had come to the truth or at least the beginning of truth.

"You continue to miss the point of the discussion." I jabbed my finger at him.

"Which is?"

"That you have already become not only a ravisher, but an extremely competent and astonishingly successful ravisher of a shy, frightened, and sexually inexperienced woman."

"I don't want to think that about myself."

"Patently, but why not?"

"Because then," he said with a gulp, "I've been wrong about myself all my life."

"Aha!" I shouted triumphantly.

"Damn you," He did grin this time, and ignored the wince of pain that came with it.

"My life is a mess, Father Blackie. I've tried to live by what I thought were good solid Catholic principles all my life and now I'm beginning to think I was all wrong."

"All that follows is that you were partly wrong."

"I tried to keep all the Catholic rules, the social justice rules too. I think I did keep the rules pretty well. I'm a fierce competitor at the exchanges, but I'm fair. No one has ever said that I wasn't fair."

"Fairest man at the CBOT," I offered.

"That's what they say. And I'm proud of it."

"No reason not to be."

"Only, it turns out, as Julia says, that the rules aren't what life is about. You gotta keep them but they're not enough."

"Sound Catholic doctrine," I agreed.

"I mean they're no good without love."

"Abandoned love."

"That's what Julia says, something like that anyway."

"So Julia tells you what is wrong with you?"

"Sure, why not?" He tried to laugh. "She's pretty good at it."

"And when she, ah, remonstrates with you, how does it affect you?"

He puzzled over that one. "Well, I guess I can say that it excites me."

And I had feared that he might flee from a tough Julia! Well, even Blackie Ryan makes an occasional mistake. In the words of Milord Cronin in my regard, "Blackwood is occasionally in error but never in doubt."

"I was a good Chicago Democrat," Bart Cain continued, "though on the left side because my father was so closely involved in the packing union—Truman, Kennedy, Humphrey. Then I got involved in the peace movement in the late sixties. I was in Korea for two years and saw what a hellish thing war is, especially for the poor natives about whom no one gives a damn. So I'm against war. I was against the Persian Gulf nonsense too. I worked for

George McGovern. He was a good man. They made a mistake throwing the mayor out of the convention, but I figured there was a new age dawning. So I got involved in everything: women's rights, animal rights, pro-choice, racial justice, the environment, minority set-asides, gay and lesbian rights. The whole package."

"Not of themselves bad causes."

"That's what Julia says."

"Ah."

"I guess"—he hesitated and rubbed his free hand across his face—"I used them as a substitute. I put all my emotions into the causes instead of into people. Or that's what Julia says and I suppose she's right."

"Indeed."

"So I bought Vin Roberts' idea of a *Commonweal* for Chicago. It seemed we needed a radical Catholic voice in the city and a Chicago Catholic radical voice for the country. And it gave my Jenny something to do that fulfilled her."

"So."

An African-American nurse entered the room. "Time for your medicine, Mr. Cain. Must be hurting pretty bad by now. I just thought you might call me early."

"Hmm? Oh, thank you, Ms. Spring. I guess I do need it."

"Marcy, Mr. Cain."

In the old days we used to offer necessary pain up for the souls in purgatory, not a bad statement of the Catholic conviction of the unity of the human species and the possibility of vicarious suffering for others. I wondered for whom Bart Cain was offering up his unnecessary pain.

"Where was I, Father?"

"A Chicago Catholic radical voice, another not unworthy cause."

"Julia says it's a silly magazine that no one reads and that Vin is a hater. I ask her if I'm a hater and she laughs and says no way. But she says that I don't want to be associated with a magazine that runs on envy and contempt and snobbery."

"Then you don't want a Chicago *Commonweal.*"

"I've been thinking about these things for a couple of years. I wonder now when I stopped being a pragmatist. Hell, maybe I never was one. I figured that it was too late for me because my life was just about over anyway. Then Julia came along and told me that I belong with you and Rich and the cardinal and Carol Braun because that's the way things got done, and I couldn't say she was wrong. We didn't make any progress when poor Harold Washington was in office."

He not only lusted for the woman, he respected her. And not for ideological reasons either. Why hadn't she told me about that? Perhaps because she hadn't noticed.

"I'm all jumbled up, Father Blackie," he said wearily. "And now the pain medication is taking over. I know I made a mess out of my family. I tried to keep all the rules and none of it worked. I can't do any of it all over again either. What I've done I've done."

Bart Cain seemed close to tears. At a later point he might try to argue with me that the medication had loosened his lips. None of us Ryans buy excuses like that.

"Messed up with Cand . . . , ah, Elizabeth?" I asked.

This time he really did smile. "No, not with her. She's a great kid, isn't she, Father Blackie? Great basketball player too. I gave up on the rules with her and she's turning out fine. I hope nothing goes wrong."

I thought of my friend Candibeth throwing her arms around a stepmother she was prepared to hate.

"You can dismiss all worries on that account," I said.

"I sure hope so . . . you see, I really didn't do anything with her. I let her go her own way."

"One cannot discount, Bart Cain, the influence of genes or of personal choice, but love is far more important than rules."

"She's the one that has always loved me." He was sinking into a stupor.

So paternal passion for a loving daughter had cleared the way for spousal passion with just the right woman.

How clever of God.

"I'll take my leave," I said.

"No, don't, not yet." He fought to stay awake. "The police say someone tried to kill me in the apartment. I'm not sure about that. Or about all these accidents. My kids are hinting that Julia is trying to get rid of me. Dave likes her, but that bitch of his won't let him talk to her—wants all the money for her kids, who are as worthless as she and Dave. They're all crazy. Julia has nothing to gain. But the cops are going to poke around to find out what's going on. I don't think they'll find anything. The cardinal tells me you're pretty good at mysteries, kind of an American Father Brown. Irish-American."

"Father Brown was based on Monsignor O'Connor, who brought Chesterton into the Church. I'm based on me."

"Would you see what you can find out?"

"You will instruct everyone to talk with me?"

"Sure. I don't want Julia or Elizabeth to get hurt."

"I assure you they won't."

As the rest of this story will show, that guarantee was more than a little premature.

Nonetheless, I returned to the cathedral rectory satisfied

with myself. I had received permission to poke my way into the mystery.

And as a bonus, I had perhaps helped God in Her odd but ingenious crusade of turning around Bart Cain.

Me and Rich Daley and the cardinal. Wait till I told Milord Cronin that!

CHAPTER 11

BART JUNIOR AND his wife Lourdes would not receive me in their Kenilworth home but they would, "since Dad-o insists," agree to meet me at the cathedral rectory. They acted as if they would lose caste by entering my first-floor counseling room, and as if it was a gesture of generous condescension to dignify me with the title "Father."

I had prepared for them by actually putting on a newly pressed double-breasted suit which by some error of the tailor's actually fit me, my pectoral cross, and episcopal ring—both of which I had managed to find in my rooms, no small piece of good fortune. Otherwise I would have had to ask one of my associates if I could borrow the back-up episcopal jewelry which he kept well hidden from me, lest I lose it too.

I had also arranged the lights in the room so they were sharply illumined and I was in a dark corner. I didn't have to draw the drapes because the rains continued to fall on the city and the early afternoon sky was sufficiently dark to raise questions about the possible advent of the end of the world.

They began by telling me about their own wonderful parish and their own wonderful pastor in tones which would have indicated that it was beyond any possible question the best parish in the whole Catholic world, instead of merely one of the richest.

Actually *my* parish was the best in the world.

But I let them babble.

"I have only a couple of unimportant questions to ask," I interjected.

"I want to make it clear, Father," Junior said firmly, raising his hand to fend me off, "that we are here under protest. We don't believe there is anything to investigate, or that if there were, a priest is the appropriate person to do the investigation."

"Frankly, Father," his wife agreed, "I am deeply troubled by this conversation."

Lourdes Cain was a plump, affected woman with vast piles of artificial blond hair, too much makeup, and strong perfume, appropriate perhaps for a younger woman at a formal dance. She was wearing a black-and-silver dress which I had seen listed in the *Tribune* a couple of weeks previously at $1500.

"Bishop," I said firmly.

"I beg pardon." She looked down her nose at me.

"My proper title is Bishop." I fingered my silver Brigid cross, perhaps the only such pectoral cross in the world. "Or, less frequently, Your Excellency or Your Grace or, in the British Isles, Milord."

They sat in stunned silence.

"My first question is about the topic of discussion at your family dinner party last Sunday night."

"We spoke about, ah, many things," Junior said airily.

"Including the future of *The Common Truth*?"

"That subject did come up, yes."

"Was it an acrimonious discussion?"

"I wouldn't say that it was."

Bart Junior had the habit of tilting his head back to one side and then to the left so that he seemed to be carefully considering a stupid question.

"You expressed strong feelings on the subject?" I asked.

He crossed his legs, tilted his head, and cleared his throat.

"As you know, ah, Bishop, I happen to bear the same name as my father and to work for his company. Our friends in Faith, Hope and, ah, our religious associates tend to identify me with what he does. This is frequently an embarrassment, especially since, with all respect to Dad-o, I rarely agree with him on either political or ecclesiastical matters."

Their parish was named in honor of the three saints Faith, Hope, and Charity. By a peculiar unconscious irony it was usually referred to by parishioners with only the first two names. Cynics, not excluding Bishop Ryan, called it "Faith, Hope, and Cadillac." Or, more recently, "Faith, Hope, and Mercedes." Their religious associates were the Opus Dei group, which did not like *The Common Truth* or anything it stood for and would have wanted to excommunicate Bart Cain if they could. In fact, Milord Cronin had already received a number of communications on the subject from Josef Cardinal Ratzinger—who naturally assumed that he knew Chicago better than its own archbishop. It was with such efficiency that the Germans won the Second World War.

"I see," I said blandly.

"Therefore"—Junior uncrossed his legs—"naturally I, ah, we think that it would be in the best interests of our family if Dad-o withdrew his support from the magazine. We did, ah, express this opinion at the family dinner, but in a friendly manner, of that I can assure you."

"It's a filthy, heretical rag," Lourdes Cain snapped.

A fifteen-hundred-dollar dress and a Kenilworth address were not an adequate veneer. She was still South Side Irish from Fifty-Fifth Street. Nothing wrong, I told myself, with that.

"Do you think you prevailed in the discussion?" I asked Bart Junior.

"Frankly, ah, Bishop, I do not believe that we did. Dad-o's style is to raise a subject at a family dinner and then listen to us. I believe that he saw my point quite, ah, clearly. But he feels quite committed to Jennifer, who works at the magazine. She has had an, ah, unfortunate life thus far despite Dad-o's high hopes for her."

"Little bitch is no better than a hooker, a heretical hooker."

I wondered how often that alliterative combination had been created in the history of the human language.

"To be perfectly candid, Bishop, I, ah, worry about Dad-o. I rather think he has tired of the magazine and I would hate to see him face, ah, ecclesiastical penalties because of his guilt feelings about Jennifer."

"Penalties?"

"I would not want to be, ah, quoted"—he crossed his legs and tilted his head—"but Father Henry, our, ah, spiritual adviser, has said that he thinks the local cardinal is remiss in his duty to the faithful by his failure to ban the magazine and excommunicate all those associated with it."

"Does he now?"

Small wonder, I thought, that this little prig was a failure on the floor of the CBOE and that all he did was shuffle papers in his father's office. Small wonder too that he was in constant financial trouble because he lived far above the generous salary his father paid him, and because he periodically ventured back into speculating, always with disastrous results.

Mike the Cop had reported on the financial condition of the Cain brothers to me that morning while I drank my ritual cup of cinnamon tea and munched on my six chocolate-chip cookies—apparently my allotment had been increased, perhaps to prepare me for the sufferings of winter.

"Bart Junior is always in trouble, down a couple hundred thousand from his last attempt to go short in oil and down at least fifty and maybe more at the end of his own fiscal year. Lourdes Hanifin Cain spends money like it's going out of fashion. The father always picks up the tab, I'm told, and will do it this time too. Usually there's a stern lecture. The last time, a couple of weeks ago, he flatly warned Junior that he would not do it again. Told him it was time that he learned to live within his income. There was quite a dustup according to the people in the firm's office."

"When did this happen?"

"Just before Labor Day."

"Why the change of heart?"

Mike had shrugged his shoulders. "Folks at the firm blame Bart Senior's new wife. They don't think she'd say a word against the family, but the marriage has awakened Bart Senior to what's been going on in the family. They like Julia, give her a lot of credit, and they despise Junior."

I was somewhat troubled by Julia Ross Cain. She obviously had a lot more influence on her husband than she had admitted to me. Moreover, for all her shy vulnerability, she was a very bright woman. I could not permit her charm to blind me to the possibility that she could be playing, could have been playing, a very sophisticated game from the beginning of her employment at B.T. Cain and Sons. The only certifiably innocent member of the family was Candibeth, for whom winning over Mother McAuley High School on the basketball courts was the most serious of life problems—now that her father was home from the hospital.

"Were they surprised by the marriage?" I had asked Mike.

"Not by the marriage as such but by the relationship when it became obvious. They figured that Bart Cain was too stern to keep a mistress for very long. Apparently she was content with the role, but he insisted on marriage."

"They did not see it coming?"

"Not for a moment. They say she was timid and quiet and he never had shown much interest in women as such."

"Repression. Then explosion."

"Oh, yes."

So if she were executing a cool and carefully designed plot, she had fooled her coworkers too.

"And Doctor Bill?"

"He doesn't take money from his father, but he's a high roller, though he can apparently afford it on his income as a doctor. Lots of travel, yacht racing, gambling, very expensive women. Yuppie playboy type. He loves to visit the casinos—Monte Carlo, Nassau, two trips to Vegas last year. Usually wins too, must have inherited some of his father's gambling skills."

"The biggest casino in the world," I had noted, "is at the foot of Lasalle Street, albeit, to apply the valid cliché, it is socially useful gambling."

"He loses sometimes, as I suppose his father does too."

"Many lose down there in the shadow of Ceres."

The last mentioned is, of course, the goddess of grain who presides over the CBOT. I daresay she's rather scandalized by the whole operation.

"He dropped a big bundle on the last Vegas trip, so he's strapped right now, not as badly strapped as his brother, but he could use a hundred big ones about now. It doesn't look like a pattern for him, not yet anyway. And as far as I can learn he never asked his father for a penny after he had graduated from medical school. On the other hand, Jenny has a regular allowance from the old man—twenty thousand a month, which she always overdraws. Her work at the magazine is 'volunteer.' "

"You don't or can't give them love so you do give them money."

"The kid . . . what's her name again?"

"Candibeth," I had murmured.

Mike had laughed. "Who gave her that nickname?"

"Some leprechaun."

Annie Casey had laughed loudly at that. "I bet I know his name."

"Anyway, she's just the opposite. She buys her clothes at discount malls and can't wait till she's old enough to get a job and earn money of her own."

"Admirable."

"The new wife has her own checking account and her own income, which has not changed since the marriage, and pays her own bills."

"Equally admirable . . . do you think she is too good to be true?"

"Maybe."

"No way," Annie had insisted as she finished wiping my glasses, something she often does.

"Downstate Protestants," Mike had said, "tend to be frugal."

"Indeed."

So in our conversation in the counseling room of the cathedral rectory I knew a good deal more about Lourdes and Junior than they thought I knew.

"Were you supported in your position vis-à-vis your sister and the magazine?" I asked.

"Not as strongly as I might have been." Bart Junior tilted his head. "Doctor Bill was on my side, of course. He feels the magazine is absurd. But he would sooner laugh than argue seriously. David has been silent at these family meetings since that foreign woman he married made him leave the firm, but I assume that he is as embarrassed as we are. She glares at us like she is from the House of Borgia and wants to poison all of us. Timmy O'Donnell, who for some reason is defined as family, is against it too—a waste of money, he says. But he usually holds back his, ah, vote until he sees how Dad-o is leaning. I thought the other night he spoke more strongly against *The Common Truth* than he had before, so I suppose we have some grounds for optimism."

The allusion to the House of Borgia was more literate than I would have anticipated.

"And Elizabeth?"

"The brat? She doesn't say anything at such family gatherings. She fidgets but does little else."

"Blows bubbles." Lourdes spat out the words. "If a child of mine did that, I'd make her spit out the gum and give her a crack across the mouth she'd never forget."

Yes, I bet you would. Just like your husband's mother unless I miss my guess.

"And the new Ms. Cain?"

They were both silent for a moment.

"Whore!" Lourdes Cain screeched.

"Now, Lourdes dear," Bart Junior said softly, placing his hand gently on his wife's arm, "that's a little too harsh."

"It is *not*!" She sniffed, and turned away from her husband, shaking off his hand. "She's fucking him for his money!"

Even from Fifty-Fifth Street that is not the kind of language a woman uses in the presence of a priest, to say nothing of a bishop, and a harmless, inoffensive one at that.

"You see, Bishop"—Junior tried and failed to smooth things over—"the whole family has been dismayed by Dad-o's marriage to a woman who is half his age and not even a Catholic. As you know I work in the same office, and it was my misfortune to watch Ms. Ross make her play, I believe the phrase is, for my father. It was vulgar and disgusting and, if I may say so, humiliating for me personally."

"Did you remonstrate with your father about the affair?"

"I'm afraid that for, ah, reasons of delicacy as well as filial tact I did not speak to him about it until it was much too late and they were rather blatantly, how should I put it, sleeping together."

"Fucking! Every night! There's no fool like an old fool!"

"Indeed," I commented, "and sometimes we become old relatively young in life."

"Dad-o," Junior continued unsteadily, "did not seem even to hear what I was saying. I raised, quite discreetly, the question of the interests of our own children, and he quite calmly reassured me that I had no grounds for unease on that point. She's changed him, Your Excellency, changed him so that he's hardly the same man he used to be. I fear for the direction of further change, if you understand my meaning."

"Whore!" Lourdes exploded again. "Someday I'll give her a good crack across the mouth!"

"Of course, we try to be civil to her for Dad-o's sake." Junior chose to ignore his wife. "But it is difficult, especially since it is impossible not to see her as a threat to our kiddies, and as a possible threat even to our own relationship with our father. I very much fear that she intends to replace us all, perhaps with children of her own eventually. It would seem to be that she may be well on her way to doing just that."

"I see. And what position did she take with regard to *The Common Truth?*"

"She tried to take a compromise position, distinguishing between the validity of a cause and the style with which one might advocate a cause. As you may imagine, that satisfied no one, with the possible exception of Dad-o."

"The causes are heretical!" Lourdes returned to the fray. "Father Henry says so."

"We refrained from any response to her, because we didn't want to, ah, offend Dad-o under the circumstances. I regret to say Jennifer was not so restrained. She used several unflattering terms with regard to, ah, Julia. Dad-o asked her not to use such words, but it had no effect. Alas, at the present time in her life, poor Jennifer cannot control her language."

"Foul-mouthed little slut."

Lourdes Cain might just belong in an institution.

"Do you think that, in the final analysis, she might also oppose continued funding of *The Common Truth?*"

"That's certainly one possible, ah, outcome." Junior tilted his head again. "She has, after all, some interest in protecting what she no doubts sees as her money."

"*Our* money."

"At the end of the evening, what outcome did you foresee to the matter at hand?"

"I was, ah, cautiously optimistic that we had made our points effectively. Dad-o is disillusioned with the journal. Whether he will be able to overcome his, ah, guilt about Jennifer remains to be seen."

"Possibly a conflict between Jennifer and the new Ms. Cain?"

"That is"—another head tilt—"a distinct possibility, Your Excellency. Yes, a very distinct possibility."

"Two whores fighting it out!"

I then asked questions about the order of departure. The Bart Juniors squabbled about that. They agreed that everyone chatted at the door as "Dad-o" shook hands, thanked them for coming, and wished them a good night. "The brat" had disappeared up to bed. Julia had stood silently in the background, and then begun to gather up the glasses in which she had served cordials. Junior thought that Doctor Bill had left first. Lourdes insisted that, no, the "gutter mouth" had departed first. They had not noticed when Dave and "that foreign woman" had left. They had been the last to leave, departing with Tim O'Donnell, who was drunk, as always. Tim had made some crude remark about Bart and Julia rushing off to bed. They themselves had driven straight home, paid the baby-sitter, and retired. Doctor Bill's "unfortunate" call had awakened them; and "of course" Junior had immediately driven back to the Near North Side, only to discover that the condition was "not serious."

This couple was being eaten alive by their all-consuming hatred. Uneasy about whether they belonged in the world into which they had moved, they saw demons threatening them everywhere. Most people in Kenilworth did not know that *The Common Truth* existed. It mattered only to their Opus Dei friends. But in a world filled with demons Julia Ross was now the chief demon. They were capable of wanting to dispose of either Bart or Julia or both. But did they have the will and the imagination to carry out such a plan?

Probably not, though one could never be sure what a weak man will do when backed into a financial corner. The attempted murder (or maiming) was crude and stupid, perhaps not inappropriate behavior for them.

Could they have carried it off?

Tim O'Donnell's testimony, if he were truly drunk, would on that subject be worthless.

"Surely you don't credit these stories about a series of accidents happening to Dad-o, do you, Your Excellency?" Junior asked. "And those ridiculous rumors about ghost phone calls?"

"About the previous events, I make no judgment, Mr. Cain, nor about the alleged ghost. However, I do believe there was an attempted murder that night, a crude, but in its own way clever, attempt."

"Someone tried to kill Dad-o!" Bart Junior threw up his hands in disbelief.

"In my judgment, the more likely target was Julia Ross Cain!"

That would give them something to think about during their ride back to SS Faith, Hope, and Lexus.

CHAPTER 12

"IN THE LAST twenty years"—Eleanor Cain's dark eyes flared in anger—"I wanted to kill that man at least once a week, Bishop. Sometimes every day."

"With poison?"

She laughed grimly. "With my bare hands."

David Cain's wife was a small woman, a slender little doll carved deftly by an artist with impeccable taste for lines. Her madonna-like face was dominated by huge and expressive brown eyes. She wore a plain dark gray business suit and light gray blouse; her long hair, tinged with white at the temples, was knotted tightly behind her head, and her only jewelry was an engagement ring with a small diamond and a simple wedding band. Her tiny, exquisite hands gestured rapidly as she talked. Her diminutive body was taut with emotion as she spoke, anger at the moment, but one (this one anyway) could imagine the anger quickly turning erotic. If she were "foreign," as the Cains seemed to think, it was because she had all the elegant appeal of a Florentine aristocrat. Paintings of women like her hung in the Uffizzi gallery, some of them doubtless poisoners.

"David is a good, kind, and wonderful man," she continued with passionate intensity. "I was twenty when I quit college to marry him. I loved him very much then and

I still do, now even more. But there were many years in between when I almost lost him. All because of that arrogant stupid brother of his."

"Ah."

"David is ten years younger than Bart Senior and has adored him from the day he was born. Bart has always treated him like he is a complete idiot, an inferior human being, not even a real man because he is gentle and considerate. David thinks that he's no good because his brother Bart says on every possible occasion he is no good. Let me tell you, he's a lot better man than Bart or those sick sons of his."

"Indeed."

She had come a half hour early for her appointment because, as she said, there were a few things she wanted to explain to me.

"Bart never liked me because I'm Italian. Eunice always referred to me as 'that Sicilian woman.' There's nothing wrong with being Sicilian, but my family was Modenese and she considered Italians and especially Sicilians to be the lowest form of human life. They both thought David made a terrible mistake when he married me, and told him so often, even in my presence. They said my children were terrible because they're half Italian. I hate them both. I'm glad she's dead."

"The new wife?"

"I hate her too! She wants to make peace between David and Bart. If she does I will lose him. I could strangle her too."

Her hands gripped one another in murderous intent.

"I hate them all!" she raged on. "All of them . . . well, except the little girl. She's a sweetheart. My daughters adore her."

"Elizabeth, a.k.a. Candi?"

Eleanor Cain's hate dissolved into a warm smile, much more appropriate for her Madonna face. "Isn't she fun? I don't see how two such terrible people could produce such a wonderful young woman."

"No argument from me on that."

Her fury quickly returned. "David became a mope, impatient with me, curt with the kids. We began to fight, and then we fought all the time. I told him his brother was ruining our life. He told me that his brother was a truly fine man and that I was blaming him for my own inadequacies as a wife. He loved his brother more than me, truly, Bishop, he did. I told him he had to choose between us and he told me he'd choose his brother any day. I filed for divorce because I thought it would scare him into changing his life. He said he'd be glad to be rid of me."

"Indeed."

Idiot.

"I went back to work because I knew that I'd need the money. He was fighting my support demands tooth and nail. He packed to move out of the house. It was all over."

"And?"

"There was a convention in New York. My boss wanted me to be there to take notes for him. David came to the meeting too, not because Cain and Sons ever needed to learn anything from anyone but to discover whether I was sleeping with my boss. I wasn't, by the way."

"Surely not."

"He didn't make a hotel reservation, the dummy, because Bart never needed to make a reservation. So there was no room for him in any of the places he would stay anywhere in the city. I told him he could stay with me so long as there was no question of fooling around . . ."

Again her eyes softened, and then drifted away from me to some far-off place.

"So the question arose anyway," I said.

"Naturally"—she smiled faintly—"because I still loved him. We fell in love again. I told him there were two conditions—we go into family therapy and he quit the firm. Surprisingly, he accepted both of them."

"Not so surprisingly," I murmured.

She looked up at me, startled. "I know a compliment, Bishop, when I hear one. Thank you."

"You're welcome."

"It hasn't been as difficult as I thought it would. We've taken a terrible financial loss, but we're happy, all of us. So money doesn't matter, does it?"

"Surely not."

"Bart never gives up. He ignores me, criticizes the children, and tells David what a failure he is—the things that always worked before."

"They don't work anymore?"

"Not so far. But he keeps trying and I keep worrying"— she clenched her fists—"that someday he will succeed. I think he is using the new wife to get David back. I'll kill her before I let that happen."

"Really?"

She smiled wryly, her anger spent, for the moment. "No, Bishop, not really. But I'd like to. She means well, poor woman. So does Bart for that matter. But he won't give up his image of David as his helpless little brother who can't survive without Big Brother's help."

"And he has proven he can?"

"He certainly has!" She became irate again. "He's very good at what he does and making more and more money. He enjoys making other people's lives secure. You don't have to be one of those macho idiots on the floor of the exchange, shouting and screaming at one another, to be a real man. David is a better man and a better husband than Bart will ever be. And a better lover too!"

"The new wife has not produced a change in him?"

"She baffles me, Bishop. She really seems to love him, unlike that horror who was his first wife. Maybe he's changing, but I'm not going to take a chance."

Megan—one of the three Megans who answers the door of the cathedral rectory in the evening after school—buzzed me. Mr. David Cain to see me.

"I would suggest that you've won your battle," I said to his wife as I went to the door.

"A draw at best," she replied. "Bart never gives up."

David Cain, in a three-piece navy-blue business suit, was as unlike Bart Cain in physical appearance and personal style as one could imagine. He was barely above medium height—five nine at the most. His hair was blond and thin and receding, his face was mobile and whimsical, and his smile, while diffident, was quick and infectious. One suspected that David Cain sang Irish songs at parties and was perhaps something of a gourmet cook.

"I'm always late, Bishop." He shook hands warmly with me. "And my wife is always early. Which gives her a chance to talk about me.

"Lea." He turned to his wife.

"David," she responded with a catch in her voice.

He winked at me, put his arm around her, and pressed his lips against hers—a kiss brief enough to be tasteful in a rectory situation and yet intense enough to leave no doubt about the quality of their relationship. She clung to him for that extra fraction of a second a woman often uses to signal that she wants more, a lot more, as soon as it is convenient.

"I only said good things," she said with a tiny gasp for breath.

"Only the very best," I added.

"The trouble is"—he chuckled and relaxed into one of the comfortable easy chairs—"I never get a chance to repay the compliment."

"I wouldn't necessarily agree with that," she said.

They both blushed and laughed, not at all unhappy about the quick picture of marital bliss they had painted for the bishop.

"What's going on over at East Lake Shore Drive?" He nodded in that direction. "Our kids come home from school with wild tales from Candi that there's a haunt in the place. It would have to be a pretty fierce haunt to take on Bart."

"Allegedly one Mary Anne Haggerty."

"So the kids say . . . the prom date."

"Do you remember that crisis?"

"I was only seven or eight then." He shook his head wearily. "Poor Bart. I remember the cops coming to our house and Mom wailing. Dad stood by Bart. But it's all a blur to me. Bart has never spoken about it. You don't believe in ghosts, do you, Bishop?"

"Of course he does," Leonora—as I must now think of her—snapped. "Everyone knows that there are ghosts!"

"The voice"—Dave Cain smiled fondly at his wife—"from the hills above Modena."

"Bah!" she exploded.

"You did not visit your brother in the hospital?" I asked.

"The family didn't tell us about it. They don't talk to us much, except for Candi, and she had other things on her mind. I read it about it in the papers and went up to the hospital after work. Our visit didn't go very well. We don't get along"—he hesitated—"since I left the company."

"The ghost claims she is punishing Bart for his second marriage . . . did the marriage surprise you?"

"Sure did. Last thing in the world I would have expected. He really seems to love her too. He deserves it. Poor Eunice meant well, but as my wife would tell you, she was a horror."

"A woman's first obligation is to her husband," Lenora snarled. "Her religious devotions should take second place. Even God would want it that way."

"Conceivably." I turned to Dave. "This one is better?"

"The family doesn't like her. I don't know what to think. Maybe all she wants is his money, but she actually seems to love him."

"She is a fortune hunter," his wife scoffed.

"Do you really think so?" I asked.

She paused to consider. "I don't know, Bishop. The rest of the family didn't like me either, and still don't. Julia tries to be nice to us, which, God knows, she doesn't have to."

"Bart does seem to be changing a little bit," her husband said, "not towards us, but kind of in general."

"He will never change," Leonora spat out.

"In the words of the late Harry S. Truman," I observed, "never say never because never is a hell of a long time."

"Never?" her husband sang from *H.M.S. Pinafore*.

"No, never!" she replied in song.

"Never?"

"Well, hardly ever."

They laughed enthusiastically.

"I'm sorry, Bishop." She regained her composure first. "I'm directing the parish musical this year and my husband has the lead."

"Admirable . . . you were of course present at the family dinner before the, ah, accident?"

"It was one of those terrible evenings," Dave said with a sigh. "Lea didn't want to go because Bart cut us out of his will when I left the firm. But I thought we shouldn't appear to sulk. I'm not sure I'll go to another."

"That silly magazine," she went on. "But it's his money and he should be able to do what he wants with it and not have to talk to his family."

"You expressed that opinion?"

"We said hardly a word, Bishop." Dave sighed. "Only Julia and Candi talked to us. Young Bill may have said a word or two."

"I will *never* go to one of those horrors again. *Never!*" Lea exclaimed.

"I see. Can you remember the order in which the guests left?"

They glanced at each other.

"I don't remember . . ." Dave began.

"We were the first ones out," his wife insisted. "I kissed poor Candi good night and we ducked out."

"That's right," he agreed.

"And you went straight home to River Forest?"

"Straight home," they said together.

"We checked on the kids," he continued. "Not that they're much of an alibi."

Silence.

"We know you have to ask these questions," Lea began.

"But we would not profit by poor Bart's death," her husband went on.

"Or lose anything because he has married again."

"We won't get any of his money."

"And we don't want it."

"Your children?"

"He'll probably disown them," Dave said sadly, "just like he's disowned us."

"He thinks they're losers," Leonora added. "Just like their mother."

Silence.

"You have to understand, Bishop," Dave said after a long pause. "Bart's a great man, generous, loyal, determined. It's just . . ."

His wife did not interrupt, did not contradict. Smart woman.

"Just that he tries to take care of people. For their own good, of course. But he takes over their lives. And with the best possible intentions, he ruins them—Junior, Jenny, even Billy, who seems so independent. Even me for years until"—he patted Leonora's arm—"my wife made me see what was happening."

"Indeed."

"Billy pretends he doesn't want any of Bart's money, but he does. I think I don't want it and most of the time I don't. But it's hard to break free even with a woman's help. You think about all you had and have lost. Only Candi doesn't give a damn about it."

"Lucky Candi."

"But he's not a bad man. God knows what he might have become if he'd had a few more breaks at the beginning or been born a few years later. He has the mark of greatness, he really does."

Dave Cain was close to tears, his winsome face twisted into a map of sadness. Leonora rested her hand on his.

"Ma messed him up, then Eunice . . ."

His wife didn't say it so I did. "He went along."

"He didn't have any choice, he really didn't."

"He seems to have been granted a second chance."

"I'd like to be friends with him. We were never friends. Maybe with Julia there will be another chance for that."

"No," his wife said flatly.

"Indeed?"

She glanced at me and smiled softly. "Not unless he really changes and respects David as being as much a man as he is, not unless he stops treating him like a gofer and errand boy, a child who can't take care of himself. Don't hold your breath, Bishop."

After they left I pondered the scene that I had witnessed. They were as appealing a couple as Bart Junior and Lourdes were unappealing. They had, it would seem, struggled with demons and tentatively won. Yet realistically, they had a strong motive for wanting Julia or Bart dead and they had no alibi. Nor was there any clear report of when they had left the apartment. They seemed to have vanished without notice. Moreover, Dave was apparently an amateur actor and his wife had, I suspected, an enormous capacity for deception. If they were acting for the bishop's benefit, they had done a pretty good job.

However, both had excellent reasons for hating Bart Cain and for wanting him dead—David because Bart had treated him like dirt all his life, and Lea because Bart had almost deprived her of her beloved and still might do so.

In terms of hatred for Bart Cain, they surely belonged at the top of the list. While David Cain was too gentle a soul to hate anyone for very long, his wife's ability to hate was apparently limitless. Hopelessly in love with her again, he might do almost anything for her.

CHAPTER 13

TIM O'DONNELL SIGNALED for another vodka martini. "Light on the martini, if you please, just a breath of it."

I sighed as loudly as I could. I was signing Mary Kate's account for the apparently endless flow of vodka that O'Donnell was gulping. Careful homemaker that she was (in addition to being a clever psychiatrist), she would bill me for costs of Tim's mid-morning refreshment. I would presumably turn the bill over to Milord Cronin, since he had assigned me to the present project. More or less.

"Mind you, Father," Tim said as he savored the last taste of his fourth martini and waited patiently for the fifth, "I say more power to Bart Cain. If you can screw a woman half your age, go for it. Enjoy life while you can. Isn't that true?"

"Eat, drink, and be merry because tomorrow we die?"

"Right! Even the Bible says that!"

I saw no useful purpose to be served by contending that the Bible did not endorse that position. Tim O'Donnell was a characteristic Irish type. He might as well have been an alcoholic priest retired before his time, a precinct captain put out to pasture because he no longer understood Chicago politics, a once-great trial lawyer gone to seed. Traces of the wit and charm which once had made him popular remained, but now as the patently despairing attempts of a has-been to re-create his past glories. Still, the stories were good, even if he were always the center of them, and the one-liners funny, even though usually at the expense of someone who had surpassed him long ago. One finally concluded that Tim, like the priest or the politician or the lawyer, was not a has-been, but a never-was.

A burned-out case, South Side Chicago Irish–style. Always burned out.

"Ah, thank you, ma'am. That looks beautiful, just plain beautiful."

Summer had only two days of life in it but it had elected to go out in golden glory. The fairways of the Beverly Country Club outside the floor-to-ceiling windows of the lounge looked like a movie set under a gentle blue sky and a warm sun. I had a crowded afternoon and evening ahead of me so I had scheduled my conversation with Tim O'Donnell at the club for ten o'clock, foolishly hoping that he would be reluctant to start his drinking that early. Tim had hung around the club for much of his adult life without ever actually becoming a member—not that alcoholism is a barrier to country club membership. He was skillful at cadging drinks and golf games from others. When worse came to worst, he could always sign the B.T. Cain and Sons account. Bart Cain would never object, but it seemed a matter of principle for Tim O'Donnell to spend other people's money whenever he could.

His nose, I observed, was larger and redder than ever and his hands trembled. He looked at least ten years older than his sixty-three. I would not have written an insurance policy on him.

"Besides," he continued, "I give Bart credit for seeing a winner. He was the only one in the office who noticed her possibilities. The rest of us never looked twice at her. But that's Bart. His secret has always been to see what other people don't see. Sometimes I've had to tell him that what he sees isn't there. And normally he listens to me, as far as business goes anyway. I'm like his senior adviser, a grand vizier if you know what I mean, an eminence grise. I had a hell of a lot better education than he did, you know. Four years at Notre Dame in the late forties and early fifties while he was struggling through night school and then fighting that goddamn Korean War. Anyway, he values my experience and education, and almost always asks me what he should do before he takes a big position in the market, get me?"

"About politics too?"

"He used to. Before he got on that goddamn McGovern kick of his. 'Course, he asked me about both his marriages. I told him it was a bad mistake to marry Eunice Slattery. I told him she was a P.T.—you know what that means, Father?"

"I am not unfamiliar with the phrase."

"She was pretty and talked a lot—never said much, if you asked me—and was a good Catholic. So he doesn't listen to me and she won't sleep with him on their honeymoon. I don't know how they ever managed to beget four children. I tell him, get rid of her. He says he's made a commitment and he'll stick by it. Hell, for the last twenty years he could have got one of those Catholic divorces . . . what do you call them?"

"Annulment."

"Yeah, well he's radical about other people's lives and goddamn conservative about his own ethics."

He sipped more of his martini. I sighed and refilled my teacup.

"She made a mess of his life and of the kids too, poor guy. I always say marriage is like a horse race. Never risk a bet unless you have a sure thing." He giggled. "I never could find a sure thing, which is why I didn't marry. Bart could have had a lot of fun if he wanted to, but not him. Won't exploit women. So when Eunice dies I figure it's too late for him, doesn't have any of the moves. I hire this dame because she's a damn good chartist, and don't even think about her as bed material for anyone much less Bart. Then he asks me whether I think he should marry her, and I says to myself, hell, she's not bad-looking after all, and I say to him, damn it all, Bart, why not. Go for it! So he does. And he's like a kid in love and she blossoms like an autumn rose, so I figure I've done them both a favor, get me?"

"Indeed."

I trust I do not have to say that I viewed Tim's account as utterly fictional.

"So it looks like he's a winner this time. 'Course he's learned a lot about life and people since he married Eunice. I'm so goddamn happy"—tears formed in Tim's bloodshot eyes—"to see him happy, it's been so goddamn long."

"He does seem quite content."

"You wouldn't know what it was like in the old days, Father. The country coming out of the Depression, all of us young, big hopes, though not big enough as it turns out. Things would get better than we could ever imagine. Lots of excitement, lots of fun, lots of great times. It slowed down with the Korean War, and it ended when he came home and married Eunice. Oh, sure, we made lots of money, but all the fun was gone. He stopped smiling. The light went out of his eyes and tell the truth, a lot of light went out of my life."

Again tears formed in his eyes.

"Yeah, those were the days. You see, in those days, Bart

was already as good at the game as they come. Not only as a floor trader—though, tell the truth, there are few better than him on the floor—but at long-range strategy. There's never been his equal, Father, let me tell you, there's never been his equal. Anyway, while he was a lot of fun in those days, he didn't have, you know, the social graces, the smoothness to fit in with people. You beat 'em on the floor, that's fine, but you gotta be cordial with them off the floor, smile at their wives, go to their parties, fit into the big world. So that's where I helped him. That and the kind of senior advice I was telling you about. I was kind of the outside man and he was the inside man, get me?"

"Remarkable."

"We had great fun at the firm, but after Eunice, no place else. Now he's having fun again but it isn't like it used to be."

"Ah."

"He could have been good at anything, Father. He had all the talent in family. His brother Dave is worthless, not worth shit, if you'll excuse the expression, Father. Worse even than poor Bart Junior. Bart has carried Dave on his shoulders all his life. Then he turns around and marries that greasy Italian broad who fights like hell to take him away from Bart and finally wins. They'll starve to death, mark my words. They're phonies, a pair of bad actors who have pretended for so long that they don't know what's true and what's not true. It breaks poor Bart's heart."

"Ah."

"You know, when Bart came home from Korea the Cains out in California—Ted Cain's cousins who made a lot of money during the big war while Ted was killing cows—wanted him to come out there and manage the wine company they were starting. They've made a bundle since then, but they would have made a bundle of bundles if he'd got the hell out of this town and away from his family and from Eunice and started a new life. I would have missed him, get me, but it would have been a much better life."

"So."

"I mean he knew. When he was a kid, back in the thirties and during the war, he used to spend a week or two out there with them in the summer. Ride out on a bus by himself. Had a great time. Ted and Mary Cain didn't like the California relatives. Didn't even talk to them after the war. Called them profiteers. I said to Bart, hell, why not go out there and start your life over again? And he says I have to stand by my parents and my brothers and sisters. So he stayed here and took care of his parents and made all his brothers and sisters so rich they haven't had to do a day's work in twenty years. But I still say he should have gone to California."

"He stays in touch with his California relatives?"

"Christmas card sort of thing. Once we started to pile up money he had no time to spend it—Eunice took care of that, though that bitch Lourdes Hanifin can beat them all at forking out a man's money. So he drifted away from the Cain Winery people."

"Would he have married Mary Anne Haggerty if she had not died?"

I had fired that volley out of the blue, hoping to catch Tim O'Donnell by surprise. I failed. Despite the substantial alcohol content of his blood, he became reserved, cautious, distant.

"What do you know about that?"

"It seems to figure in these recent accidents. Someone calls after each of them claiming to be Mary Anne Haggerty's ghost."

"No shit!"

"I have not heard any of these calls personally, but the alleged spirit is said to play a record of 'I'll Dance at Your Wedding.'"

A grim mask descended on Tim O'Donnell's face. "That was a long time ago. Why bring it up now?"

"Someone has brought it up. It will almost certainly appear in the media in the next few days."

"There's no point in digging up that story. It's dead and she's dead."

"Nonetheless, it will come out."

"Bart Cain never killed anyone, not even gooks when he was in Korea."

"There's no statute of limitations on murder."

"They'll never find any evidence of murder; they didn't find any then and they'll not find it now."

"Arguably."

"She just vanished. We'd stayed up all night at the cottage and eaten breakfast. No booze. I wanted to bring some, Bart wouldn't permit it. We all wanted to get an hour or two of sleep before the sun got high in the sky. All except Mary Anne. She said she wanted to take a little walk so she could think about how wonderful her first prom was. She never came back. We searched for her till late in the afternoon and then called the police. They dragged the lake and used bloodhounds to search the whole area. They never found anything."

"So I understand."

"Would he have married her? I don't know. She was a little doll. Sweet as they come. With the craziest parents on the whole South Side, and that covered a lot of territory in those days." He paused thoughtfully. "I don't know what would have come of it. She was only fifteen. But she sure would have been a lot better wife than Eunice."

"Bart was in love with her?"

"Out of his mind. First love. Adored her. Wanted to protect her from her parents. That year we were seniors he talked about her all the time. Who knows what would have happened? Who knows anything?"

There was a tone of something more than bitterness and despair in Tim O'Donnell's lament. What was it? Perhaps awareness of a knowledge that he would never share with anyone.

"I see."

"You'll never find out anything about that, Father." He shook his head sadly. "And there's no ghost, get me? Forget it all."

"There are phone calls and there have been murder attempts."

"Nothing to do with Mary Anne, believe me." He jabbed his martini glass at me defiantly. "Ask any of the others: Pat Collins or Jane Reedy—Roger's gone now, God be good to him. But you won't learn anything more about what happened forty years ago. It's over and done with, get me?"

"Forty-five years ago."

"Regardless. It's finished, been finished since that day."

"I understand."

But I did not understand. Something strange had happened at LaGrange Lake that June day in 1947, something that the survivors had kept to themselves in a code of silence much stronger than the *omerta* of the Outfit, something which I had begun to suspect had had a powerful and pervasive influence on the rest of Bart Cain's life and, to a lesser extent, on the lives of the other four young people who had been there with Bart and Mary Anne Haggerty.

It had to have been powerful to have sobered Tim O'Donnell so quickly.

I would not let go of it.

I signaled our patient waitress to cut off the vodka spigot. "I suppose this marriage will have little effect on B.T. Cain and Sons?"

Tipsy again, Tim O'Donnell rolled his eyes. "Maybe, and then again maybe not."

"Oh? He'll lose interest in the firm?"

"Worse than that. He may retire, get me? The new missus says he works too hard and doesn't need any more money. He should travel, relax, play a little. She wants him for herself, I suppose. Can't blame her, but I think she's wrong. Take B.T. Cain and Sons away from Bart and he's nothing."

"And the firm?"

"The firm's nothing either. He's the show, Father Blackie. Take him away from us and we're worse than nothing. The way he feels about those kids of his, he'll have to turn the firm over to Bart Junior and Junior isn't worth watery shit, though he's a little better than Dave, who, thanks to be God, is gone already. Everyone else will pull out. Me? I've been grand vizier for Bart so long, I don't think I could work for anyone else, even if someone else wanted me."

"Surely you have provisions for retirement?"

Mike Casey had assured me that Tim was devoid of capital resources and in debt—lots of unpaid small bills for gourmet food, expensive liquor, and costly suits—and had run out of credit.

"A little bit, Father, a little bit. And Bart always says I have nothing to worry about, so I suppose he'll take care of me. But that's charity, get me? I wouldn't have anything left to do."

For thirty years he had not done much and lived off Bart Cain's charity, and it had not bothered him.

"Mind you," he continued, "I can't blame the missus. She's new in the company. Doesn't know any of us all that well. No reason why she should care. She's got her meal ticket, too bad for us."

"You think she married Bart Cain for his money?"

Tim O'Donnell leaned back with an inebriated-man-of-the-world smirk on his tired face. "Why the hell else would she marry him, Father Blackie? Sure, she likes him. But I don't imagine she gets laid too often, not from a man my age who's been out of practice all his life, get me? Nothing wrong with it. She spots a good futures contract and takes a position. She ends up a rich woman. Too bad, like I say, for the rest of us, but that's life."

"You do not see Bart Cain as a successful lover?"

"Love? What's that? Anyway, whatever it is, Eunice Slattery cured him of it long ago."

Tim was a defeated and envious man, a lifelong friend who had watched Bart Cain rise to the heights and resented a success which he thought should have been his. Oh, he was loyal, all right, and would protect till death the secret of LaGrange Lake. But he didn't like the marriage, indeed, was offended by it since, despite his version of it, Bart Cain had surely not consulted him.

However, his resentment was mostly passive. It was not like the hatred of Junior and Lourdes, which was murderous, or possibly that of Dave and Leonora, which might be even worse because it was better hidden. Tim lacked the energy for attempted murder. In the depths of his drunken invidiousness he might have thought about it and even chortled about it, but he would not end up actually doing it.

By himself. Part of a conspiracy? It could not be ruled out, though why would conspirators want this drunken and probably unreliable phony in their plot?

"You were of course at the family dinner last week?"

"Week ago last Sunday?" His voice was blurred now. "Yeah, I was there. Right before he fell down the steps. Wouldn't be surprised that he had a small stroke. Kind of thing that happens when a man his age tries to get it up too often. Dumb meeting about that magazine of his."

"Your position on that subject?" I glanced at my watch. I had better end this mostly useless conversation soon.

"Bart is fed up with it and, tell the truth, with that bitch of a daughter. He'll end it, but he'll have to agonize a bit longer before he does it. The new missus wants it to go too. *The Common Truth* is finished, you can take my word for it."

"Aha . . . one last question. Can you tell me the order in which the guests departed that night?"

"Hey, Father Blackie, you give me credit for having a better memory than most old men have. Let me see, all I can remember is that I rode down with Junior and his nutty wife. Almost suffocated on that perfume of hers. Would never want to sleep with that fat bitch, get me. Then I drove straight back to my townhouse here in the neighborhood over on Prospect Place."

"Dave and his wife?"

He frowned. "Tell the truth, I can't remember. They just kind of disappeared like they always do. They're so useless no one even notices them."

"Indeed."

"Anyway, Father." He rose with me and offered me a weak, tremulous hand. "Thanks for the drink and the conversation. Nice to talk to you. Reminds me of the conversations I used to have with Ned."

My Old Fella, God be good to him, had an infinite capacity for patience with bores, and infinite skill at avoiding them, two characteristics that I lack, as is patent.

More than one drink and conversation with Tim O'Don-nell, Ned would not have had ever in his life.

As I hastened to the door of the club, the small portable phone in my jacket pocket beeped. As usual I looked around in search of the offending computer. My siblings had presented the phone to me as a Christmas present so that they could "keep track" of me. It was not a wholly successful tactic because I usually forgot to put it in my jacket pocket.

"Father Ryan," I said as, having discovered that the beep was coming from my own person, I flipped on the phone.

"Sean, Blackwood. What the hell is going on!"

Milord Cronin. When he uses his first name he is in high dudgeon, a state he enjoys enormously.

"The twentieth century I believe."

"You know I don't want any ghosts in my archdiocese, and particularly in my own cathedral parish?"

"I believe I have heard you remark on that subject, yes."

"So this morning's news programs report that there have been four attempts to murder Bart Cain, each of them accompanied by a phone call from the ghost of a woman who died in 1947."

"One Mary Anne Haggerty."

"How could you permit this to happen?"

"A very intractable spirit, Milord . . . do you recall any memories of her death?"

"Kid went for a walk by herself at a prom party, fell in the lake, drowned."

"No body ever recovered."

"You think Bart might have killed her?"

"I think it improbable."

"There really have been attempts on his life?"

"It would seem so."

"More likely on Julia's, huh, Blackwood?"

Not for nothing had Sean Cronin risen in the Church.

"Precisely."

"Yeah . . . you protecting them?"

"To the best of my very limited ability."

He laughed. "You know who's doing it?"

"I entertain certain scenarios."

He laughed again. "I don't want anything to happen to either of them, understand?"

"Perfectly."

"And, Blackwood . . ."

"Milord?"

"I don't want that ghost hanging around my parish. See to it, Blackwood!"

He hung up before I could reply.

CHAPTER 14

"SHE'S A CONNIVING cunt," Jenny Cain shrieked. "She's fucking my fucking father for his fucking money."

I have a remarkable tolerance of obscene and scatological language. As I remark in my book on James Joyce, the Irish are the poetic practitioners on such expressions the likes of which the world has never seen before and will not see again. I am no more offended when ingenious Dublin women manage to work the expressive Anglo-Saxon verb which stands for sexual congress into a sentence three times than I am offended when men do the same thing— which is to say not offended at all. As I also remark in my book on Mr. Joyce, the Dubliners mean no harm by it, indeed they mean practically nothing at all by it.

However, the shrill venom in Jenny Cain's expletives was grating, not to say shocking, even when it was alliterative, as in the opening words of her comment quoted above.

"That does not seem to be consistent with the spirit of sisterhood," I said mildly.

"Fuck sisterhood!" she shouted. "That woman is objectifying herself for money! She's encouraging male oppression! She's subjecting herself to fucking male oppression. She's no sister."

"Ah."

"She's part of the problem," Sister Miriam chimed in, snubbing out a cigarette, "not part of the solution."

The day after my session with Tim O'Donnell, I found myself in a dilapidated garret in the Hyde Park neighborhood, hard by The University (as it is locally called). Rent for the apartment, the "editorial offices" of *The Common Truth*, was not necessarily inexpensive, and its tattered state was hardly in keeping with its value. However, it was required for a would-be "intellectual" publication like *The Common Truth* that it lay indirect claim to the cachet that The University provides, and for its pose as a radical journal identifying with the poor and the oppressed that its office look like a set for a contemporary staging of *La Boheme*—even if rental for an apartment at Fifty-Third and Kenwood could easily exceed a thousand dollars a month—unless the apartment was owned by The University, which subsidized housing for students and junior faculty.

Jenny Cain had insisted that she would meet me only with Vin Rogers and Sister Miriam, a nun who was a "colleague" on *The Common Truth*. Sister Miriam was a well-known and outspoken feminist and a member of a local group called, I believe, "Nuns for Free Love" or something of the sort. She was distinguished only for her ability to repeat clichés at a high decibel level. In person, she was an older woman with white hair and the gentle face you might have expected in your favorite grammar school teacher, which is what she had once been.

"You want to know who's trying to fucking kill that old asshole, why do you have to bother us when we're trying to put the book to bed," Jenny said, continuing her tirade. "Anyone with half an ounce of brains—which is a lot to ask from a celibate priest—would know that it's her."

Jenny Cain was turning thirty, a pretty woman when her face wasn't twisted in rage, a scaled-down and slightly haggard version of the incomparable Candibeth—who doubtless was also part of the problem, and this despite the fact that she had scored twenty points against Trinity High School the night before. Jenny's anger was deep, outspoken, free-floating, and dominated the rest of her personality. Jennifer Cain was potentially angry at everyone and everything. I assumed that the prime target of her rage had been her pious mother—admittedly a worthy target. She had attended Northwestern School of Journalism, and left after two years as part of a feminist student protest, the subject matter of which had escaped me if I had ever known it, and had for a decade drifted from bed to bed and cause to cause, always with a generous subsidy from a guilt-ridden father. When he had founded *The Common Truth* at the suggestion of Vin Roberts, she'd promptly climbed on board the magazine and, if reports were to be believed, into Vin's bed as a substitute for his wife, who had remained on Staten Island, which, I believe, is part of New York City, with his three children.

"This conversation," Vin sneered in his low and intense voice, "is a classic example of oppression of the weak by the powerful. And you're the classic example of the kind of ecclesiastical appointed by the Polish pope as part of his effort to restore nineteenth-century traditionalism."

Vin always sneered. A short, fat man with dark skin, only marginal amounts of hair, and a self-satisfied smile, Vin might have been less angry if he were three or four inches taller and twenty pounds lighter—the latter condition over which theoretically he had some control. He was by far the brightest of the three, an A.B.D. (all but dissertation) student of the humanities (whatever they may be these days) from N.Y.U. and a writer of invective of some originality, persuasiveness, and power; a "Philip Nobile from Staten Island," he had been dubbed by another Catholic journalist (referring to the writer who had journeyed from *Commonweal* to *Penthouse*). Vin Roberts (né Vincente Roberto) had bounced from one Catholic publishing position to another, always seeking the top job and always leaving because he could not get along with whoever had the top job. He would depart from employment usually with a blast at the editor as an oppressive reactionary. He had enjoyed a stay of some duration at *Commonweal,* utterly convinced that he could run a better magazine, and walked out (without notice and with an appropriate blast) when he had persuaded Bart Cain to give him a chance to do just that in Chicago. *The Common Truth* might appear late, but at first it was a well-edited, attractively laid-out magazine with lively and intelligent writing—save for Jenny Cain's unintelligible poetry and obscure literary criticism. Only as time went on did a shrill tone emerge, and as more time went on a content that was recklessly angry and frequently libelous. Vin Roberts had been self-destructive in small ways as an assistant editor. Now he was self-destructive in spectacular fashion as an editor-in-chief.

"Doubtless," I said in reply to his absurd charge that I was typical of anything, "even the learned Polish pope makes an occasional mistake, save in matters of faith and morals."

"I've already answered your question," Jenny said, continuing her tirade, poking a finger which was curled around an unlighted cigarette at me. "I left that disgusting place as soon as I could get out of there and took a cab right to my apartment in Lincoln Park. I turned off the fucking phone. I have a witness but I'll be fucked to death before I tell a goddamn priest who I was with."

"Bishop."

"What?"

"Goddamn bishop."

Lest I give the oppression that I was surrounded and outnumbered by this angry threesome, I must confess that while not exactly having the time of my life, I was rather enjoying the conversation. Milord Cronin has remarked on numerous occasions, arguably with some exaggeration, "There's nothing Blackwood enjoys more than baiting ideologues. That's because, beneath the episcopal purple, he's your quintessential machine pol."

I believe that I occasionally responded to the effect that it takes one to know one.

"I know nothing about fucking phone calls from fucking ghosts." Jenny ranted on. "You don't have to be a fucking genius to know what happened. She pushed him down the stairs. First she fucks the poor old asshole, then when the doorbell rings and he goes down to answer it, she sneaks up after him and pushes the dumb prick down the steps."

"Was there not some risk that, er, Elizabeth might have seen this?"

"That brat? She couldn't even see her cunt if it wasn't fucking attached to her."

I let pass the improbable biology of her response.

"There's no fool like an old fool," Sister Miriam said, repeating her wisdom.

"Was not the future of *The Common Truth* discussed at the family dinner?" I pursued my inquiry with a pretense at meek patience.

"It would have been more appropriate"—Vincente stretched his tiny hands smugly across his very large belly—"in a place like that to discuss why one man and his woman should have such a home when tens of thousands of homeless wander the streets of this city."

Bart Cain had not purchased respect with his grant to *The Common Truth*.

"Doubtless . . ."

"The rich get richer and the poor get poorer," Sister Miriam added.

"What was the tenor of that conversation, if I may ask?"

Jenny answered in her own way. "Those fucking assholes want to silence us. They want Daddy's money for themselves. Well, they won't get it. He's so guilty about me that he'll do anything I want, despite his young hooker."

"Even Doctor Bill is opposed to your work?"

"That prick? He's opposed to everything that doesn't help him fuck his expensive women. Sure he's against us. He's into submission and objectification. Dermatology? Can you imagine any worse pimple on the ass of capitalism?"

"He's not part of the solution," Sister Miriam agreed, "he's part of the problem."

"I understand . . . so you feel that your publication is not in jeopardy, even from the intrigues of, ah, Ms. Julia Ross Cain."

"Don't be naive, Bishop," Vin Roberts sneered as he lighted a cigarette. "Even someone in your position in the power structure must know that the supporters of the poor and the oppressed, women and minorities, gays and lesbians, are always in jeopardy. Nonetheless, we will say what we have to and publish what we have to and take our chances with the future."

"We shall overcome!" Sister Miriam assured me.

I turned back to Jenny. "Did you happen to notice whether Doctor Bill was still there when you left? There seems to be some disagreement as to his departure."

"How the fuck should I know what that prick did!"

"But you were the first to leave?"

"Didn't I say that already?" She paused to light her cigarette from that of Vin. Now there were three of them pumping carcinogenic pollutants into the atmosphere of the room.

At the cathedral rectory smoking is forbidden. Everywhere.

"Yes, I believe you did," I told Jenny.

"You're just wasting my time, typical male exploitation."

"Time is money," Sister Miriam warned me.

"Let's get this straight, Ryan." Vin Roberts leaned forward, presumably so that I might better see his face in the nicotine haze. "We know what you're up to. You're working for that bitch. You're trying to pin these murder attempts on us. Well, you won't get away with it." He frowned ominously. "I'll have every journalist in the country after your balls if you try to take away our freedom of expression."

"A terrifying possibility . . . now I must ask, Ms. Cain, whether you have ever heard your father mention Mary Anne Haggerty?"

"That cunt he poked when he was a kid? What the fuck do I care about her? She was just another victim of male oppression who asked for it by letting men objectify her. I don't believe in ghosts—they're a capitalist trick—but if she's come back to haunt him, more power to her."

"Pie in the sky when they die." Sister lit a Marlboro from the stub of her previous cigarette.

"And you're confident your father will continue to support *The Common Truth*?"

"Like I said to you before, asshole, I know how to twist Dad-o's prick so the money will keep coming."

Poor Bart Cain. He holds in his arm a newborn

daughter. He already has two sons, so this tiny girl-child is someone special. Life can't be all bad if someone like this comes into the world. His heart is filled with love for her. He dreams wonderful dreams about watching her grow up. He sees nothing but grace in her life and from her life for him. Little does he realize that the child will turn into an angry, spiteful woman who ridicules and manipulates and exploits him. What goes wrong? What has happened to little Jenny which makes her so enraged and so contemptuous? Why has she slipped into the postures of hippie rebellion which went out of fashion fifteen years ago? What did someone do to her and who was that someone?

The standard interpretation would be that her mother punished her constantly because of jealousy of her father's affections. It wouldn't be the first time. Cannot one hear Eunice Slattery Cain demand that her husband return the child to her own arms because he is not holding the baby right? Does not one hear her already warning the child's father that she won't let him "spoil" the little one?

But what kind of a weak, wife-dominated husband permits such abuse?

And Candibeth?

By the time of her arrival her mother might no longer have cared. Even if there was only a modicum of father-daughter love, Eunice did not prevent its flowering.

Blame Eunice, poor unfortunate woman?

Blame her husband, who, presumably dominated by his stern and angry mother, traded the mother in for a stern and angry wife?

Blame an immigrant culture which taught that you had to control the lives of others by limiting the love you gave them, so limit it, in fact, that you forgot how to love?

Leave them all to heaven, Blackie Ryan. God judges, you don't.

You only try to clean up the mess.

"We will not permit ourselves to be dominated by capitalist money." Vin Roberts drew himself up to his full height and laid down the law (or the party line). "If Bart Cain betrays us, it is all we can expect from a capitalist exploiter of the poor and women and the minorities."

"And gays and lesbians," I added sotto voce.

"Where there's a will, there's a way," Sister Miriam reminded me.

"There's always prayers to St. Jude, Sister," I replied. "Or St. Anthony. Or the Infant of Prague."

Bart Cain would agonize a little longer and then find a moral principle that would force him to do what he wanted to do—cut *The Common Truth* off. Shortly thereafter Jenny would be ejected simultaneously from Vin's staff and bed. And shortly after that, the magazine would disappear without a trace and Vin would return to Staten Island. The Chicago media would lament its passing, praise its honesty and vigor, and heave a secret sigh of relief that it was gone.

What would happen to Jenny?

Not clear. At some point Bart, perhaps reassured by Julia, would curtail Jenny's allowance and warn her that if she intended to continue her lifestyle, she would have to get a job. Which might be the best possible thing that ever happened to her since he had held her as a neonate in his arms.

One could even imagine a marriage to a lawyer or a doctor or even a commodity trader who had tired of the bed-hopping single life, and the inevitable pilgrimage to the North Shore, the Republican Party, and the Opus Dei. She would not be the first radical young woman to make that journey.

"Are you finished with your fucking questions, *Bishop*?"

she sneered. "Do you mind if we put the book to bed now?"

"If you can find room for it in this place." I rose.

"You're the enemy, Ryan," Vin Roberts warned me. "We'll get you eventually."

"Doubtless."

"You're part of the problem, not part of the solution."

"Arguably . . . Oh." I paused at the door. "I should like to recommend a possible article on an oppressed group in our society with whom you might want to identify."

"Such as?" Vin sneered yet again.

"Such as nonsmokers who must endure carcinogenic hazes like this." I waved at the room and quickly ducked out the door before they could bombard me with the ideological justifications they had found to rationalize their addictions. The nice thing about ideologies is that to the truly committed they provided rationalization for almost any vice one could name.

Exit Bishop Ryan, part of the problem indeed, but still, as often is the case, with the last word.

To be fair, I think I did hear Jenny Cain yell "fucker" after me, but as the door was already closed, that hardly counted.

On Kenwood Avenue I breathed deeply the air of Hyde Park, refreshed at the moment by a brisk northeast wind blowing off the lake a few blocks away. It had been an exhilarating conversation.

There was enough anger in the offices of *The Common Truth* to generate a score of murders—though poor Sister Miriam could no more kill anyone than she could swat a fly or rebuke an unruly third-grader. It did not follow, however, that this anger would ever turn anyone in that

smoke-filled room into a murderer. Oh, if a revolutionary
party should take power and they found themselves on a
committee of public safety, they could check names on a
list of counterrevolutionaries to be "eliminated" with
serene consciences and indeed great glee. But personally
they were probably harmless, no matter how violent their
rhetoric. It would be those who read their rhetoric and
pushed it to its logical conclusion who might be dangerous
to the life and limb of target groups, once Jews, now white
male heterosexuals.

Under ordinary circumstances Vin Roberts would lack
the personal courage to dispatch a capitalist to his eternal
reward, no matter how much he might defend revolutionary violence in the pages of his magazine. Jenny might
despise her father and hate her stepmother, but the sight of
blood would probably terrify her. Two more unlikely
killers or would-be killers on my list—which, alas, didn't
seem to include anyone else.

Yet under extraordinary pressures intellectuals and
would-be intellectuals could turn violent and blow up labs,
libraries, and administration buildings with little concern
for the technicians and librarians and administrators that
might go up in smoke with the destroyed buildings.
Usually such seemingly random acts of violence were the
result of a man and a woman egging each other on with
taunts that the other was not consistent enough in his or
her principles—or not politically correct enough, in the
cliché of the day. The taunts would be merely verbal until
the last minute, when it was too late to turn back from
destruction and possible murder. Thus could two ordinarily
harmless and inconspicuous creatures destroy millions of
dollars of equipment and research and maybe an occasional
human life. Moreover, since they were inexperienced at

destruction and clumsy in their plotting, they would quickly be caught and fall apart under the pressure of the criminal justice system, of the stupid cops to whom they felt so superior—just as did the unfortunate Raskolnikov of Fyodor Dostoyevsky. All of this would happen, presupposing that, unlike the hapless Weather Persons of inglorious memory, they didn't first destroy themselves.

So it was not impossible that Jenny Cain and Vincente Roberto might gibe each other into a clever but crude murder. Perhaps she could find a way to slip him into the penthouse before she left. Then my tentative scenario could play itself out—though it would require a patience and a discipline neither seemed to possess.

Their rhetoric was dangerous. Might they not also be personally dangerous to oppressors—virtually the rest of the species, cigarette smokers presumably excepted?

As I was pondering this possibility and walking towards my car—easy enough to spot so long as I was on the right street—my tiny phone beeped again. This time I recognized the source of the sound after only perhaps six or seven beeps. Well, perhaps ten.

"Father Ryan."

"Bishop," said a mild voice, "I'm sorry to disturb, but the cardinal gave me your number. I wonder if I could have a word with you after supper. Outside. On the sidewalk. I don't want to alarm Julia."

"Surely," I said. "You're able to walk outside?"

"With a walking cast and a crutch," he said. "Not very long or very far."

"Seven o'clock?"

"Under the canopy of the Drake?"

"Excellent!"

As I closed the phone, I wondered if Bart was about to tell me the truth about the Mary Anne Haggerty mystery.

While I was driving down the drive towards Evanston and the home of Ms. Patricia Hurley Collins, fog began to drift in off the lake, an appropriate symbol for the day.

I had lots of scenarios and no evidence. And one elusive image to which I could not quite give a name.

CHAPTER 15

"I SAW IN the paper," Patricia Hurley Collins said softly, "that Bart had remarried. I'm not surprised. He was not a man to live alone. She seems much younger than he is. Tell me, Bishop, is she nice?"

"She seems to me to be very nice," I said cautiously.

"And is he happy?" Patricia Collins was a diminutive woman with carefully arranged white hair, a sad face, and bright kindly eyes which sometimes sparkled gleefully, a graceful and cultivated woman who had withdrawn from the human condition, yet was still concerned about those who remained in it.

"Those who have known him say that they've never seen him so happy," I replied.

"I'm so glad!" She clapped her tiny hands. "He's not had such a happy life. I'm not sure that Eunice was the wisest choice for him."

"Arguably."

"Some," she continued, "should remarry and some should not, even if the first marriage was quite happy. As for myself, I can't imagine being married to a man other than Roger. But I wouldn't say that anyone else should follow my example. I find no difficulty in living alone."

Ms. Collins perhaps did not quite live alone. Her late husband was not altogether absent from the large home on

Sheridan Road, only a half block away from the lake. One imagined that she kept it just the way it was the day her husband left, as he had many on many mornings, to catch the El and ride to his bank office in the Loop, never to return, interrupted in his daily routine by a sudden and massive heart attack which sent him, already dead, into the path of an oncoming train. The pictures of children and grandchildren, the tasteful paintings and statues, the carefully chosen antiques, even the golf clubs by the hall closet next to the stairs to the second floor—all suggested that nothing had changed in this refined and conservative house. Except that with his heart attack, the heart had gone out of it.

"The Spirit," I said, "has chosen to make each of us different."

"Quite right, Bishop, quite right. But can you tell me something more about this, ah, Julia Ross that he married other than that she's quite attractive? I could see that from the pictures in the papers. Is she Catholic?"

"No, she isn't, but she goes to church every Sunday, of her own volition, I would add. And she gets along nicely with Elizabeth, the youngest child, who is not quite sixteen."

"That's remarkable, a tribute to both of them, I suppose. Well, that's very good news indeed . . . is she from a straitened family background?"

"Definitely. On the other hand, she has been successful at her work and apparently insists on spending her own money instead of Bart's. Protestants, you know, can be much more frugal than we Papists."

She laughed easily. "Tell me about it, as my grandchildren would say. I do live in what is still an old-fashioned Protestant suburb. On the whole I'm rather glad I'm Catholic . . . tell me, Bishop, if you would permit a nosy old woman one last question, do you think they are really in love with one another?"

"As far as an inexperienced and unperceptive priest can tell, they are passionate lovers and are likely to remain so. In the Holy Spirit's plans the age difference does not seem to matter."

"I'm so glad to hear that, Bishop Ryan. So glad." She sighed and sank back into her enormous easy chair, indeed almost vanished in it. "Bart was a passionate young man and he is entitled to a passionate spouse. I'm afraid . . . but I was about to be uncharitable, I fear."

"You can ask another question if you want."

She chuckled. "What do you think I want to ask, Bishop?"

"A question about the youngest daughter?"

She nodded and her eyes sparkled. "Inexperienced and unperceptive priest, indeed. I understand that the other children might not have turned out as well as Bart would have hoped. But this sixteen-year-old, might she be different?"

"She directs my teen choir, Ms. Collins, and scored twenty points last night for St. Ignatius's girls' . . . excuse me for an enormous blunder . . . *women's* basketball team."

"Enough said, Bishop, and more than enough . . . now, I understand you want to ask me some questions about Mary Anne Haggerty, a result of this disgraceful publicity in the media."

Her kind eyes became guarded, just as had had Tim O'Donnell's bleary eyes.

"If you'd care to answer them."

"First of all"—she sat up straight in the chair and spoke with quiet yet firm authority—"it is nonsense to think that if the dead return, Mary Anne Haggerty would come back to haunt Bart Cain. She loved him, Bishop Ryan, just the way I loved Roger. Neither love was teenage foolishness, though naturally all of us had a lot to learn about life. I'm not saying they would have married, but they were completely unselfish with each other. Again, if the dead return, Mary Anne might have haunted him about Eunice, but not about a May-and-September love which might warm his heart and his bed in the later years of his life. She would celebrate it just as I do, with no jealousy, none at all. I trust I make myself clear."

"Remarkably."

"She was a lovely child, Bishop. A sweet, bright little thing—though she was taller than me even then—who had somehow managed to escape unscathed from a simply terrible family situation. She worshiped Bart Cain—a sophomore looking up at a senior date—worshiped the ground he walked on, the air he breathed. And big, quiet goof that he was, he worshiped her back."

The standard portrait of Mary Anne Haggerty, and delivered with standard enthusiastic voice and guarded eyes.

"I see . . . and can you tell me about the day she disappeared."

"I'm sure that such a famous priest-detective—*excuse me*—bishop-detective has already read all the newspaper clippings. There is really nothing to tell. We had a wonderful prom and I had decided that I would marry Roger and that was that. We had driven up to my parents' little cottage at LaGrange Lake—outdoor plumbing, would you believe, Bishop Ryan. The rest of us, who had been running on nervous energy for several days and nights, wanted a bit of a nap. Mary Anne was too excited to sleep and said she'd take a walk around the lake. She never came back."

"Had she been at the lake before?"

"No, Bishop, she had not. But, it was a very simple little lake and there was no danger in walking around it—I loved that cottage so much but my parents sold it the next summer. Compared to the house Roger and I have in Dorr County it was very unimpressive, but I have always mourned it."

Despite the nostalgia in her voice, Patricia Hurley's eyes hid behind a mask.

"May I be quite candid, Ms. Collins?"

"Of course, Bishop. Why not?"

"I don't believe a word of that story."

"You do shoot from the hip, don't you?" She smiled. "Bishop Blackie is not the meek little man he pretends to me."

"Arguably. But you haven't responded to my comment."

"No, I haven't." She sighed. "And I won't. If I am not telling you the whole truth, Bishop Ryan, I assure you that you will never learn the whole truth. Never. Moreover, there is no guilty person at large who should be punished for a crime committed long ago. More than that I will not say."

Despite her firmness, she had given me a very useful hint—if only I could figure out what it was.

"I have every intention of discovering the truth, Ms. Collins."

She considered me carefully. "Perhaps you will after all. I admire your doggedness and your concern about Bart. But in the very unlikely possibility that you do learn it, Bishop, I guarantee you that you will do nothing with it."

"Arguably."

"No, Bishop, *certainly*. And I would add that, as you

know as well as I do, Bart Cain would never kill a woman."

"About that, Ms. Collins, you'll get no argument from me."

I had been warned off and assured of what I already knew was true. Moreover, I had been told that even if I solved the Mary Anne Haggerty mystery, I would do nothing with my solution.

The woman was sweet and cultivated and smart. But she didn't know her Blackie Ryan if she thought she could dangle that kind of puzzle in front of his myopic eyes and expect him to forget about it. Bart Cain's life was in danger. Someone had warned him in the name of the mysteriously vanished Mary Anne Haggerty. The media had picked up the story. The morning *Sun-Times* had informed us:

POLICE TO REOPEN CAIN
MYSTERY MURDER
INVESTIGATION

"We're not going to find anything," John Culhane had said to me. "But the media will eat us alive if we don't make the effort. Hell, we'll even have a hard time finding the files."

And Mike the Cop had added, "If they couldn't solve it forty-five years ago, Cousin Blackie, we're not going to solve it now."

But a shadow had been cast over the lives of two people I cared about, Candibeth and Julia—and now even Bart Cain. I had to know more about that shadow before I abandoned any effort to remove it.

As I struggled against the northbound rush-hour traffic on Sheridan Road and then the Drive, a few of the pieces began to fit together, but I couldn't quite grasp the whole picture.

Nor did I comprehend yet which mystery was the more important, the presumed attempts on the life of Bart Cain or the presumed murder of Mary Anne Haggerty.

CHAPTER 16

"I CAN'T BELIEVE anyone would want to kill me, Bishop Ryan," Bart Cain insisted. He stamped his walking stick, a sturdy Irish blackthorn, on the sidewalk. "I've made enemies, but I'm not important enough to murder. And how would they have carried it off, anyway? John Culhane—good cop, by the way—showed me those marks on the stair posts. But anything could have made those marks. And the apartment was empty. There was no trip wire when Julia and I walked up the stairs. Elizabeth was already sound asleep—poor kid despises those dinners. Who could have put that wire across the stairs?"

"Someone did."

"Obviously, but who, how, and why?"

We were standing in the thick fog near the canopy of the Drake Hotel. Chicago was shrouded in deep fog and darkness on this day of the equinox. Lake Michigan, just across the street from us, was silent and invisible.

"If we knew the answers to those questions we would no longer have a mystery, Bart . . . you normally answer the door, do you not?"

"No." He hesitated. "I don't. When Irene Jones is here, she answers it, of course. Otherwise, either Beth or Julia answer. Julia says it makes sense to establish that routine because I am so often trading on the computer and that is a minute-by-minute, second-by-second matter, while on the other hand preparing a chart does not labor under such extraordinary time constraints. Beth says she can push the pause button on her rap record when she runs down the steps."

"This is generally known to those who visit you?"

"Well, since we've been married it would have been apparent to our perceptive guests. Besides, I take it that two young women are far more attractive at an opening door than an aging commodity trader."

"A matter of gender . . . Julia answered the door for your dinner guests that Sunday evening?"

There was a moment of silence in the darkness.

"I presume so. I know I didn't let any of them in."

"Yet you rushed down the stairs later in the evening?"

Silence again.

"Well, I was impatient. My children are prone to leave things behind. Then they come rushing back regardless of the time of day. Highly undisciplined behavior."

"Indeed . . . was the bell from the elevator at the elevator vestibule of your apartment or from the lobby?"

"I couldn't tell, Bishop. The two bells sound practically the same from our second floor. I don't remember anything after I started to charge down the stairs, but I am told there was no one at either bell."

"It would seem that that was the case."

"It is kind of creepy."

"And kind of evil. Contrary to custom, you did answer this bell, however—three quick rings, I'm told."

"And you want to know why?"

"If you want to tell me."

"You know enough about my relationship with Julia, Father Blackie, to guess that we were not asleep. Our, well, our foreplay that night was particularly, ah, vigorous.

As soon as the last guests left, Bart Junior and Lourdes, I believe, we . . ."

He trailed off.

I remained silent.

"We, uh, begin our preliminaries right there at the vestibule. We can't keep our hands off each other. It gets worse every day. I know why I can't, but I can't understand her compulsions."

I did not comment.

"Anyway, we were pretty far along. When the bell rang, we were at the stage where it was easier for me to suspend the game for a few minutes than it was for her."

"Ah."

"You don't disapprove?"

"Of loveplay? God forbid that I should disapprove."

More silence.

"He wanted to kill Julia!"

"Kill or maim."

"All the accidents were aimed at her!"

"It would seem so."

"But the limousine?"

"Probably a real accident."

"That phony ghost called just the same."

"When he or she found out about the accident."

"Why would anyone want to kill poor Julia? She has never harmed anyone! I can't believe it."

"Come on, Bart Cain, you know better than that. Can't you imagine the possibility that one of your guests that night saw your wife as a threat to their expectations?"

"Which one?" he shouted at me.

"We don't know."

"How did he do it?"

"That's less of a problem than which one."

"Julia is in danger . . . I've got to get back."

"Relax. I think the danger is temporarily suspended. There's been too much publicity over the accidents. Our ghost will lie in wait for a while."

"There is no ghost," he said firmly. "It's someone real and, like you say, someone in my family . . . but none of my children would do something like that! It's impossible."

Bart Cain was overwrought. I did not want him shouting on East Lake Shore Drive in the fog.

"Calm down, Bart, and let's discuss it for a few minutes. Quietly. I assure you that Julia is in no immediate danger."

An assurance which was profoundly mistaken.

He drew an audible deep breath. "OK, Bishop, you're right, of course. As usual. But how could anyone think Julia is a threat to their inheritance? She's the one who forbids me to change the will."

"That could be seen as a dodge."

"She pays her own bills, buys her own clothes, takes care of her own expenses, won't let me buy her any jewelry or perfume—I guess Protestants are kind of funny about jewels. She even wanted to pay for half the honeymoon, and I drew the line at that. She says if we go off on vacations she'll pay for half or she won't go. She's even talking about paying me rent."

"And what do you say to that?"

"That then I'll pay her for sleeping with me."

"And she says in response?"

"That she should pay me!"

"Protestants do tend to be more frugal than we are. Nonetheless, some would say those are dodges too."

"I told them all when I announced our marriage that no one would suffer because of the change in my life."

"Someone obviously thinks they might."

A deep breath again in the dark. "You're right, of course."

"Moreover, Bart Cain, there is always the possibility of more children . . . has this been discussed?"

"By Julia and me, of course; not with the others . . . we hope to have children. Both of us want them. It's a chance, but then so is life. Maybe I can do better as a father the second time around."

"You think those with expectations of inheritance would not be aware of that possibility and see it as a threat? You cannot be that naïve!"

"I'd be lucky to live long enough to see a couple of new kids get to college. But if we have any, I'll set up trust funds to pay for their education and give them a start in life. They'll probably be better off if they don't expect a big inheritance. Julia certainly believes so."

"Does she?"

"Very strongly."

Again I faced the possibility that Julia had not described to me accurately her influence on her husband.

"Those who are worried about their inheritance might well believe that such a promise is also a ploy and Julia will persuade you to abandon it eventually."

"Do they want me to die, Father Blackie?"

"They want your money and they want to protect their share of it, a not unnatural reaction in those with expectations."

"There's nothing Julia can do to win them over?"

"Not a thing."

"They are so jealous they want to deny me happiness even though I tell them that Julia won't cost them any money?"

"The would-be killer, at any rate."

"One of my children?"

"One of the guests at dinner that night."

He groaned. "Dear God, what have I done wrong?"

"Like most of us, probably a lot of things, but that issue doesn't seem to be relevant just now."

"Not Elizabeth!"

"Hardly."

"Well, I didn't fail with all of them."

"You did your best with all of them. People have the freedom to choose their own agenda of concerns, regardless of a parent's best efforts."

Not once did he suggest what was patent to everyone else: Should there be blame for what his children had become, it was more his first wife's than his. Bart Cain absorbed guilt as though it were his as a matter of personal right.

"She didn't marry me for my money, Father Blackie. I know that. I'm convinced of it. There's no doubt in my mind. Am I wrong?"

"I think it safe to assume that you are not."

I had one or two questions that I needed some answers to, but at that point in time, as they say in the nation's capital, I felt the assumption was safe.

"Is God, trying to punish me, Father Blackie?"

"Not my God, at any rate," I responded, trying to control my impatience with his obsessions on guilt and punishment.

"He could be teasing me with happiness and then take it away."

"She does not play the game that way," I insisted.

"I constantly feel guilty about how much fun I'm having with Julia. It's so good its got to be wrong."

"Spoken like a true Irish-Catholic puritan. Bartholomew T. Cain, will you please do me the great favor of shutting up and listening to me? I am Bishop John B. Ryan, Doctor of Philosophy and Doctor of Divinity, the latter admittedly *honoris causa*. More to the point, I am your parish priest, or to make a perhaps necessary concession to canon law, vicar to your parish priest, our mutual friend, Milord Cronin. Are these points clearly understood?"

He chuckled, knowing well what was coming.

"Yes, Bishop."

"Therefore, with my full Apostolic power, and I note for the record that according to traditional Catholic teaching I am counted a successor to the Apostles—we will not speculate as to which one—I command that all this foolishness about guilt and punishment come to an immediate end. Moreover, subject to immediate and automatic excommunication, I further command that you are to permit yourself only two reactions vis-à-vis your passion for your wife—joy and gratitude. Are these commands clear?"

He was laughing heartily. "Yes, Bishop. Where were you when I was a kid?"

"Unborn or a neonate, presumably. Nonetheless, you may be assured that I speak for our heritage and that anyone who has suggested different reactions to Julia smacks of heresy."

He was laughing so hard that he could only gasp in response.

"Indeed, not to rejoice in such a lover as her would be both blasphemous and sacrilegious, is that clear?"

"Yes, Bishop," he gulped.

"Excellent. Now that we have settled that, tell me about the disappearance of Mary Anne Haggerty."

Dead silence in the fog. I sensed his battered body tightening up next to me.

"That was a fast pitch, Father Blackie."

"Perhaps."

"I told you," he continued with some asperity, "that there's no ghost involved."

"The would-be killer would make us think there was."

"The killer doesn't know anything about Mary Anne Haggerty, not a thing."

"Indeed."

"She was a lot like Julia. Hell, I don't know whether that's true or not. It's only an impression. She was sweet and good and fragile and shy and smart and loving and generous and I loved her. Maybe that's the only similarity. I can't even remember anymore what she looked like. Still, the first time I saw Julia at the office—I mean *really* saw her and began to want her—I thought of Mary Anne. She's not the kind that would come back from the dead to punish anyone. She'd probably tell me the same things you did about love, tell me to enjoy it and be grateful for it."

"Indeed."

"Is there no way I can convince you of that?"

"Convince me? I accept that Mary Anne Haggerty seemed to you when you were seventeen to be that kind of person. Why should I doubt that?"

"I didn't kill her, Father Blackie. I couldn't hurt her little finger, I loved her so much. The cops accused me of trying to rape her. They said that I killed her unintentionally when she resisted me. That's not true, there's no truth in it. It's all over the papers now and it hurts a lot more people now than it did then. But it's not true. And there's no way they can prove it's true."

"I understand they never found her body."

"They can't prove murder unless they find her body. They won't ever do that."

I could not see his face or his eyes, but I knew that the same mask had descended that I had seen on the faces of the others. The same story, not necessarily untrue, but not the whole truth either.

"What exactly happened?"

"I wonder how many more times I will have to tell the story on this go-round. It's a very simple story. It was my first prom and hers too. We had a wonderful time. She was a great dancer and I didn't notice how bad I was. If she did, she didn't say anything. We drove up to LaGrange Lake in Tim's family Packard. We were all exhausted. The five of us wanted to take a nap. Mary Anne was too keyed up. She said she'd walk around the lake and wake us up. I watched her pick her way through the underbrush and went to bed. She didn't wake us up and never came back. That's all there is to it."

"I don't believe that."

"You suggest that I lie?" He bristled.

"Not in fundamentals, perhaps in some trivial accidentals. I merely suggest that you have not told me the whole truth."

"You'll never hear any more of it from me. Or from any of us, for that matter. Or from that fake ghost."

Strange that a man who felt guilt about so many things, including about enjoying the body of his new wife, showed no guilt about Mary Anne Haggerty. Ought he not be saying that if he had walked around the lake with her, she'd still be alive?

"Bart Cain, I have been assigned by Milord Cronin to solve all of these puzzles. You may assure me that the disappearance of your first love is unrelated to the threat to your present love. They may very well be unrelated, but I cannot accept that on your word alone. I propose to solve both mysteries."

"You're welcome to try," he said curtly.

"I shall indeed."

We had both become very formal.

"If you should learn any more about what happened that day, I know you will never use it."

"Perhaps."

So I had a second admission within a few hours that there was more to be said about the disappearance and presumed death of Mary Anne Haggerty.

One shouldn't challenge Blackie Ryan that way, especially when the picture in the back of his head is beginning to emerge ever more clearly from the elevator which runs down to his unconscious.

"He could have killed any one of us," Bart Cain exploded suddenly.

"On Sunday night? Certainly. He assumed that Julia would be the victim, but of course he could not be sure, nor could he know whether the fall would kill or merely maim the victim, whoever the victim might have been. The same would hold for the curious matter of the falling chandelier. Our criminal seems oddly indifferent to outcome."

"Why would he feel that way?"

"I suppose because he wants to get rid of Julia one way or another. If it falls out that she is killed, so be it. If, on the contrary, she runs away, well, that meets his needs too."

"And if I die?"

"Then Julia inherits nothing and the killer's problem is solved."

"And if Elizabeth is the victim?"

"Should she be injured, perhaps Julia is frightened off. As you are aware, your wife gives the impression of being easily terrorized. Should Elizabeth die, well, perhaps the same result would occur and there would be more inheritance for the schemer."

"He must be mad!"

"In a certain sense the killer *is* mad, but very clever, Bart Cain, very clever indeed."

"It could be any of my older children—Junior, Bill, or Jenny. They all hate me."

"And perhaps Tim O'Donnell and Vin Roberts—though the latter was only represented at the family dinner. It could be any one of those five. The only ones who are excluded are Julia and Elizabeth. I do not exclude David and Leonora, who surely have motives aplenty despite their charm, and the intelligence and wit to carry out such a crime."

"Yet it doesn't sound like any of them. You overestimate David, though that wife of his would be capable of anything, but I doubt that she could bring him along; Junior is a pompous fool, Bill is bright but lazy, Jenny . . ." He hesitated. "She's infected with rage, but it's mostly talk. Vin Roberts is too bright to try such a fool trick, and Tim O'Donnell, who wanted Mary Anne Haggerty for that prom date, has half hated me ever since."

"I see."

"Could it be Tim? We've been friends for so long."

"He seems to lack the physical resources for such an effort."

"Don't let him fool you, Father Blackie. He's a great faker, always has been. It's in his nature. He lies for the fun of it."

"I believe some member of my family who knows him from the club has suggested the same thing."

"He'd be my prime suspect, but maybe because I don't want it to be a member of my family."

"Yet he seems always to have been loyal."

"Yeah, in his own curious way." He hesitated. "It couldn't have been Dave, could it, Bishop? I mean, that wife of his has turned him against me. She's a schemer, a really dangerous one. I think she'd stop at nothing to get her hands on my money."

Rather than commenting, I changed the subject. "Do you have any recollection of the order in which your family left the apartment that evening?"

"Is that important?"

"It might be."

"Let me see if I can put it together. As I have said, Elizabeth promptly went up to bed. The rest lingered for a few moments of idle and I must say uncomfortable conversation. Julia was trying to be friendly; they were rebuffing her and talking only to me. I presume that Jenny and Doctor Bill left first because I do remember Tim O'Donnell and Junior and his wife getting on the elevator together. Lourdes—Junior's wife—has the habit of being the last one to leave, presumably so that no one will talk about her. I remember Julia sighing with relief as the elevator door closed. Lourdes is a terrible woman, to be perfectly blunt. I believe that I may have said that to Julia."

"I see. And Dave and his wife?"

He was silent for a moment. "I don't know. They were so quiet I hardly noticed them all evening, not that Dave ever has much to say that matters. They must have left as they always do, maybe with Doctor Bill."

"Indeed."

"As I said, poor Dave is a harmless failure. But she's a hater. Just look at her eyes sometime."

"I think," I said, concluding the conversation, "we'd better get you back to your wife's ministrations. I hear you shivering from the damp."

"Not a bad idea," he said. "I wondered when you were going to suggest it."

I assisted him to the lobby of his building. He was obviously still in pain. And still, I presumed, avoiding pain pills.

"Thank you for suggesting Doctor Murphy to my wife," he said rather formally at the entrance to his building. "He's proving very helpful."

"Remarkable."

"I should probably arrange for security for her."

"It has already been arranged."

"By you?"

"Arguably."

I helped him to the elevator. The doorman rang Julia and said, "Bishop Blackie has delivered your husband back, Miz Cain. Yes, ma'am." He chuckled. "I'll send him up right away. No, ma'am, he doesn't look like he's caught his death of cold."

I noted that there were three elevators at the back of the lobby in an alcove, two of them on the right which served the apartments in the building and a smaller one on the left and some distance away from the other two. Moreover, if the doorman was at his desk at the door, he would not be able to see the elevator bank, save through one of the line of TV security monitors in front of him on the desk.

Interesting.

Then I returned to the fog, which, appropriately, was thicker than ever.

CHAPTER 17

"I HATE INDIAN summer." Doctor Bill glanced out of the window of his office at the bright sunlight which washed the grim stone buildings of the Northwestern University Medical Center. "It's nothing more than a tease. Winter is upon us whether we like it or not."

"Lamentably," I agreed.

We were in a tiny office he kept in the Passavant Pavilion of the center, a metal desk and two metal chairs its only furnishing. A prescription pad and a pen rested on the center of the desk. William Cain wore a white hospital coat with his name embroidered in red above the pocket.

"Do you sail, Bishop Ryan?"

"I have ventured on sailboats. I do not attempt to operate them."

"I do a lot of sailing during the summer." He smiled genially. "That's one of the many advantages of my specialty—I have time for recreation."

"A wise policy."

"But when I bring my boat through the locks and up the river to be demasted and stored for the winter, which is what I will do next weekend, I wonder why I don't live in San Diego instead of Chicago—it's a melancholy parade of boats, like a funeral procession."

"And you bury them in stacks along the river just as they bury bodies in New Orleans?"

"Nice metaphor. Yes I bury mine at the Henry Grebe Ship Yard at Belmont and Western . . . have you ever gone up the north branch on a boat, Bishop?"

Ours had been a desultory and amusing conversation—mostly because Doctor Bill Cain was a desultory and amusing man.

"Only as far as Chicago Avenue."

"It really gets interesting further up. At Goose Island the old Columbia Yacht Club is sunk to the waterline. The Coast Guard wants to get it out but can't find the owner. There's a few little piers along the river with boats tied up—a long way from the locks and the lake but a nice summer mooring. Some people risk keeping their boats at the piers all winter long. The river hasn't frozen solid for the last several years. Global warming or something of the sort, I suppose. The underbrush is so thick on both banks that sometimes you could imagine you weren't in a city but out in the country, someplace quiet and peaceful. I love it, even when the ride up the river is a funeral procession for summer . . . well, I suppose you want to talk about my family?"

"If you would."

"Not much to say. I was lucky to be number two. Poor Junior protected me from my mother, just like Bart protected poor Uncle Dave from their mother."

"Ah. And what about Uncle Dave?"

Bill Cain shrugged indifferently. "He's trying to escape, finally. I don't think he'll make it. Too late, poor guy. Still, I don't quite buy the family theory that he's a totally weak man. You have to have something in your balls to cope with that little Florentine bitch he's got on his hands. Really hot, that one. And the Madonna face, Bishop. Have you noticed that? She could be in a Raphael fresco in the loggia outside the Sistine Chapel, don't you think? Most of them were hookers, I'm told."

"More likely in the Uffizzi in Florence, unless I'm mistaken. Some of them were killers."

He paused. "Yeah, you're right. She does kind of look like Lucrezia Borgia at that."

"High compliment."

"Eunice was truly a terrible woman, Bishop. One hates to say that of a mother, but we must be clear-eyed about our antecedents, must we not?"

"Indeed."

"Dad-o—her name for him, by the way—couldn't have cared less about our career choices. He named the firm B.T. Cain and Sons in case we wanted to join it. And we both have some kind of paper function in it, in addition to Junior's being a vice president, which is, to be honest, not much more than a paper function. But my mother absolutely insisted that Junior go to work with his father. The poor man is utterly unqualified for the role. I don't know what he'd be good at, but he's certainly not good at financial services, that's for sure. He never had any other choice."

"You escaped those pressures?"

"Pretty much, though Mom always lamented that the final 's' on Sons was not accurate. 'Maybe Doctor Bill will change his mind after he's made his money as a doctor and join the family firm,' she'd say to people. In my hearing, of course."

"Why?"

"God knows, you should excuse the expression. She had her vision of the kind of family we ought to be, all intimate togetherness, and it was beyond discussion. As far as Dad was concerned we could go our own way as adults. I messed around with drama when I was at Grinnel, really loved it. Dad said if I wanted to go into the theater it was fine with him. He's an odd one, Bishop. Liberal and permissive in some ways and a stern old-fashioned Catholic in others. But I'm sure you've noticed that."

"You did not, however, choose the theater."

"You know what that life is like. Out of work and impecunious most of the time. Dad would have picked up the tab, but I didn't want to be dependent on him. I'm the only one of his children who supports himself. If I sound proud of that fact, it is because I am."

"Not without reason."

Doctor Bill loved to hear himself talk. So I listened.

"Funny thing, I probably would have been good down at the exchange. I'd love the excitement and, like Dad, I'd win." His eyes were shining. "I go off to Vegas for a couple of days each winter and love every second of it. I almost always win, I guess because I inherited Dad's mathematical mind. I lost a bundle the last time around, but that goes with the territory and it doesn't happen often. Dad lost on occasion at his casino too. But it's only an amusement. Winning can become an addiction, just like losing. Dad's addicted to the game. He should have got out long ago and taken life easy, but he can't."

"A pity."

"Yet," he said, continuing to wax enthusiastic, "I certainly understand his love of the game, the toss of the dice, the moment of risk and revelation, the danger and exhilaration. The ultimate thrill, I suppose is Russian roulette—a game, I hasten to add, Bishop, I have never played and never will play. However, if I were working down at the exchange with Dad, the whiff of contest might seduce me too. I might be more addicted than he. So I stay away from there and get my kicks by sailing and climbing

rather safe mountains and my occasional jaunts to Vegas
and such-like."

"A wised restraint."

"One doesn't get addicted to dermatology"—he gestured at his prescription pad—"that's for sure."

Doctor Bill seemed to be the most normal of the Cain
children, though perhaps his casual and rueful style was a
carefully constructed defense against family pressures.

"I must say that you could have knocked me over with
a puff of wind when he introduced Julia to us. I had been
after him to slow down and take it easy, but I would never
have thought of recommending that he sniff around for a
woman because it was so unlike him. Then he introduces
us to this woman half his age and tells us that they're
going to be married. It was clear from one look at them,
him especially, that they were already getting it off
together. I almost laughed out loud. The rest of them, none
of whom can live without his money, looked like they
were at a wake and I wanted to laugh."

"Indeed. You approve of the marriage?"

"Why should I approve or disapprove? What business is
it of mine?" He lifted his hands off the desk. "Dad's of age.
If he wants a woman to screw, that's his business."

"You don't accept the dictum that there's no fool like an
old fool?"

"He's in good health. He could last twenty more years
easily. The rate of intercourse goes down with age, but
there are lots of men in their eighties who can still get it up
several times a week. If you can do it, why not do it?"

"Does the rest of your family agree with you?"

"Come on, Bishop." He chuckled. "You know better
than that. Of course they don't. They see their meal ticket
diminished and maybe their inheritance lost. Well, the kid
doesn't; she seems to get along with Julia—even calls her

'Mom,' but that's because she's too young to grasp the implications for her life. All she seems to care about is her basketball. Another family addiction, you see."

"Conceivably. You do not feel threatened by the second wife?"

"Why should I? Look, I'm making enough money now for a good life. Enough even to support a family if I ever get married. Carol, my current companion, wants to get married, and I don't see any reason not to. Dad-o's not going to cut us off without a cent. So he gives Julia half the money. There's still a lot in the other half, even if you split it four ways. It's different if like Jenny and Junior and Timmy O'Donnell you can't earn your own living. Lourdes could buy only five-hundred-dollar dresses." He threw up his hands and laughed. "What a tragedy!"

"I am informed that the new Ms. Cain forbids a change in the will."

"Damn good ploy if you ask me. Look, I don't care if she married him for his money, so long as she's good to the poor old guy. He's entitled. Mom and he slept in separate bedrooms as long as I can remember. I'll be damned if I can figure out when and how they conceived Elizabeth. She must have been drunk. She got kind of kittenish when she'd had too much to drink. Anyway, Julia is good to him whatever her motives might be, so I don't begrudge her any money. Why should I? It's only money. As long as you have enough, who needs more."

"I am told it's never enough."

"For some people, you know, but, Bishop, that's crazy."

"A valid point."

"I mean, I was almost as astonished at Julia when I met her as at the reality that Dad-o was humping a woman."

"You were not impressed?"

"Why should I be impressed? She's a nerd and a hayseed—you catch that Carbondale accent?"

"Centralia."

"Whatever. She looks a lot better now that Dad-o's got her dressed up. I admit that she's something more than a bed warmer on cold winter nights. But I still wonder what the hell he saw in her. I guess I would have been surprised by any kind of woman because I had never even speculated about the kind of woman he might get the hots for. Still, yeah, Julia was a surprise."

"I see."

"Mind you, she's perfectly pleasant if you can forget the accent. Certainly not a bimbo. If she turns Dad-o on, what the hell! She's not my type"—he chuckled—"but then I'm not sleeping with her, am I?"

"Indeed not."

"Again, I kind of admire Dad-o. He finds this hayseed with remote possibilities and turns her on. Not many men could do that. I wonder if he was practicing back when Mom was alive. I can't see him doing it, but you never know."

"So you think Julia is attractive now?"

His eyes glowed faintly. "Like I say, not my type but interesting. Fire-and-ice kind of woman. Exudes a sort of low-key sexual appeal that might poleax a lot of men."

"So."

So Julia intrigued him sexually. Well, welcome to the club.

"It's hardest on Jenny," he continued. "I mean, she fought Mom for Dad-o all her life and lost, mostly because Mom was bigger than her for the first fifteen years or so. Now she's got another woman to fight, one that's only a couple years older than she is and who is sleeping with

Dad, which Mom almost never did. Jenny is insane with hatred."

"So it would seem."

"It's Mom's fault, actually." He shook his head in mild dismay—all Doctor Bill's emotions were mild. "She didn't want a girl. From day one she defined Jenny as a rival. The more Dad-o doted on her, the meaner Mom was to her. The result? Today's Jenny. Not a pretty sight at all, poor kid."

"You survived, however?"

"I wasn't the first one for whom she had special plans—including marriage to that perfectly awful woman who was her high school best friend's daughter—and I wasn't a pretty little rival. As for Elizabeth, Mom didn't want her either but hardly ever noticed her. So she kind of dragged herself up, at least so far. I can't figure how she and Julia are such good friends—that doesn't make much sense. But then Freud didn't explain everything, did he?"

"Presumably not."

"So there it is, Bishop. A nice family mess, not untypical for your devout Irish Catholic, although the new wife makes it a lot messier."

"Tim O'Donnell?"

"A toady, a gofer, a hanger-on. More useless than Uncle Dave and Junior. Delusions of grandeur."

"I see . . . and did you take a position at that dinner party about the family publication?"

He laughed again. "What a nonissue! No one reads it, except Junior's right-wing friends and some editorial writers. Pure trash. Vin Roberts belongs in a mental institution. Dad-o had grand ideas about what it would become. Now he keeps it going only for Jenny's sake. He ought to dump it and he will eventually and I said as much, though gently, because I didn't want to hurt Jenny any more than she's been hurt already. She was crying and cursing and poor Dad-o was wincing every time she'd say 'fuck,' which meant a lot of wincing. Every time Julia would open her mouth, Jenny would go into another paroxysm of rage. Bad scene. I hate all the dinners, but this was the worst one yet. When Dad introduced Julia as our forthcoming stepmother it was bad enough—the room temperature dropped way below freezing—but this was much worse."

"And Jennifer?"

"She'll find a new game to play."

"And you?"

"I won't lose a night's sleep over it. I'll keep on writing my prescriptions"—he gestured at the pad again—"and sailing and traveling to Europe, maybe Ireland again in the spring—fascinating and violent people, by the way—and sleeping with Carol and indulging in a profitable little fling at Vegas now and then. Maybe I'll get married."

"A pleasant enough life."

"Doesn't lack for much, does it? Life is short enough without ruining it over money."

Bill Cain presented a perfectly plausible self-portrait, the easygoing, relaxed middle child and second son. An aging playboy perhaps, but not an irresponsible one. Was he not considering marriage and family? Almost a textbook-case middle child. Nor did there seem to be a valid reason yet to question the basic outline of his story. He had not accepted money from his father since he had graduated from medical school. While he had lost money on his last trip to Las Vegas, he was usually a winner and his loss was not of the dimension which would cause a major problem in his life. He even admitted the loss to me, somewhat ruefully. Indeed he even hinted at the possibility that his gambling was a kind of low-key competition with his father. He had very cleverly made a case that he had no motivation for mayhem. But as far as one could determine, he really had no motivation. I would have to seek more information about this "Carol" whom he might marry, perhaps because she was threatening to move out on him unless he did. After a while everyone in the single bars is much too young. Or rather, they think you're much too old. The logistics of finding a woman for the night or for the week become too difficult to maintain indefinitely. Why not get married?

"Do you recall in what order you left the apartment the night of the dinner?"

He frowned, pondering the question.

"Well, I don't know why it would make any difference. I'm sure I left before Junior and Lourdes. She's always the last one out. She fawns over Dad-o and shows him the latest pictures of the 'kiddies.' It's disgusting. She does not speak to Julia, pretends she doesn't exist, scarlet-harlot kind of thing. And of course she didn't show her the pictures. Lourdes will be picking butterflies off the wall if Julia gets pregnant."

"Will she?"

"Why the hell not? If I were her, I would. Dad-o is too besotted to say no."

"Indeed."

"As to these accidents the media are making so much of, I think the whole business is nonsense. Same for the ghost. Some old crank who remembers the newspaper stories from a half century ago."

"Ah?"

"So Dad-o is getting it on and he hears a bell and trips down the stairs. Is he the first human being that's ever tripped on stairs? Is it the first time that a doorman ever rang the wrong bell? Is it the first time someone has made a mess out of installing a new chandelier, particularly a heavy one? I admit that two accidents coming so close together is a little much, but the chandelier could have fallen any time, so it wasn't necessarily aimed at Dad-o. Then some cop tells the media about this woman from the past . . . what was her name, Bishop?"

"Mary Anne Haggerty."

"Right. So it's wonderful copy. Maybe the great Bart Cain, a paragon of social concern and radical advocate of rights for women, actually raped a kid a half century ago and killed her! What bullshit! I'll tell you one thing, Bishop: Dad-o is incapable of killing a woman. Otherwise he would have killed Mom a long time ago."

"Arguably."

"So I don't know that I've been any help to you, Bishop. You've probably figured out our family already. Believe me, we're all crazy one way or another, but none of us have the courage to be master criminals. No one is trying to kill Dad-o."

"Or Julia?"

He paused and became serious, very serious. "Well, there are a couple of them who would kill her if they could, but I don't think they could carry it off."

Doctor Bill was the most likely suspect, I reflected, in terms of the imagination and discipline to be a killer. But he seemed to lack any reason for bothering with such a dangerous threat to his relaxed and satisfying life.

"Tell you what, Bishop," he said as he shook hands with me, "if Carol and I decide to set a day, we'll stop by and see you, OK?"

I assured him that it was; I did not add that I would not hold my breath.

"Call for you, Bishop Blackie," the young person at the

desk informed me as I entered the Wabash Avenue door of the rectory ten minutes later.

"I'll take it in my office."

I turned on the computer, an automatic gesture when I enter that room.

"Father Ryan."

"Mike, Blackie. The Michigan State Police have found a body, apparently that of a young woman, in a field on Michigan 60 just outside of Cassopolis. Ten miles or so from LaGrange Lake. She's been in the ground for a long time."

"Mary Anne Haggerty."

"They're scrambling for dental records. They'll have a hard time finding any after forty-five years."

CHAPTER 18

"I ASSURE YOU, Father Blackie," Bart Cain said calmly, relaxing on a huge easy chair, his walking cast stretched in front of him, "it was not Mary Anne Haggerty's body they found. Or if it was, I didn't bury her there. How could I have? They found no trace of a body in Tim's Packard. Even with the rather crude state of forensic medicine at that time, they would have discovered something. How else would we have carried the body ten miles?"

I marveled at his confidence. He had wanted to go on TV and deny knowledge of the body. Fortunately, his lawyer and his shrewd media adviser, May Rosen, had talked him out of it. "Even if you deny it," she'd said, "they'll think you're hiding something. You should have no comment at all."

"In and of itself," Joe Houlihan of Bender and Rock, a sometime United States attorney and perhaps the best trial lawyer in the city, had said, "the body, even if it should be the body of Mary Anne Haggerty, proves nothing."

We were in the spacious parlor of the Cain penthouse and had just finished watching the evening news—an hour and a half of it—flicking from channel to channel. The anchorpersons and the field reporters were having a grand time of it. Some of them already had Bart Cain on death row. Pictures of Mary Anne Haggerty as an eighth-grader were juxtaposed with pictures of the skeleton, apparently discovered by a farmer plowing a long-unused field. Clips of Julia and Candibeth fighting their way into their apartment were juxtaposed with wedding shots of Bart and Julia. Both women were pale and tearful and had a hard time even saying, "No comment." As in:

"Elizabeth, do you think your father killed a girl your age forty-five years ago?"

Or:

"Julia, do you believe Mary Anne Haggerty's ghost has come back to haunt your marriage?"

Or yet again:

"Lizzie, how do you feel about your father being accused of murder?"

No one had accused him of murder yet, but that was irrelevant.

At that question, Candibeth almost lost it. Like, totally, you know. She turned on the small male reporter like she was about to tear him limb from limb, a fate he richly deserved. However, she replied, "No comment" with dignity beyond her years.

"Bastards," Joe Houlihan murmured.

In the background of one clip on Channel 7, you might have seen, if you looked closely, a brief image of an inoffensive and practically invisible little priest in a rain-soaked Chicago Bulls jacket sneaking through the crowd.

Candibeth and Julia now sat on a sofa, arms around each other protectively, while Houlihan strode impatiently back and forth in front of the now-black large screen (*very* large, larger even than the large one I tolerate in the community room of the cathedral rectory).

The women were pale but now in control of their emotions. Bart Cain's tranquillity was unearthly.

Bishop Ryan, for his part, was virtually invisible.

"If it wasn't for the ghost stories last week," May Rosen, sitting at a table near the screen with her notes, observed, "they never would have made the linkup."

"It could be anyone's body, even an American Indian from a couple of centuries ago," Houlihan argued.

Hardly, unless the particular field had an unusual chemical content, unusual, that is, for a field in Michigan.

"It isn't Mary Anne Haggerty," Bart said, repeating the position he had taken since the crisis began.

I wondered how he could be so certain. I also wondered how the other survivors of that party so long ago would react when the media discovered them.

"There will be a story every day," Ms. Rosen predicted, "until they make an identification with dental records."

"What if they can't find any records?" Julia asked.

She was wearing a severe, but not unbecoming, gray suit, while her stepdaughter was clad in the St. Ignatius blazer and skirt. The fearsome rain which obscured the dark and turbulent lake beat against the vast windows of the apartment.

"Then the story will gradually die out—unless they can find more evidence."

"That's not too probable." Joe Houlihan stopped his pacing. "If the cops didn't come up with anything forty-five years ago, they won't now. It's all a media blitz."

"They have to earn a living, I suppose," Bart Cain said calmly. "Still, I hate to see my wife and daughter be victimized by the way they do it."

"Vultures," said the obscure little priest in the corner.

"I deeply regret this." Bart turned to the women in his

family. "I'm afraid we're going to have to live with this for the next couple of days."

"If I didn't lose it out there," Candibeth said firmly, "I'll never lose it. But I want to get that guy some day."

"Elizabeth," her father said mildly.

"I didn't say I would." She sniffed.

"We can live with anything," Julia said. "Even an indictment."

"There won't be an indictment," Bart said firmly. "I assure you of that."

"I'm inclined to agree," Joe Houlihan said. "But I wouldn't be absolutely certain. Heaven only knows what the Cass County prosecutor might decide to do during an election year. You have grounds for optimism, but not unrestrained optimism."

"It seems to me"—the harmless little priest finally managed to get a word in edgewise—"that the worthy media persons may have missed an important detail."

Everyone in the room turned in his direction, as if they had been unaware of his presence.

"Oh?" Joe Houlihan frowned impatiently. "What?"

"The skeleton is repurted to be a shorter woman, perhaps, they said, five feet two or three. They assert that the late Mary Anne Haggerty was also short, but that assertion is on the basis of no testimony from anyone who knew her. It is rather only a projection of her eighth-grade photo in which she stood in the first row, as we short persons usually are constrained to do. Assuming, however, that such a photograph was taken in the early days of the eighth grade, as they usually are, almost three years would have intervened, in which she might have grown several inches. I have been given to understand that, though the adjective 'little' is often predicated of her, Mary Anne Haggerty was in fact by no means tiny."

Everyone in the room stared with something like awe at the aforementioned harmless little successor to the Apostles.

"She was about Julia's height." Bart Cain smiled at me. "Maybe even Elizabeth's."

"Not five three"—Candibeth grinned and clapped her hands—"that's for sure!"

"Do we have evidence?" Houlihan demanded.

"Do you remember that snapshot you showed me, dear?" The color had returned to Julia's face. "She certainly seemed a tall girl to me."

Bart Cain's eyes roamed the room, carefully taking in all our faces. "Tim took a flash on prom night, all of us except him. I've kept it ever since."

"Could we see it?" Joe Houlihan asked.

"I suppose so," he said shyly. "Nothing wrong with seeing it. Julia's the only person I've ever shown it to in all these years. I'll get it."

"I'll get it for you, dear. You can't climb those stairs."

"You remember where it was?"

"In the bottom left-hand corner of your desk."

"Totally cool." Candibeth was herself again. "Really excellent."

The picture was passed around the room, and arrived finally for the inspection of the inoffensive priest.

Everyone was silent, perhaps out of respect for a young woman whose life was cut short at the age of fifteen going on sixteen. Only Candibeth, herself the same age, commented.

"Oh, Daddy, she's *cute*. Even beautiful. You were kind of cute then too. Still are." She raced over and hugged her father.

The five children in the picture were incredibly young in their old-fashioned formal dress and hair arrangements. There was no doubt that Bart, who towered over Roger

Collins, had already reached his six-feet-one-inch height and that his date came up to his shoulder. Moreover, it was the same face as the one in the eighth-grade picture.

On the back of it someone had written in ink that had long ago faded, "Bart Cain and Mary Anne Haggerty, St. Leo Prom, June 14, 1947."

It was a woman's hand, presumably that of Patricia Hurley, now Patricia Hurley Collins. A curious kind of memorial card, but the only one that Mary Anne Haggerty would ever have.

"This will do it," Houlihan exulted. "Even if they can't find any dental records, not even a crazy prosecutor would seek an indictment once he knows we have this. It should be real easy to date too."

"Can we release it to the media?" May Rosen asked. "It'll end it all."

"I'd rather not," Bart said, "It's . . . it's very personal."

"Not yet anyway," Houlihan agreed. "Let's keep it in reserve. I might pass on a discreet word to the state's attorney's office here and he can alert his colleague across the lake that it's someone else. Let's hold it in reserve till we're sure there's no dental records."

"It's almost sacred." Julia spoke slowly. "It would be a shame to desecrate it."

"Kind of like a sacrilege," Candibeth chimed in.

They had both waived their rights to freedom from media pressure, and so we agreed.

"Isn't she pretty, Father Blackie?" Candibeth bounced over to me and showed me the picture again.

"Indeed."

Two young women had died in the vicinity of Dowagic, Michigan, I thought. Two lives ended before they had begun. But so it has often happened in the tragic history of our species.

In the picture all of the young people were smiling. Mary Anne Haggerty's smile was gentle and tentative, no premonition of doom there.

Something about all of this, I told myself, was completely wrong. Something was missing. Something crazy.

The TV channels were back with more pictures. The obscure little priest was quite invisible.

But the lead was sensational:

"The Cass County pathologist told reporters early this evening that there was a crack in the skull of the woman's skeleton found in a farm field near Michigan Highway 60 today. The crack, he said, was consistent with her having been struck on the head with a blunt instrument. That increases the likelihood that the body may well be that of Mary Anne Haggerty, who disappeared in the Cass County area after a prom date forty-five years ago with commodity tycoon Bart Cain."

CHAPTER 19

DID CAIN KILL
PROM DATE?

"BULLSHIT!" SAID MIKE the Cop as he threw the newspaper aside. "We need either tougher libel laws or more responsible journalists in this country."

The article answered the question with a cautious "probably yes," though it did admit that the prosecutor in Cass County had said that it was too early to say whether there was enough evidence to seek a grand jury indictment.

"Too early!" Mike shouted. "He doesn't even know it's the girl's body, much less what might have happened."

"If Bart was not a celebrity, no one would pay any attention," Annie said, echoing her husband's sentiments.

"It goes with the territory," I said with a sigh. "The American public, whatever its many virtues, revels in the destruction of the rich and famous." I then told them about the prom picture.

"That's that." Mike rubbed his hands in satisfaction. "That kills a case."

"It does not follow, alas, that the media will not pursue it until the authorities either find dental records or inspect the picture."

201

"If Joe Houlihan says there's grounds for cautious optimism, then it means he has airtight evidence."

"It was reported on the morning news," I observed, "that no dental records for Mary Anne Anne Haggerty have been discovered. It would appear that no one even knows who her dentist was."

I munched on one of my four chocolate-chip cookies. Clearly the increase in my allotment had been temporary.

"It would be a lot better"—Mike picked up his paintbrush and began to clean it—"if they could find the records. That's conclusive evidence. It ices the story instantly."

"After a lot of harm has been done to innocent people, like Julia and Beth," his wife said sadly. "Here, Father Blackie, give me your glasses, they look terrible."

"When I go out in the rain, they will only become obscured again."

"Shame on you!" she exclaimed. "Shanty Irish!"

Meekly I handed over my Coke bottles.

"You should wear contacts. Then people could see your lovely blue eyes."

An admonition I hear from my three female siblings at least weekly.

"These glasses are required for the persona," I said.

They both laughed.

"I am missing something, Mike," I continued, "making some unconscionable error—that comes of trying to solve two unrelated mysteries at the same time."

"You are convinced that they are unrelated? What about the ghost?"

"A red herring, I think."

"Did anyone in the family know about Mary Anne Haggerty?"

"They all deny it, all except Julia, to whom he showed the picture, the only one who has seen it all these years."

"Still carrying the torch."

"Or the memory. It is a measure of his passion for her that he shared that memory with her, which patently he did not share with his first wife."

"Then Julia might, theoretically at any rate, be responsible for the calls?"

"And she might, theoretically at any rate, have sent him down to answer the bell so that he would fall over the trip wire which she, by some miracle, stretched across the staircase while they were in the bedroom."

"She might have slipped out of the bathroom into the adjoining bedroom." Mike pointed at the floor plan I had laid on his paint table.

"Perhaps."

"But not very likely . . . your friend and neighbor Tim O'Donnell knew about Mary Anne and her disappearance. He might be the ghost."

"Bart Cain believes that he should be our prime suspect, not without some reason, I would add. However, in his cups he might have told the story, totally embellished with winks and hints, to anyone in the family. Or to anyone willing to listen and perhaps buy him a drink."

"We're not even sure, are we"—Mike put down his paintbrush—"that the person responsible for the accidents is also responsible for the phone calls."

"Not absolutely certain, no."

"You wanted information on Carol Clifford, Bill Cain's current squeeze, as the columnists refer to such persons?"

"What did you find?" I asked.

"Nothing much that would surprise you. About thirty. *Very* attractive. Socialite model, which is a nice way of saying she's on the edge of being a high-quality party girl.

She's been around and has been passed around too. But not all that tarnished. No longer models. Claims to be an 'interior designer' and has a few clients, though not enough to sustain her lifestyle. Been with Doctor Bill for eighteen months. Time is running out to get a husband. Betting is that he's sufficiently hooked on her to marry her. Money would be very important to her, naturally. But I don't think she's worth killing for."

"Indeed."

"And from your evaluation, Doctor Bill is not the kind of man who would kill just to guarantee the money a future wife might want, especially when there's a lot of other women around who would not want so much money and would be slightly less tarnished."

"He does not seem to be such a one."

"So how does your list of suspects shape up."

"One must begin"—I sighed loudly, picking up the memo I had typed out before I strolled over to the Reilly Gallery—"with the acknowledgment that this is a peculiar kind of crime. Brilliantly executed as far as the locked-room puzzle goes . . ."

"I don't see how he got away with that."

"Blackie does," his wife announced. "He just likes to keep his little solutions secret till the last minute."

"Arguably," I continued. "It is a crime which is ingenious in its execution but highly problematic in its effect. Let us say for the sake of simplicity that only the chandelier and the trip wire are actual attempts to kill or maim. Let us also assume that Julia Ross Cain, prairie nymph, is the target of these attempts. Anyone in the house, however, could have been the victim, as Bart Cain was in fact on the Sunday night in question. Even if the falling Irish crystal was only intended as a warning, it could have injured anyone in the family or the good Irene

Jones or any other person or persons who might have been in the house. The weapons, if you will, only make sense if one assumes that the criminal's paramount purpose is to frighten, though he does not mind if his means of terror also injures or even kills."

"A strange sort of person," Mike agreed.

"Let us therefore consider the suspects:

"One: Julia Cain, a very bright and resourceful woman with corners of her soul that remain quite unexplored. She knows about Mary Anne Haggerty. Of all the possible suspects, she is the one that is most likely to have the skill and the courage to carry out such a plot, though I cannot imagine her trying anything so convoluted. But what would her motive be for killing her husband? She stands to make no financial gain from his death at the present time. Moreover, her love for him does seem authentic. Perhaps she wants merely to remind him of his mortality, so he will insist on changing his will so as provide for her. But why such a convoluted approach to what should be easy to accomplish through countless other ways? I'm afraid she goes to the bottom of the pile for the present.

"Two: Elizabeth Marie Candace Cain, a.k.a. Candibeth. And the pope is a Southern Baptist."

Mine host and hostess laughed.

"Three: Bartholomew Cain Junior and his ineffable wife Lourdes Hanifin Cain. Both hate Julia Cain with considerable ardor. The latter will not even speak to her or acknowledge her presence. They are in a constant state of negative assets, brought about by Lourdes Cain's addiction to shopping malls. They have lived off the elder Bart Cain's largesse for all their married lives; indeed they have pretended to North Shore gentility. It is not clear that Junior could earn an honest living if his life depended on it. Presumably the father is not unaware that his son is a useless failure. Presumably he will not abandon him while he lives or in his will. But unless I am mistaken, they keep careful track of the elder Bart Cain's net worth and what they think is their reasonable share—by their standards—of that net worth should he die tomorrow. There is no way that they can fail to perceive that Julia Ross Cain is a threat to their just expectations. So they have both the motive and the hate—for Julia especially but for the elder Bart Cain too—to sustain a murder or mayhem plot. Yet it would be hard to imagine that they have the ingenuity and the nerve to carry any such plot off, and especially anything this ingenious.

"Four: William Cain, M.D., a man who has adopted a mask, not totally inauthentic, of the relaxed, tranquil playboy of the world. Life, he will tell you with apparent sincerity, is worth too much to worry about an inheritance when you already earn all you need and know your father will take care of you anyway. He does not depend on his father for income and has not done so since he graduated from medical school. He disliked his mother intensely, but seemingly bears no ill will towards his father. The only sign of competition with that parent is an occasional gambling bout at Las Vegas, which he admits he enjoys. Even though the last such was unsuccessful, his losses were not prohibitive and he usually wins. He may soon take unto himself as a wife one Carol Clifford, of whom it might be said that she has been no better than she has had to be. This person might expend substantial amounts of money, but one would have to be sure that she was insisting on guarantees of exact sums before marriage. On the face of it that's improbable because of her precarious position in the marriage market and because she seems to be one who is pressing for marriage. On the whole, then, while Doctor Bill certainly has the imagination and the savoir faire to carry off a complex crime, one cannot find the slightest trace of a motive."

I paused to finish my tea and demolish the remaining half of chocolate-chip. Annie Casey replenished the tea-cup but did not replace the cookie.

Thus refreshed, I continue. "Five: There is no absence of motive, however, in his younger sibling Jennifer Cain. The woman is consumed with free-floating rage. She lives on a hair trigger and is capable of almost any wild, heedless action. If looks or words could kill or maim Julia Ross Cain, Jennifer would have killed her on sight, because of jealousy of her father's love if for no other reason. Moreover, she sees her current lover and her current cause in jeopardy. It is hard to tell whether she would shrink from murder. She could easily find an ideological justification for it, as she can for anything she wants to do. In a fit of anger she is capable of almost any dangerous and destructive behavior. But a planned and organized plot seems to be to beyond her emotional condition. Plenty of motive but, as I see it, no competence.

"Six: However, both motive and competence can be found in her lover and employer at *The Common Truth*, Vin Roberts, né Vincente Roberto. He is a cunning man who sees the world through an ideological prism that filters almost any event anywhere into oppression, and especially capitalist oppression, of him. He is capable of planning an elaborate conspiracy and persuading himself that it is not only morally legitimate behavior, but indeed the only morally legitimate behavior. Moreover, he sees his first venture as editor-in-chief, a position for which he has schemed and connived all his life, in grave danger. Thus he has ample motive for trying to kill or maim or frighten Julia Ross Cain. On the other hand, he is a lazy and self-indulgent man, more interested in personal survival than even being an editor-in-chief. In a few years it is conceivable that he could do a Michael Novak and sell out to the American Enterprise Institute or some other such conservative think tank. Hence, he is a survivor, and an intelligent enough survivor to comprehend that for all their stupidity, the capitalist police system usually apprehends and punishes those who kill or maim important capitalists and their families. He may be so enamored of the fair Jennifer as to be egged into crime by her, but I rather doubt it. In my observations he is already weary of her, which would be an appropriate reaction."

I sipped from teacup and observed, wonder to tell, two more cookies.

Should I ask for more? Ah, no, that would spoil the persona altogether.

"Seven: David Cain and his wife Leonora Cain, Eleanor to the Cain family, and Lea to her husband. An attractive couple, hard to dislike. Yet he has multiple motives— resentment, greed, envy, and above all the need to salvage what he can from his once-great expectations from his brother, if not for himself, then for his children. The woman of the family is a powerful hater and an intelligent one. They are capable of conceiving and carrying out an elaborate plot. Moreover, it is not clear when or even if they left the apartment. So motive, and perhaps both resourcefulness and opportunity.

"To conclude. Eight: Timothy John O'Donnell, lifelong friend of Bart Cain, business associate, and virtual member of the family. O'Donnell has played phony games for all his life and is probably incapable of separating reality from fantasy, fact from imagination, truth from falsehood. He pictures himself as the intelligence and charm behind Bart Cain's success, but cannot be unaware that he is now and probably always has been dependent on his friend's largesse. He knows that Cain no longer needs him, if he ever did. He also knows that Cain will never abandon him, if only because he has never done so. However, his self-image demands that he be seen as part of B.T. Cain and Sons. Should the firm fold, he no longer would have a position from which to claim dignity and honor. Indeed he would be seen by all as a dependent of Bart Cain and nothing else. Everyone sees him that way now, but he can at least pretend to himself that he is still perceived as an important man of business. Moreover, his lifelong role as second fiddle to Bart Cain has stirred deep resentment in him. His anger may be passive-aggressive but it is still powerful. He has the motive and imagination, therefore, to be the criminal, but, I should think, hardly the physical strength or the sobriety to execute a plot. He is, it should be noted, the only one who does not have an alibi for the time after the dinner party. However, I judge that none of the other alibis—Lourdes and Junior for each other, Jenny and Vin also for each other, and Carol for Doctor Bill—are worth that much.

"Thus on a basis of a combination of motives and skill, no one seems to have been the criminal. Yet, if my scenario to explain the locked-room puzzle is correct, it had to be at least one of them that drew the trip wire across the staircase.

"I do not reject the possibility that some of these suspects might have been acting in concert. Junior and Lourdes might have allied themselves with Doctor Bill, and Vin of course with Jenny. But I have no evidence for such alliances."

I cast aside the sheet in disgust.

"As we used to say in the seminary of the glory days, 'Ergo, meathead!'"

"So you don't know who did it," Annie Murphy said in some surprise.

"Oh, yes," I said, "I know who did it. I think I know how. But I can't prove it."

"You know who did it?" Mike the Cop looked at me suspiciously. "Who?"

"When I have explanation and proof you will be the first to hear."

"Then Julia Cain is still in danger?" Annie's eyes widened in horror.

"I think not."

But as will be seen, I had reckoned without the imagination of the criminal.

CHAPTER 20

"IT'S LIKE TOTALLY gross, Father Blackie," Candibeth protested. "I mean totally, but it's also kind of neat."

To emphasize the ambiguity of the situation she produced a particularly large bubble-gum bubble.

I heard her expression of ambivalence in my office after teen choir practice on Tuesday evening. I had succeeded in making "Blackie's Folly" at least moderately user-friendly, and was about to summon the troops to rejoice with me when Candibeth bounced in. The target of her ambivalence was not the continued media assault on her family, but the "totally gooey" affection between her stepmother and father.

The "Cain Murder Mystery," as it was now called, continued to preoccupy the anchorpersons. Men and women who had attended the prom forty-five years before were dragged before the camera to say either than Bart Cain was a "quiet and likable kid" or a "sullen nasty kid" and that Mary Anne Haggerty was either "pretty free with herself, if you know what I mean" or "a nice quiet little thing." Psychologists answered questions about how a man could live for forty-five years with guilt for such a terrible crime and still be a successful businessman. Most of those who knew or claimed to know Mary Anne said that she was a "tiny little thing." Only one bright-eyed woman said flatly, "*Well*, she was *tiny* in the eighth grade, but she grew three or four inches in high school and she wasn't tiny at the prom."

Her observations were ignored.

Meanwhile the search for dental records continued.

An "internationally famous" professor of physical anthropology from The University (of Chicago, a specification not usually added by those who are associated with it) offered as his informed opinion that on the basis of "an admittedly cursory examination of newspaper pictures of the skeleton, it has been in the ground a lot longer than a half century. Moreover," he continued cheerfully, "some details of the skull suggest Asian origins rather than Indo-European."

"Are you saying, Professor, that it could be a Native American skeleton?" The reporter seemed shocked—as if she had heard heresy, perhaps even politically incorrect heresy.

"One might draw that as a tentative conclusion. It would take several weeks of careful examination to arrive at a firm conclusion."

"But you think the body has been in the ground for at least fifty years?"

"For a lot more than fifty years, I'd say."

"But the only conclusive determination requires dental records?"

"If you want a very quick identification, you can't beat them. Given a couple of weeks I could exclude certain possibilities. But it looked to me from the picture like the deceased didn't have any dental work at all. That's not your typical Celtic-American."

"But you cannot say conclusively that the Cassopolis skeleton is not that of Mary Anne Haggerty, the prom date of Bart Cain forty-five years ago?"

The professor considered the reporter as though she were a person with two heads. "I couldn't say anything conclusively unless I had examined the skeleton. But my personal opinion is that it is not."

Just so there would be no doubt in the mind of the audience, the anchorperson repeated the theme. "It must be remembered," he said solemnly, "that the professor was expressing only his *personal* opinion."

Meantime the various police jurisdictions were reported to be conducting feverish investigations.

"Neither the state police or the Cass County police can even find their files from 1947," Mike Casey the Cop said contemptuously. "And they have no leads. It's all smoke and mirrors, Cousin Blackie. The media have made something out of nothing and only because they've got a celebrity for a victim—Feminist Mogul Suspected of Rape and Murder. They're leaning on my guys to do something. Poor John Culhane keeps telling them that it's out of our jurisdiction, but they think he should be digging up witnesses."

"So he tells them that his cops are cooperating fully."

"Which means that he has five guys sitting on their asses waiting for the phone from Cassopolis to ring."

But gradually the media interest waned, and Candibeth no longer needed security guards to get into the car to be driven over to St. Ignatius and more guards in front of St. Ignatius. The Jesuits sternly put a lid on conversations between reporters and her classmates, some of whom—of both genders—had informed the reporters that they were assholes.

So one afternoon she ambled over to the rectory at my request to discuss the party before her father fell or was pushed down the steps.

"I'm worried about Dad," she began. "It's totally a downer."

"Ah?"

We were, I thought, in for another scenario in which we talked around a subject and I was responsible to figure out what it was.

"I mean he's a different man. I want him that way always. Does it have to stop?"

"Does what have to stop?"

"I mean all the screwing . . . It's really good for Dad, you know?"

Well, that was not quite talking around a subject, though perhaps in her world in this era it was.

"I am told that it is good for most people, especially when they love one another."

"Of *course*, but what if it stops? Then will Dad go back to being the way he used to be? What will that do to Mom? I mean she has to like it a real lot, you know? Women have passions too, Father Blackie. What if Dad gets tired of fucking her all the time? You should see the look in her eyes after they've done it to one another! Awesome, like *really*!"

No, not indirect at all.

"Such things go in cycles with most people, Candibeth. I would suspect that there will be downturns for them too, but the downturns will not be too steep. They will not, I think it safe to say, ever tire of making love to one another."

"Totally excellent."

So that was what she was worried about. Does love fade? My answer that it often regenerates was enough.

"I couldn't believe they kept it up when Dad had that cast on his leg. I thought it would be like, you know, impossible. Then I figure she's fersure giving him head and she's probably pretty good at it, you know."

"Candibeth!"

"Well, I mean, if they're in love and they're married and they can't do it any other way, why not?"

I did not tell her that the Vatican would probably disapprove because that wisdom was lost on her generation.

"I figure like someday, when I'm a lot older, I'll like go hey, Mom, can you tell me how you do some of those things. And she might look shocked, but she'll tell me. Maybe demonstrate with a Coke bottle like Madonna in *Truth or Dare*. Fersure."

"It is unwise for me to speculate on those matters, Candibeth."

I was on the verge of losing it to wild laughter utterly inappropriate for a bishop. In any event, Candibeth was living proof that ignorance is not required as a precondition for innocence.

"She's a great mom, Father Blackie. A totally great mom—like, you know, I wanted to go where Riverview used to be after I watched that outstanding videotape you sent over? And she drove me over and we stood in the parking lot and had a good cry together?"

"A good cry?"

"Because of all the fun people had here for so many years on the Bobs and all and now they don't anymore."

"But you can always go to Great America,"

"It's not the same."

I know when I encounter a manifestation of womanly sensibility with which it is futile if not dangerous to argue. So, with the wisdom that comes from age, I changed the subject.

"Can we talk a little about the night of the dinner party?"

"Yuck. Total *yuck*."

"Why *yuck*?"

She giggled at my imitation. "Jenny is like totally gross, you know. I go, Mom, she lost it years ago if she ever had it. I'm like you're afraid to say anything because she might hit the ceiling. Daddy should stop her."

"And Mom says?"

"She's like your dad loves her and I'm like then let's not have any more family dinners because some night I'm going to totally lose it and smash her."

"Invite me. I'd like to watch."

I took it as almost certain that the prophesied smashing, in all probability nothing more than verbal, would surely occur. I hoped that Bart Cain would have the sense not to take sides.

"I *mean* it, Father Blackie. I'm up to here with her." Candibeth put her hand on the top of her head.

"What else?"

"I'm also up to here with Aunt Lourdes. She is like totally disgusting and she treats Mom like total shit. Won't talk to her, won't answer her questions, pretends she's not there. I might just"—she grinned impishly—"smash her too."

"A scene fit for the Roman Colosseum."

"I totally *mean* it. And Uncle Junior is such a *wimp*!" Her bubble this time was small and derisive.

"Indeed."

"They're arguing about that stupid magazine. You know, the one that asshole Jenny is sleeping with edits? And I'm like why not give the money to the homeless instead of to people who just write about the homeless, you know?"

"You actually said that?"

"No." She grinned again. "But I *thought* it, all night long. If I like said it poor Jenny fersure would be picking flowers off the wall, you know."

"And Uncle Dave and Aunt Lea?"

"They're like totally quiet. No one talks to them or listens to them, you know? And I think they're nice and she's real cute too, for a woman that's like totally old."

"Indeed. What conclusion did the family draw at the end of the meeting about the fate of *The Common Truth?*"

"They never draw any conclusions, Father Blackie. Daddy says he'll think about it, we never like take a vote."

"And what will your father do?"

"*Well,* before Julia he would have been, like, guilty about poor sick Jenny and kept on giving the money. Now he'll talk to Julia and she'll be like it's not helping Jenny to support something that artificial and maybe he'll agree with her. He sure does listen when he asks her something."

"As well he might . . . so you wouldn't bet on the future of *The Common Truth?*"

"Like totally no way."

Did the others know of Julia's rising influence? Did Jenny know? Could she see the handwriting on the wall?

"Then what happened?"

"Well, I kiss Aunt Lea good-bye and scoot up to bed because like we have to play St. Viator's the next day and if I stay around while crazy Aunt Lourdes slobbers over Daddy and shows him pictures of her yucky kiddies and insults Mom, I'm probably going to totally lose it, you know? So I fall right to sleep because I'm already zonked out."

"And then?"

"*Well,* then I hear this terrible sound and a scream and then Mom screaming and so I run downstairs and there's

Dad lying on the floor, kind of strange-like, and there's blood all over and Mom has like *totally* lost it, I mean she doesn't have any clothes on and she says Daddy is dead and I take his pulse and it's all right and I tell her and then I call 911 and tell them to send an ambulance over right away and I get a robe for Mom and I take Dad's pulse again and it's still all right and I check his breathing and it's all right and I make Mom calm down and she's fine after that and she tells me that someone rang the doorbell and I look at the door and the elevator isn't even there and I call downstairs and Ivan—that's the doorman—he says he didn't ring it and I tell him to let in the ambulance people and pretty soon the fire department shows up and they're real nice and real gentle with Daddy and we go over to the hospital and he's all right and then that creepy ghost calls and Mom gets her and I wish it was me because I'd bash her too and I don't want it to ever happen again and, Father Blackie, who did it?"

"I don't know for sure, Candibeth, but I'll find out."

"Like real soon?"

"Indeed."

"Well. I'm glad to hear *that*! I think it's Jenny."

"Maybe."

"Anyway, Dad goes like I did a real good job and he's proud of me because I didn't lose it and Mom laughs and says it's a good thing *one* woman in the house kept her head and I'm like really grossed out, you know?"

"Indeed you did real good, Candibeth."

"You should say 'very well,' Father Blackie." She giggled. "It's all right for me to talk funny. But you're a bishop. You shouldn't develop bad syntax habits."

"I stand corrected. Is there anything I don't know about the ghost that I should?"

She frowned. "Daddy says it's a crank, not a ghost, and

Mom asks then who rang the doorbell and blows my mind too . . . do you know how he rang the bell?"

"I'm sure I do."

"Excellent . . . yeah, one other thing. Daddy is like totally sure that the skeleton isn't that poor kid. I believe him but I wonder how he knows. It's like he knows where she really is."

"I'm sure he's not a killer, Candibeth."

"Fersure."

"You'd better get home before your parents start to worry about you."

"The limo and the guards are out front"—she turned up her nose—"just in case there's one of those reporter assholes waiting for me. We got to get rid of them, Father Blackie."

"We will, Candibeth, we will. Real soon."

I was far too optimistic.

CHAPTER 21

"YOU CATHOLICS *ARE* idolaters." Julia Cain's eyes sparkled with laughter. "Our minister told us you were and he was right."

Wearing a green-and-gold Notre Dame warm-up suit with a matching green ribbon in her hair, she was sitting at the computer station in her office on the second floor of their penthouse. Sun was streaming in the window, and across the drive the lake was stirring up vigorous white-caps to celebrate the first cool, crisp autumn day of the year.

"A Notre Dame Saturday convinced you of that?"

"Did it ever! I've never seen such an orgy of symbolism in all my life. It was insidious and seductive and beauti-ful!"

"Ms. Cain is up working on her computer, Bishop," the good Irene had told me. "She says you go right on up and I'll make some tea for you."

"Cookies?"

"Sure. You sure do have a sweet tooth, Bishop."

"Arguably," I had admitted.

"Better than football Saturdays at Charleston?" I said to Julia Cain.

The glow in her eyes faded. "You don't miss much, do you, Father Blackie?"

"I try."

"When I was there I went over to Champaign a couple of times." Her good humor returned. "They do big productions, but it's not like Notre Dame."

"They invented it."

"Bart had a grand time. Did you know that he had always wanted to go there as a boy but his parents wouldn't let him because they said the Depression was coming back?"

"So I'm told."

The good Irene arrived with Earl Gray tea and a plateful of assorted cookies.

I sighed contentedly.

"And he's had those tickets since 1955," she continued when Irene left. "And he hasn't gone to a game since he had that fight with Father Hesburgh about immigration legislation."

"A good cause."

"You don't take sugar or milk, do you? As black as midnight on a moonless night, right?"

"Indeed."

"Even if he didn't like the immigration bill, I told him it was just plain silly not to go to the games and that I wanted to go. So we went and we had a wonderful time, despite the cane he's still using. His friends were so happy to see him again."

"Did they like you?"

"They seemed to."

"You were of course wearing the warm-up suit . . . and the ribbon."

"Father Blackie." She blushed. "You must think I'm terrible."

"Merely adroit."

"I brought it across the street at 900 North Michigan, at

Candibeth's insistence. It was sinfully expensive. First time I ever went into that building. Never again."

"Or until you need something to please your husband's friends."

"Fersure." She chuckled. "I think the cloud is lifting. For awhile it looked like it would never go away."

Julia Cain had good reason to be happy. Mike Casey had called that morning. "They've found the dental records. The Dowagic police keep open files on all the unsolved murders in their area, three or four in the last fifty years. No one thought of looking in them until last night. Sure enough there were the dental records. Their pathologist is doing the comparison today. There's no doubt about the outcome. They had a physical anthropologist from Ann Arbor down last week and he told them that the skeleton had been in the ground for over a hundred years and that there was no dental work on it at all. They've been quiet about it because their local media like ours are screaming cover-up and will accept nothing but dental records. So a family is kept under a cloud for two weeks."

"Call Bart Cain and tell him the good news."

I had awakened that morning with the vague impression that something Candibeth had said the night before was enormously important and that I had missed it. I was still groping for it.

"Do you often tell your husband what to do?"

In accordance with the potent words of the Wise Man, "Waste not, want not," I was devouring the cookies. Destroying them altogether, as the Irish would say.

She shifted uneasily on her chair. "I worry about whether I'm becoming a scold. When we were first married I waited for him to ask what I thought about something. Now I just tell him."

"He agrees?"

"Most of the time. Practically always. I mean, I told him it was silly not to go to Notre Dame games and he thought about it for a moment and then said I was probably right. So I went out and bought this"—she waved at her warm-up suit—"and he was very pleased when I came home and put it on. *Very* pleased. And yet"—she grew serious—"Eunice was a scold and I don't want to be his second dominating wife."

"You do not mind, however, that he be putty in your hands?"

She blushed again and lowered her eyes. "No, Father Blackie, I don't. I know I'm good for him. The advice I give him is good advice . . . I don't want to destroy the putty, though."

"A delicate balance?"

"Very." She looked up at me, frowning. "No easy answers, huh?"

She refilled my teacup and consumed the one cookie which her Methodist heritage permitted her to indulge in.

"None," I said. "There never are easy answers to complex problems of human intimacy. Whoever suggests that there are is either a charlatan or a fool."

"Well"—she dismissed the problem with a wave of her hand—"we'll work it out. He doesn't have to agree with me all the time."

"Only when you're right."

She laughed. "He can disagree even sometimes when I'm right. Not too often."

So Bart Cain was learning that his passionate discovery also had a mind and a will of her own. Thus far the discovery had not troubled him. Excellent. It was not that Eunice was manipulative and Julia was not. Rather, Julia's manipulations were straightforward and candid—and of-ten, I suspected, blunt.

So she would become shortly, if she was not already, the most important influence in his life, much to the dismay of his already jealous and resentful family. There would be more trouble with them.

"Doctor Murphy is wonderful." She changed the subject abruptly. "I'm so grateful to you for recommending him. He makes me work hard, but I guess I have to. I should have seen someone like him long ago."

"Indeed."

"You've figured out—because you figure like totally everything out—that I was molested as a girl. By my father and by our minister. It turned me off on sex and religion. I hated the thought of a man touching me." She rushed on, eager to finish the sad story. "They were such creepy, mousy, sneaky little men. Ugh."

She shivered and paused.

"So I thought I would never marry. I was used and used up, a paper plate thrown away after a picnic. No man would want me and I didn't want to be wanted because it meant snide laughter and pain and degradation. When a boy wanted to kiss me at the end of a date—and I didn't have too many dates—I froze up completely. So I convinced myself that I did not feel any sexual desire. I would live with my charts and my math"—she gestured at her computer screen—"and that was that."

"Only it wasn't."

"When I saw desire"—she was crying—"in Bart's eyes, it was so different from the way my father and Pastor Paxon looked at me, similar and yet different, that some-thing just tore loose inside of me, all the loneliness and need and hunger which had been locked up for so long. I didn't *want* to respond to him, but I was carried along by my own emotions. I knew he wouldn't hurt me."

"An accurate judgment if you ever made one."

"Fersure. I knew I was marrying a father figure, but a kind one, a father who would, well . . ."

"Cherish?"

Alas, all the cookies were gone. Naturally I could not ask for more.

"Oh, yes, cherish me and desire me at the same time. I know enough about Freud to realize that it might be very unhealthy but I didn't care. I said I'd work that out later. So I guess that's what I'm doing now."

"You've told your husband about your childhood experiences."

She nodded. "It was the most difficult thing I've ever done. I knew he'd still love me but I was so afraid. Doctor Murphy said I'd have to do it eventually, for my own sake, not his. So I did."

"And?"

"And Bart Cain held me in his arms and cried with me."

"Bart Cain wept?"

"I know." She giggled despite her tears. "Isn't that amazing?"

"Totally."

"And then we made love, no, I made love to him and I knew it would be all right . . . No, that's not true, Father Blackie it will never be all right. Those memories will never go away. But I'm all right and my marriage is all right and that's what matters."

"*Indeed!*"

Lady Wisdom's grace was a firestorm in this apartment. Unfortunately She expected me to take care of the minor details of cleaning up the mess which Her bright schemes had produced.

"So"—she wiped away her tears—"that's the story. I'm glad I told him. I'm glad I told you, though, like I say, you know everything anyway."

"So it is said, but with some exaggeration. Now you must tell me what this attractive object is on your twenty-one-inch super VGA screen."

"Chaos."

"Ah, so it would seem."

"You know what chaos research is?"

"The search for an explanation of higher-order order in seemingly random events, why each snowflake has a different design, why the two worst hurricanes of the century come within a single month, how does a heartbeat rhythm emerge from a mass of cells."

"Precisely." She became an academic, indeed, an academic mathematician. "You know about fractual math?"

"A bit."

She began a brief lecture. "There is some persuasive evidence that even chaos in not completely chaotic. So we try to find not the order in chaos, but the order behind chaos and the order in front of chaos. You know I'm working on my doctorate? I didn't tell you, but I'm sure you know about it."

"I haven't read your thesis proposal."

"I *knew* you knew . . . anyway, what are the patterns in seemingly random weather events, in the coming and going of ice ages, and, as you might guess, in long- and short-term fluctuations of the commodity markets. I'm not talking about charts here." She pushed a macro combination on her keyboard and a fairly complicated graph appeared. "Nor about super charts." She produced a far more complex three-dimensional design. "But hyper charts, not only three-dimension but n-dimensional."

The third graph did not look like a chart at all but like

a painting of forested blue mountain ranges with orange rivers flowing through them and occasional clown faces staring balefully at the viewer.

"Probing the mind of God?"

"As far as He regulates the grain market," she said solemnly, "yes. I can't call God She yet, Father Blackie. Maybe if I continue to hang around with you idolaters I will."

"She doesn't mind because She is both male and female and neither male nor female."

"Does He mind what I'm doing?"

"Hardly. Otherwise He would not have given us minds like His own. Or passion like His own . . . what advice does this wondrous artifact give me about the grain market?"

"It tells you that, despite George Bush's attempt to peddle American grain this autumn as a help to his reelection campaign, you should go short on wheat."

"Which your husband knows already?"

"That's the point! Why does the human organism understand in some deep level of instinct how to deal with chaos even though it is only now beginning to understand what chaos is? It must be that humans somehow participate in or at least resonate with the plan in chaos."

"And Bart says of this research?"

"He loves me so much, Father Blackie"—she sighed—"that he thinks everything I do is wonderful even when he doesn't know what I'm talking about. And he never patronizes me."

"Wise man."

"These have been a hard couple of weeks," she said, turning off her computer system. "They've brought us closer together. I am astonished by Bart's self-restraint under pressure. I suppose he wouldn't be a good trader if he were not like that. But he's taken a terrible beating, first physical and now psychological."

"Indeed . . . especially the strange matter of Mary Anne Haggerty."

"He keeps saying that he did not kill her and that the body they have found is not hers."

"In the second matter he is now proved accurate, though it may be doubted that the media will let it go."

"I suppose . . . he never says a word about what happened that day. It's all buried in a deeply private part of himself that I can't penetrate and don't want to because he doesn't want me to."

"I see."

"I asked him once if he had any idea who might have killed her. And he said that no one killed her, she just disappeared. Strange answer . . . I'll be glad when they finally release the dental report today."

"Indeed."

"The family has been terrible these last two weeks, except for Bill, who thinks it's all kind of funny, which I suppose in a way it is. Lourdes is in a hospital. Junior blames us of course, me especially, like I was the farmer who discovered the body. Jenny calls every day and shouts obscenities."

"Nothing from Tim O'Donnell?"

"No. Not to me at any rate. He might talk to Bart at the exchange or call him on his private line in his office. He was there of course, wasn't he? On that mysterious day? It was his car they drove in."

I remained silent.

"He's a strange little man, isn't he? I don't see why Bart puts up with him except that he's an old friend and you Irish are loyal to old friends. I don't trust him. He's a sly fox. I think he enjoyed Bart's accident."

"Accident?"

"If you don't believe in ghosts, it had to be an accident, didn't it? I do believe in them, so I think there was some sort of ghost here in the apartment that night."

"A ghost strung the trip wire?"

"Who else would have done it, could have done it? There certainly wasn't any trip wire when we went up to bed after the last of the guests had left. Beth was sound asleep. Bart and I were in each other's arms. Yet someone laid that horrid trap."

"Someone else might have been in the apartment."

"No one was there. Everyone had gone home."

"A servant or a caterer who had remained?"

"They all left after dinner while we were having drinks in the parlor. I gave them each an extra tip and I had exactly the right number of twenty-dollar bills."

"In what order did the family leave?"

"Well, as you've probably heard a hundred times, Beth went up to bed first. She was tired and she had a big game the next day. She was also very angry. Then I suppose that Bill and Jenny left, not together because they can't stand one another. Junior and Lourdes and Tim hung around. She was gushing over poor Bart and showing him new pictures of her kiddies. I thought she'd never leave."

"She didn't show you the pictures?"

"As far as Lourdes is concerned, I don't exist. The three of them left together."

"And David and his wife?"

She frowned. "They're so quiet you hardly notice them. But they're nice, sweet people. I wish we could be friends. But she's so afraid that Bart will take her husband away from her. I wish I could tell her that I won't let him. But I suppose she wouldn't believe me."

"But when did they leave?"

"I really don't remember, Father Blackie." She paused. "And that's strange because I always try to be nice to her."

"Indeed . . . then after all the guests had left?"

"I peeked into Beth's room to make sure the evening had not made her sick. Bart turned off all the lights from the control panel at the head of the stairs—he's fussy about electric bills, a holdover from the Great Depression, I guess—and we went into our bedroom and closed the door. Sometime later the bell rang . . ."

"Which one?"

"They sound so much alike I can't even tell when I'm on the first floor of this place. Bart said that Jenny probably forgot something again, she usually manages to do that, and he would answer the door. He threw on a robe, opened the door, flipped on the lights, and ran down the stairs. I saw him fall and ran after him. As Beth would say, I kind of lost it. I thought he was dead. She was as cool as a cucumber. Called 911, calmed me down, tried to find out who rang the bell . . ."

"A good person to have around when there's an accident."

"You think someone was trying to kill or injure me and got Bart by mistake, don't you?"

"Arguably," I said with a sigh.

"I certainly answer the bell usually . . . take-charge-wife type."

"Any suspects?"

She thought for a moment.

"Jenny and Lourdes would like to kill me. If looks or hostility could kill, then I'd be in the tomb." She rubbed a hand across her face. "I must be a terrible threat to them. Is there anything I can do that will change them?"

"No. Except die."

"I was afraid of that . . . but even if they wanted to

kill me, how could they have done it? They had left the apartment before we went up to bed. How could they have come back and set the trap?"

"Do any of them have keys to the apartment?"

"I don't think so. The building association is very strict about giving out keys. Even if they wanted to come back up, the doormen are under strict instructions to *always* ring before they send someone up, even if that person has just come down. The older people in the building scare easily. I guess I will too from now on."

"Doctor Bill?"

"He kind of gives me the shivers. He's the one charming person in the family, besides Candibeth, of course. But he's always sizing me up, wondering what I'm doing with his father. No, speculating on it, depicting it and smirking. He's a predator with women, I suppose, though definitely not a pushy one. It's mostly evaluation, but also just a touch of sly invitation to find out if I'm interested. Needless to say, I'm not. Some men are that way, I guess, and it's not their fault."

"So it is said."

"Actually"—she hesitated—"he did make one pass, light and quick—and he backed off immediately."

"Indeed!"

"I suppose that I'll have to become accustomed to that sort of thing now that my husband has made me seem sexy to men. I haven't yet figured out when to be flattered and when to be offended. Though obviously from my stepson I am offended, but not violently so."

She was more puzzled than either offended or flattered. My conclusion would have been that for Doctor Bill to take that kind of risk—even granting that he liked risk-taking—he must have been powerfully attracted by his stepmother.

"But other than that, and a woman gets used to that sort of fantasy in men, he's perfectly pleasant to me, the only one that is."

"What do you think will happen in the family?"

"You mean when it all calms down? I think Bart has had it with Lourdes and Junior and Jenny. He might put them in their place. Which," she added crisply, "is long overdue if you ask me."

My questions and doubts answered, I took my leave and she went back to her quest for the mind of God, who apparently does play dice with the universe. For the fun of it, if you ask me.

Something she had said teased my mind, a bare hint which fit in with other things I knew or ought to know. There was an explanation for the Mary Anne Haggerty affair and it was just beyond the tips of my fingers.

CHAPTER 22

"LATE THIS AFTERNOON," the breathless anchorperson began in a tone appropriate for the launching of World War III or the coming of the Last Judgment, "authorities in Cass County, Michigan, released their findings on the skeleton uncovered in a farm field there two weeks ago. Our Rod Stone is there with the story."

"Well, Della, it would appear that the skeleton of a young woman with a possible skull fracture that was unearthed here two weeks ago is not that of Mary Haggerty, the missing prom date of commodities tycoon Bart Cain forty-five years ago. An analysis of her dental record establishes conclusively, according to the sheriff of Cass County, that the body is not Ms. Haggerty's."

Cut to the sheriff, a handsome, polished black man.

"As a point of fact"—the sheriff talked just like John Culhane at his press conferences, the educated articulate cop—"we now estimate that the skeleton has been in the ground for at least two hundred years. Moreover, while there were several missing teeth, there was no evidence of any dental work as we understand it."

"Was it a Native American, Sheriff?" our Rod Stone, always politically correct, demanded.

"Possibly, though it could have also been the body of an early settler. It is our judgment that she was not the victim of foul play but died of natural causes."

"The crack in her skull . . ."

"Is recent and was probably caused by contact with the farmer's machine."

"Does this conclusively prove that Bartholomew Cain did not kill Mary Anne Haggerty?"

The sheriff made a face. "All our findings prove is that this skeleton was not that of Ms. Haggerty."

"So the murder investigation is still open?"

"We don't know that there ever was a murder. There's a missing-persons file which is still open."

"Are you going to question Mr. Cain?"

The sheriff, who wanted to be free of the case, frowned. "We have no new evidence that would justify reopening the investigation. Should we find such evidence we might want to ask Mr. Cain some questions."

"Are you actively pursuing an investigation?"

"The file on the case is still open."

Back to Rod Stone in front of the Cass County Court House.

"So you see, Della, Bart Cain can relax a little tonight. The woman buried in the farmer's field near here is not his 1947 prom date. But the mystery of her murder remains unsolved. Apparently the local authorities are not going to devote much time and work to an investigation of a possible crime committed by a rich and powerful Chicagoan almost a half century ago. Yet there remains one crucial unanswered question: Did Bart Cain rape and murder Mary Haggerty? It is a question to which Mr. Cain has yet to give a convincing answer." Dramatic pause. "Rod Stone, Cassopolis, Michigan."

"Black sheriff?" Milord Cronin asked me.

"Majority black county. Terminal for the Underground Railroad, which smuggled slaves out of the South before the Civil War."

"Hmm . . . they're not going to let up on Bart, are they?"

"Rod Stone sure isn't."

"They get the evidence they've been expecting for two weeks and it's suddenly not conclusive any more."

"A rich and famous man is fair game."

"He practically accused Bart of rape and murder and demanded that he prove his innocence."

"The American way. Bart didn't have to become rich and famous, did he?"

"By the way, Blackwood, what did happen to Mary Haggerty?"

"At the present time, I do not know."

"Don't you think you'd better find out?"

"Arguably."

"Then see to it, Blackwood!"

CHAPTER 23

WHILE EATING BREAKFAST the next morning after Mass I saw to it. And saw it. The pertinent remarks of Julia and Candibeth converged. The elevator door from my unconscious opened and the full picture came tumbling out.

I sat there in a half-trance, an English muffin doused in raspberry jam in my hand. It could not be possible. No way.

I ran through a number of scenarios which made it possible. Then the one which made sense came tumbling out of the elevator too.

I checked the two pictures which were rapidly emerging against the data at hand. Everything fit. Dear God, what a story!

Not, however, for Rod Stone.

"You OK, Boss?" one of my associates demanded.

"Mm."

"Are you having a religious experience, Blackie?" a resident cleric asked in the voice of one who has seen two moons in the sky instead of one.

"Of a sort."

I ran through the facts again. Oh, yes, it all fit. I would have to take certain actions to test my theory, cautious, careful actions.

"He's solving a puzzle," another associate said calmly. "It happens every once in a while. Nothing to worry about."

I swallowed the English muffin in a single bite. "Excuse me," I said to my colleagues, "the game's afoot."

I spent the morning making phone calls.

It would be necessary for me to make a brief trip.

I hunted up my senior associate. "Gus, the place is yours for a day or two. Don't do anything reckless."

"Hey, wait a minute," he shouted after me as I departed from the door to his room.

I called Milord Cronin's direct line at the pastoral center. "The game's afoot," I informed him.

"And you're catching a train from Padington Station?"

"O'Hare."

"You'll be back when?"

"A day or two. Don't say anything rash to Milord Ratzinger before I come back."

I packed a few things and caught a cab for the airport without ticket or reservation. One of the many nice things about living in Chicago is that you can fly almost anywhere in the world almost any time you want.

There was indeed an empty seat on a flight to the place I sought.

I was away from the cathedral for the better part of three days. When I finally arrived back in my rooms at midnight on the third day, I was in agreement with those who said that even if I found out the full story of Mary Haggerty I would not make use of it.

It did not follow that someone else might not make use of it.

That eventuality, however, was not subject to my decision.

CHAPTER 24

THEN MATTERS TOOK a spectacular turn.

At eight o'clock the next morning I walked over to East Lake Shore Drive. I would tell Bart Cain that, as promised, I had solved the mystery and, as he had predicted, I would do nothing with my solution.

I never did get to deliver that message.

It was a chill, gray day with a wintry wind blowing off the lake—though it was only mid-October.

I walked along Michigan, huddling in the shelter of the Drake Hotel, and turned the corner onto East Lake Shore Drive.

Then it happened, as if in a slow-motion NFL game replay.

A black Lincoln Town Car pulled away from the Cains' building, their car doubtless taking Candibeth to school. A large van pulled in front of it and blocked the street. Another limo turned behind it and blocked its retreat. Two black-clad figures with hoods over their heads emerged from each vehicle. All four cradled automatic weapons in their arms, either Uzis or Walthers.

They fired short blasts at the Cain car. The Lincoln ground to a halt as if exhausted. One of the figures shot open the lock on the front door, pulled out the driver, and threw him to the ground. Another reached in and opened all the doors. Two of the gunmen stood ready with their weapons, one facing the car, the other moving the gun barrel back and forth with an obvious message: Don't anyone try anything or a lot of people will die.

Terrified pedestrians screamed all around. I stood motionless, frozen at the entrance to the Drake, paralyzed and powerless.

The first gunman pulled open the back door and threw Candibeth to the ground next to the driver like she was a useless sack of potatoes. Then he and the other one near the Lincoln jumped in the front seat. The two remaining terrorists, for such surely they must be, held their weapons in the air and fired off several volleys, like they were Lebanese militiamen in Beirut. Then they jumped back into the van and careened down the street. The Lincoln followed close behind. As the Lincoln roared by me, I caught a glimpse of Julia in the backseat, a weapon buried under her chin.

They barreled through the red light at Michigan and Oak as though it wasn't there. Several cars spun around and bumped into one another. The van continued west on Oak, running interference for the Lincoln in complete disregard for oncoming one-way traffic. It smashed through double-parked cars and moving cars coming towards it and brushed them aside like tiny toys. It turned north on Wabash and disappeared from sight, the Lincoln right behind it.

It indeed was a bravura performance, both "professional" and reckless.

I became conscious of terrified screams all around me.

As I rushed to comfort the fallen Candibeth, two thoughts rushed through my mind.

One: Why take the wife and not the daughter?

Two: I would get those bastards no matter how long it took.

CHAPTER 25

"IT LOOKS LIKE we're dealing with Irish terrorists." The FBI agent in charge sounded greatly pleased with himself. "That's good news and bad. The good news is that while they kill British soldiers and civilians, they rarely kill those they kidnap. The bad news is that they are almost diabolically clever and insanely reckless. Their actions this morning show both characteristics."

Tell me about it, the obscure little priest sitting in the far corner of the Cain parlor murmured to himself.

The parlor was jammed with various at present ineffectual defenders of public order: Chicago police, Illinois State Police, and very much in charge and disdainful of all lower forms of police, the Federal Bureau of Investigation, acting under the provisions of the Lindbergh Law.

A number of higher-level Chicago cops were bustling around the room, having been photographed by TV cameras as they entered the 207 building, but John Culhane of Area Six was obviously directing the Chicago effort, and was the only city cop with whom the FBI deigned to deal. Mike Casey was huddled with Bart Cain and a grim and tearful Candibeth, her head bandaged to protect the cut opened when she'd hit the street.

"Let's kill those fuckers," she had said to me when I had pushed my way to her side on street, "kill them, Father Blackie."

"If necessary, by all means."

"How did they know that this was the first day we didn't have security guards in the car?" Bart now asked for the tenth time. "How did they know Julia would be in the car with Elizabeth?"

"Those are important questions," the special agent in charge responded. "We'll get to them in due course."

I did not know his name because when he had entered the apartment, he had announced himself thusly: "I am the Special-Agent-in-Charge." Apparently we were supposed to fall on our knees. He was a tall, angular man with a hatchet face, thin lips, and cold blue eyes. They obviously picked their men to fit the film stereotypes. Fact imitating fiction.

It should have been obvious to anyone and everyone that they knew about the passengers in the Town Car because someone in the family had talked to Julia the night before and pried the information out of her. Or possibly Candibeth.

In due course I would find out who that person was.

No one from the family was with us during the next two days, though Doctor Bill at least had offered to come to the apartment. Bart Junior had called to remonstrate with his father about the terrible effect on Lourdes. We had heard not a word from Jenny or her lover. Tim O'Donnell had spoken with Candibeth on the phone and promised his prayers. He was not feeling very well, he'd told her, or he would have come right down.

"He's totally blotto," she had confided to me. "He's like totally lost it again."

"He lost it fifty years ago."

"Do we know the names of these terrorists?" John Culhane asked.

"I don't think there's a need to know that," Special-Agent-in-Charge said.

"Bullshit," John replied. "Our guys have got contacts in the Irish-American nationalist community in Chicago. I want to know their names."

"Well," Special-Agent-in-Charge temporized, "I suppose there's no reason to keep their names secret. They use many aliases, of course. But we have reason to believe that they are Ed MacSweeny, Sean McGrail, Nessa O'Connor, and Siobahn Gallagher."

He pronounced the last name like it was See-oh-ban.

"Shevaun," said the virtually invisible little priest, in a stage whisper.

"Why haven't we heard from them?" Culhane asked.

"Apparently, they do all their communications through the media. Calls more attention to their cause."

"Channel 5 at five o'clock," the aforementioned harmless priest observed. "Highest ratings."

"What will we do?" Bart Cain asked, his fear under iron control.

"We'll wait to see what they want. They may ask for an exchange of certain of their people for your wife. As you know, the Government of the United States of America does not negotiate with terrorists."

"Except when it does," Mike the Cop complained bitterly. "Are they IRA?"

"Some fringe group."

"The local IRA supporters would hate them. Maybe . . ."

"All in good time," Special-Agent-in-Charge admonished Mike. "We have to find out what they want before we do anything."

The van and the Town Car had been abandoned at North and State, in front of the cardinal's mansion, to which Milord Cronin rarely withdrew. A nice touch. They then had sped off in another car, make unknown, headed west on North Avenue.

Trail lost.

One of the many phone lines which had been rigged in the apartment rang. "Channel 5, Commander. They've just had a tape delivered from the terrorists. Five o'clock news."

"Turn it on," Special-Agent-in-Charge ordered.

There was no anchorperson. Rather, we saw a man in a black turtleneck and hood with only the center of his face appearing.

"Good evening. Bart Cain," he said genially in a patent Cork brogue. "I am a Commandant in the Legitimate Army of the People of Ireland. I know you support the cause of freedom around the world. But to tell you the truth, I'm a little disappointed that you haven't contributed to the cause of your own people in Ireland. Sure, 'tis the way it is with you Yanks. Make a few dollars and you forget how close you still are to the bogs. Well, what me friends and I intend to do is to give you a chance to make a small contribution. Two million of your Yankee dollars in unmarked hundred-dollar bills if you please, and not in any serial-number arrangement either, if you take me meaning. If you're willing to show us that you are a patriotic Irishman after all, why, then we will give you your pretty young wife back none the worse for wear. If you're not cooperative, well, I would hate to tell you what might happen to her. And as our friends from the FBI and the CIA have already told you, we have a record of not harming people, unless they're Brits, of course, and we're at war with them. So I'm giving you twenty-four hours to collect the money. And I'll be back tomorrow night to tell you where to leave it, understand?

"Ah, is it that you want to make sure that your dear Julia

is still alive? Well, sure, we'll let her talk to you in her own words."

The camera moved jerkily to Julia's face. Her eyes were wide with fear, her mouth bandaged shut.

"Now, since we can take these video things over and over again, we're going to let her tell you that's she's fine in her own words—and warn you that it'll be a mite hard on her if you don't cooperate. And, oh, yes, poor lass doesn't know where she is. Never been here before in her life."

He carefully removed the bandage and jammed a nine-millimeter semi-automatic under her chin, the latter presumably for effect since they were taping the whole scene.

"How are you feeling, my dear?"

Julia licked her lips and spoke in an unsteady whisper, passive and lifeless.

"I'm all right, Bart," she said. "Sort of sick from the ride like I was in a roller coaster. Please do what these people ask exactly the way they tell you. They are determined Irish patriots and they'll kill me if you don't cooperate. Give my love to Beth."

Doubtless they had shot tranquilizer into her, probably as soon as they had changed cars.

"So you see," MacSweeny, for that was a Cork name, continued, "everything will be all right if you just do the right thing by the people of Ireland. Talk to you tomorrow."

The screen went blank for a moment, and then there was a babble of reporters and anchorpersons.

"Find out how that tape was delivered," bellowed Special-Agent-in-Charge.

There was a long discussion about whether the terrorists should be paid. The FBI thought it was a mistake. Bart

Cain understandably disagreed. Joe Houlihan, who had drifted in, and Mike the Cop insisted that the money be paid.

"She's worth a lot more than two million dollars to me," Bart said.

"Totally." Candibeth spoke for the first time.

"I don't think the Government of the United States of America can cooperate in such an effort," Special-Agent-in-Charge said.

"Get the Director on the phone," Mike the Cop snapped, "and let me talk to him."

I did not hear Mike's sotto-voce conversation with the Director, who of course knew him, as did every major law-enforcement official in the land—through his books and articles, if not personally. It was evidently decided that Bart Cain could ransom his wife and the FBI would help him.

"Do you have that money available?" Special-Agent-in-Charge asked Bart.

"Of course."

"In unmarked hundred-dollar bills—that's a lot of hundreds. Let me see . . ."

"Ten thousand of them." Candibeth had done the calculations. "Two hundred packs with a hundred each in them."

I mentally repeated her calculation. Right on.

"No." Special-Agent-in-Charge was counting on his fingers. "Two thousand packs; that's a big package."

"Two hundred," Candibeth said firmly.

"See, Chief"—one of his flunkies rushed up with a hand calculator—"it is two hundred."

There ensued an angry conversation between the two agents, which was finally settled when Special-Agent-in-

Charge announced, as though it was his position all along,
that it would be two hundred packs.

"Two large attaché cases, that's all we'll need. Now Mr.,
uh, Cain, do you have that money available?"

"We can get it from the banks and the Fed," Joe
Houlihan told him, "can't we, Bart?"

"Of course, but we'd better begin now. It will take
time."

The "Fed" was the Federal Reserve Bank.

The three of them, Bart, Mike, and Joe, each grabbed
phones and began making calls.

"Special Agent Cooper," I said meekly to Special-
Agent-in-Charge when he happened to walk by me.

"Are you talking to me, uh, Reverend?"

"Most Reverend, actually. I know how you can get the
money a lot easier than that."

"How?" He laughed as though he were talking to a
harmless fool.

I told him.

"Why would we want to do that?"

I told him.

"That's the craziest idea I have ever heard."

"Arguably."

"We would never do anything like that! Absolutely
not!"

"Let me talk to the Director."

"I would never bother the Director with such a lunatic
scheme."

"Mike." I summoned the retired police superintendent.
"Would you please tell Special Agent Cooper here that the
Director wants to speak to me."

"My name is *not* Cooper!"

"Ah."

So I did speak to the Director.

"Blackie, I figured you'd show up eventually."

I told him my idea.

"Why?" he asked sharply.

I explained my reasoning.

"That's the craziest idea I've ever heard."

"Indeed . . . but you'll do it."

"Naturally."

So it was arranged. Steal one of my parishioners out from under my nose, would they?

Tipperary men are a match for Cork men any day in the week.

CHAPTER 26

I SHUTTLED BACK and forth between the cathedral and East Lake Shore Drive that evening and the next morning. I said Mass on the dining room table for Bart and Candibeth and the cops who wanted to attend. We prayed that God would protect us from evil and bring Julia Ross Cain safe and sound to her family.

That evening, however, a strange event occurred. The doorman rang. Candibeth jumped to the phone before anyone else could. "Send them up," she said, as one having authority.

A few moments later, the elevator door opened and Dave and Leonora Cain entered the apartment. He hesitated at the door. She did not. Rather she ran to Bart, threw her arms around him, and weeping, buried her head against his chest.

Startled, Bart Cain nonetheless accepted the grace of the moment and held her close and wept with her. Then, even more astonishingly, he stretched out one of his arms and included his brother in the embrace.

They added a new and more gracious dimension to the crisis. Leonora helped Beth in the kitchen (not exactly taking over) and kept a steady supply of northern Italian pasta available. Dave remained by his brother's side making quiet suggestions and offering calm hopefulness.

Bart accepted both as if his agreement with his brother was a matter of course.

Now, Lady Wisdom's ways are wonderful and inscrutable, but cynic that I am, I suspected that on this occasion She'd had some notable human assistance.

I cornered my suspect in the kitchen, her hands covered with pasta flour.

"Nice going, young woman," I informed her.

"You mean Uncle Dave and Aunt Lea?" She nodded towards the front room. "*Well,* I call them and go get your asses right over here. I'm like you want a reconciliation, you'll never have another chance like this. Dad like totally needs you."

"And they came."

"Totally."

At Mass the next morning the second two sections of the Seventeenth Psalm seemed an appropriate prayer:

> I call upon you; answer me, O God,
> Turn your ear to me, hear my prayer.
> Show your wonderful love,
> You who deliver with your right arm
> Those who seek refuge from their foes.
> Keep me as an apple of your eye;
> Hide me under the shadow of your wings
> From the violence of the wicked.
>
> My ravenous enemies press upon me,
> They close their hearts.
> Fill their mouths with proud roaring.
> Their steps even now encircle me;
> They watch closely, keep low to the ground,
> Like lions eager for prey,
> Like young lions lurking in ambush.

Rise, O Lord, confront and cast them down,
Rescue me so from the wicked.
Slay them with your sword;
With your hand, Lord, slay them,
Snatch them from the world in their prime.

"Amen!" Candibeth agreed enthusiastically with the bellicose psalmist.

Hoping to catch the messenger who delivered the second tape, the FBI had agents at all the media outlets in Chicago. The terrorists outsmarted them and sent the tape to Channel 9 for their noon news by Federal Express— using the FBI's own account number.

"Good morning to you, Bart Cain," MacSweeny began cheerfully. "Sure, aren't we all hoping you had a good night's sleep, even though, as you probably figured out, we're recording this the night before, you see. But there's no reason for you not to have slept peacefully if you've made up your mind to follow our instructions to the letter. And don't listen to those assholes from the FBI who can't even protect their own Federal Express account number, if you take me meaning. They don't know how to deal with folks like us.

"Anyway, this is what you do: You have your friend Commander Culhane close down Lake Shore Drive from top to bottom between midnight and five A.M. Not a car anywhere on it, understand? Not a car in sight and no one in the park either. You walk across Grant Park past Buckingham Fountain and down to the embankment at the edge of the lake with your contribution to the people of Ireland in two attaché cases. There's a little landing ramp there, concrete falling apart. Just put the bags there at three-fifteen and then turn around and walk back to where you came from. You're by yourself, of course. And if any police sharpshooters try anything, just remember that they'll be killing your wife.

"I hope that's clear. If you keep your part of the agreement, we'll be back with our final little message tomorrow sometime. We'll tell you exactly where you can find your wife. So long as you do exactly what you're told and don't let them assholes try anything, little Miss Julia here will be perfectly safe, if you take me meaning, and you'll have her back in bed tomorrow night, as simple as that. Isn't that true, dear?"

Julia again, terrified, confused, almost incoherent.

"It's true, Bart; please do what they say."

"Are we hurting you, dearest?"

"No, you keep me tied up and gagged but you give me food and drink and you're not hurting me."

"And do you know where you are, dearest?"

"How could I? The only view that I have is of the roof of this place."

"All right then." MacSweeny again. "Just one more thing. Tell those FBI assholes we don't want any boats out on the lake watching us either. Is that clear? And if any of you bloody capitalists who own boats of your own try to mess with us, we'll blow you out of the water."

End of the tape.

"She's not even trying to tell us anything," Special-Agent-in-Charge lamented. "Not a thing."

"Would you?" Mike the Cop demanded ironically.

Somehow I thought maybe she had, but I couldn't quite figure out what it was. Or how she could communicate in words that we would understand and they wouldn't.

There was a furious argument among the usual suspects about whether the terrorists' instructions should be followed exactly. The Bureau wanted a police boat out on the lake to shadow whatever boat the terrorists might use. The

Chicago cops refused to cooperate. Then the Bureau wanted a Coast Guard helicopter from Glenview to hover over Grant Park. They refused to cooperate. Finally there was another appeal to the Director and he ordered compliance with the terrorists' instructions.

So at two-forty-five A.M. Bart, Candibeth, and I were standing, under umbrellas, in the rain with John Culhane and Mike the Cop on Michigan Avenue, next to an unmarked police car. We were just south of the Art Institute waiting for the next act of the drama to begin. Across the street, barred by mounted police, were the media and thousands of curiosity-seekers.

I was dressed in jeans and a black leather jacket and cap, the kind of bishop that no TV camera would recognize.

"We've cleared out the park," John said, "shut down the drive, controlled all those bloodsuckers across the street, closed the harbors, and chased a few boats off the lake. We're as ready as we ever are going to be."

"It might be a trap," Mike the Cop added. "But I don't think so. In their own crazy way they honor their agreements, though you have to watch for the card up their sleeve. Just cross the drive, put the attaché cases on the old ramp, turn around, and come straight back."

"What will they do?" Bart asked.

"I presume they've pumped up an assault boat somewhere. They'll put-put down the lake, pick up the cash, and depart quickly. They'll come ashore somewhere else and vanish. It's risky but it attracts the maximum publicity to their cause."

"Time," I said.

Bart hugged his daughter, shook hands with me, said, "Pray for us all, Father Blackie," and began his walk across the park, still limping from the injury to his ankle.

The four of us said the Rosary as we waited. The crowd across the street was silent.

Twenty minutes later we heart the faint put-put of an outboard motor. It grew louder and then softer again. A few minutes after that, Bart reappeared in the gloom, his limp much worse.

The crowd cheered him as we got into the car.

"You heard the boat?" he asked.

"Indeed. You didn't see it?"

"No, I was already across the street and into the park."

Our driver reported to Culhane as soon the car pulled away. "We got a report from our man with the night scope over at the planetarium, Commander. He says he saw two subjects in a small rubber boat. They went straight out into the lake till we lost them in the rain."

"Shit," Culhane muttered.

"That's what they figured to do," Mike the Cop said. "Beach it somewhere close, maybe sink it, slip across the drive to a waiting car, and be off."

"We'll be watching for them as best we can so we can follow them, but we're not likely to spot them. Maybe it's just as well if we don't find them," Culhane said.

The media would raise bloody hell with the cops if the terrorists were not caught. Terrorism happened in Europe, not in Chicago. They didn't count the gang wars in the drug neighborhoods, which were far more dangerous that Belfast.

Or Sarajevo.

The TV crews were waiting for us on East Lake Shore Drive, demanding comments from Bart and Candibeth, both of whom were too tired and worn even to be angry.

So Mike and I and the two Cains went upstairs and watched for the dawn.

CHAPTER 27

DAWN WAS NOT much, a faint gray in the eastern sky. The five of us waited grimly in the penthouse, drinking coffee and munching on the rolls which Annie Casey had produced from the deep freeze. Annie kept Candibeth occupied with a proposal that as soon as she was sixteen, she might work at the Gallery a couple afternoons a week. "Not during the basketball season, of course."

That prospect was described as "totally bonkers."

"When do you think we'll hear from them, Daddy?" she asked after she had lost that temporary enthusiasm.

"The noon news, surely."

"I wouldn't count on that," Mike the Cop cautioned us. "They'll want time to get away. They'll probably have some of their Chicago help deliver it for the five o'clock news."

I had little doubt about that. I knew in my heart of hearts that something was going wrong, badly wrong. Ed Mac-Sweeny and his bunch of crazies had a last trick up their sleeve. They had played us for fools.

"I can't help but thinking that God is punishing me for my self-righteousness and meanness," Bart Cain said to me at mid-morning.

"Better that than punishing you for enjoying yourself too much."

He smiled wanly. "Maybe I'm growing up a little . . . will we get her back, Father Blackie?"

"We can but hope."

My own hope just then was at a very low ebb. We were at the mercy of monstrous people, men and women who, because they possessed a few weapons, could control the life of a city and destroy the life of a family. I recited the psalm to myself again.

We waited and we waited and we waited.

The phone rang and rang and rang.

Nothing.

There was much about the kidnapping on the noon news. But no message from the kidnappers. Nor on the evening news. Nor on the ten o'clock news.

A rubber assault boat had been found half sunk under the Michigan Avenue bridge, at that time under repair. So they had climbed the sea wall and dragged the boat over it. Then they had abandoned the boat and climbed into a car on the lower level of Wacker Drive. Clever and reckless. And clumsy of them not to have sunk the boat completely.

The Caseys and I went home for some sleep.

Mike woke me up on the phone at five to six in the morning.

"Someone threw a tape at the door of Channel 7 just a few minutes ago. It'll be on the local news and then on *Good Morning America*. It doesn't sound good."

"I didn't think it would."

I turned on my TV. The funereal expression on the Channel 7 anchorperson did not offer much hope. Ed MacSweeny appeared on the screen in his usual black garb. I turned up the volume.

"Top of the morning to you, Mr. Bartholomew Thomas Cain," he said with his usual charm. "I hope you find this a happier day than yesterday. First of all I want to thank

you for your kind contribution to the cause of the people
of Ireland. The Republic, one and indivisible, thanks you
with all its heart.

"Secondly, in the interests of justice, we've had to make
a slight change in plans. You see, there's one thing about
this whole matter we haven't told you before. Your lovely
young wife is a conspirator with us, don't you know? She
cooperated in her own kidnapping. That's why we took her
instead of the child. She told us when and where we could
make the pickup, if you take me meaning. The idea was
that we'd split the money with her. Sure I wouldn't want
to be asking what's wrong with your marriage, since that's
none of our business at all, at all, is it now? Maybe you
weren't giving her enough money and if that be the case,
I'd say shame on you. Or maybe the old saying is true that
there's no fool like an old fool!

"But I'm rambling on, am I not? The point of this is
that, you being so nice and cooperative with us, it'd be a
shame to cooperate in such treachery. So this is what we're
going to do. We're going to bring all the money back to
the people of Ireland. And we're going to leave your wife
right here where we've had her all along, right in the city
of Chicago. If you want her back, you can just come and
collect her. If you don't want her back, well then, just leave
her here. We're keeping her tied up just like she's been, so
you won't have all that much time to find her."

The tape cut to a shot of an almost lifeless Julia,
breathing, it seemed, but just barely, bound and gagged on
a narrow bed.

"How long do you think a human can survive tied up
like that without any food and water? There'll be spasms
and cramps, won't there now? And difficulty breathing
too, I suppose. Twenty-four hours? Thirty-six? Forty-eight

at the most. So if you want her, you'll have to hurry, won't you now . . . what time is it?"

He glanced at his wristwatch—an Omega, I noticed. Nothing but the best for the Legitimate Army of the People of Ireland.

"Let's see, it's sixteen hundred hours the day before you see this tape. That's four o'clock your Yank way of telling time. So if you figure that after twenty-four hours it gets dicey for our pretty friend here, you'll have, oh, maybe ten hours after you see this tape for the first time.

"So that's all sorted out then. Oh, yes. Just to make it interesting we're not going to tell you where she is. You and those asshole cops and FBI agents are going to have to find out for yourselves. We sincerely wish you good luck. God bless you all!"

There was a brief shot of Julia and then the tape ended.

CHAPTER 28

I PUSHED THE rewind button again.

"Nothing?" asked Sean Cronin, who was sitting on the other side of the community room, offering moral support as I played the three videotapes over and over again.

"Nothing," I murmured. "I know something is in there, but I can't seem to pry it out."

"You need some sleep. That might clear your head."

"My head is already clear, that's the problem, so clear that it is empty."

"I have a Confirmation up on the North West Side."

"Where?"

"West of the expressway on Belmont."

"Drive carefully in the rain."

"Never fear. You'll have it solved before I get back."

"Maybe."

It was the coldest autumn day yet, high in the middle forties. Rain was pouring down relentlessly. Chicago was cloaked in funereal gloom.

There was one more mad development.

At eleven o'clock Mike called again. "Turn on the tube, Blackie. There's bound to be a news break in a few minutes. Our friends ran out of luck. About an hour ago they encountered a roadblock near Harvard, Illinois, out in McHenry County. Local cops looking for some punks that knocked over a bank in Woodstock. One of our friends got nervous and fired first. Two cops wounded, maybe one terrorist. Police radio says they're holed up in a farmhouse out there. No one home, thank God, so there's no hostages. I'm going out there with Bart to see if we can negotiate with them to find out where they've hidden Julia. I'll have my portable phone. Annie's staying here in the apartment with Elizabeth."

I turned on the smaller TV which we use when there is an obligation to watch two NFL games, or a Cub and a Sox game. I watched for a news break while I continued to play and rewind the tapes, over and over and over again.

About eleven-forty-five the news breaks appeared simultaneously on all channels—live shots of a very old farmhouse, surrounded by nothing but barren trees and hundreds of cops, cops of every variety—McHenry County, Illinois State, and FBI—the latter wearing blue raincoats with "FBI" in large yellow letters stenciled front and back. Presumably so that the TV audience would know which cops were America's finest. The rain continued to fall in torrents, so that both the media types and the cops who were reporting minute-to-minute looked like they'd been swimming.

The FBI, it was reported, was negotiating with the terrorists, although Special-Agent-in-Charge, now fully in charge, repeatedly told reporters that the Government of the United States of America does not negotiate with terrorists.

As far as one could determine, the terrorists were demanding medical help for their wounded colleague and guaranteed free passage to Cuba. When they were on the plane they would reveal the location of Julia Cain and not before. Special-Agent-in-Charge in charge was offering them "consideration" from the American Government if they surrendered voluntarily and revealed where they had left Ms. Cain.

"Fock you, asshole," MacSweeny's rich tenor voice replied—on a phone line into which the video sound systems had somehow been plugged. "The same kind of *consideration* you gave Manuel Noriega, I suppose. Look, man, we're Irish patriots and we're not afraid to die. We'll take a lot of you fockers with us and that bitch Cain too. Now wise up or we'll come out shooting."

Both sides were bluffing, but neither side seemed ready to move yet. By the time they did get down to cases, Julia might well be dead.

The media finally got a comment from Bart Cain, who now looked his age and much more, a tough warning. "I have the impression that the special agent in charge is more concerned with the image of the FBI than he is with the life of my wife."

Ouch. That would go national—the networks were already cutting in—and D.C. would start wondering how the FBI looked live from McHenry County. Someone would arrive from Washington to take full charge and Julia would be already dead.

Sorry about that.

Reporters repeatedly speculated about MacSweeny's claim that Julia had conspired with the terrorists. The most common opinion was that she "had" to have been part of the plot because it was the only explanation of how the terrorists knew when to strike.

Idiots. There were scores of other possible explanations.

The cameras panned around the stockade the cops had constructed out of a ring of police cars, a reversal of circling the wagons in the old Westerns. Behind each car several cops crouched, rifles, handguns, and automatic weapons at the ready. A ring of firepower underneath the rain. Everything but crossbows.

At last I didn't *see* any crossbows.

Many of the cops were probably worried whether their rain-soaked weapons would work when and if the shooting actually started. As the TV coverage continued they began carrying the weapons under rain slickers.

Well, except for the real addicts, it was probably an interesting, one-shot change from the afternoon soaps.

Periodically some of the stations, those which still in a time of economic cutbacks had enough personnel to cover all the sites of this "unfolding story," would switch to the Area Six Detective Division, where an exhausted John Culhane would be telling the increasingly belligerent reporters that the CPD was "moving heaven and earth" to find Julia Cain before it was too late. That live shot would be followed by clips of Chicago cops in "house-to-house searches" occasioned by flimsy tips, none of which had been true.

The press corps was convinced that Julia Cain would not be found alive and was probably dead already.

Finally I turned off the volume on the smaller TV set and concentrated on the tapes.

Over and over and over again.

Nothing, nothing, nothing, and more nothing.

I took off my glasses and covered my eyes with my hands to rest them for a moment.

At that moment the light exploded in my brain. I ejected the third tape and inserted the first. When I came to the passage I was looking for I played it over a couple of times. Yep, just what I thought. I played the second tape. Again I played the decisive part a second time.

No doubt about it.

I grabbed for my phone book and looked up a certain address.

Yep. 3250 North Washtenaw. Right where it ought to be!

I sat for a moment in stunned silence. Now everything made sense. I knew now who the criminal was and why. Moreover, within certain clearly defined limits, I knew where Julia was.

I reached for the phone to make a call.

No, it would take too long to get that show on the road.

I made another call.

"Annie, put the kid on . . . Candibeth, be at the corner of the drive and Michigan in five minutes. We're going to go get your mom."

Please God, before it's too late.

CHAPTER 29

RAIN STREAMING FROM her trench coat, and bubble gum exploding nervously from her mouth, Candibeth popped into my 1955 blue Impala. "Fersure, Mom is still alive, Father Blackie. She's in great condition and she's a strong woman."

"I think so too, Candibeth. We're in time and have some time to spare, for which thank God."

I wasn't sure how much time. The drugs the terrorists had pumped into her veins might have weakened her constitution.

"I mean, like she doesn't smoke and only sips at drinks and works out in our exercise room every day and is careful about what she eats. Totally healthy."

"That will certainly help."

I cut across from the corner of Oak and Michigan into the Inner Drive.

"Tell you what, Candibeth. You keep on saying the rosary that you have in your hand and I'll think. There's a number of details that must be worked out before we get up there."

"Where?" She began to finger her beads.

"You'll understand everything when we get there in just a few minutes."

I followed the Inner Drive into Lincoln Park and turned

north on Stockton. I avoided the usual mess at Fullerton, slipped into Sheridan Road, via Lake View and Canon Drive, and turned left on Belmont from Sheridan.

"This is faster than coming on Lake Shore Drive," Candibeth exclaimed, popping a bubble enthusiastically. "When I'm legal, Father Blackie, you gotta show me how to do it."

"Naturally."

The rain had diminished but the streets were slippery and the city was dark. I picked my way west on Belmont, past Clark and then Lincoln. The traffic eased west of Ashland. It required only thirteen minutes to make it from East Lake Shore Drive to Belmont and Western. I turned right there, going north alongside the concrete viaduct, turned against the red light at Roscoe, and then barreled into the parking lot which served the large shopping center, not quite a mall. On one side was DeVry Technical Institute and on the other Lake Technical High School. I kept right on going through the DeVry parking lot.

"Hey!" my companion exploded. "I've been here before! This is . . ."

"Riverview!"

"Right! Totally bitchin', Father Blackie! Where's Mom?"

"We should know in a few minutes."

I turned right on Campbell, which ran along the far side of the parking lot. I wasn't sure how to get there, but the trees which lined the other side of the street marked the course of the Chicago River. After ten or fifteen yards I swerved right again on to a narrow asphalt trail. It curved into a paved lane, marked by concrete benches on either side, which ran along the trees that edged the riverbank. On my right, through the trees, I saw boats lined up three and four deep, like subs alongside their tender in the old war films. Not here. Too many people.

I drove north along the lane till it came to an end beneath the Belmont Avenue bridge. A perfect secluded place for removing a comatose person from a car.

I stopped the car and jumped out, making sure that my pocket phone was in my Chicago Bulls jacket.

"You don't have a raincoat, Father Blackie," Candibeth protested, as Irish women always do.

"It's stopped raining . . ."

The river level was about ten feet below the steep tree-covered bank. I pushed through the first row of trees. Sure enough, the Henry Grebe Ship Yard was just across the river, fifty yards—half a football field—away. 3250 Washtenaw.

I looked upriver and downriver for a pier and a boat.

No pier. No boat. There had to be a boat.

"Look, Father Blackie! A boat!"

Then I saw it, a very old and very dingy boat—the kind that Humphrey Bogart used in all those old Caribbean films—parked up against a small pier cuddled parallel to the shore and hidden by trees on which some rose and golden foliage remained. On its stern the name *Regina* was painted in fading letters.

"Down there!" I pointed, and began to run down the bank.

With notable lack of dignity I slipped on the mud and almost tumbled into the river. My sturdy companion grabbed me by one hand and pulled me to my feet.

"Be *careful*, Father Blackie," she warned me. "We can't afford to lose you in the river."

"Perhaps."

Later I would learn that the river at Belmont Avenue was twelve feet deep, more than enough to dispose of a clumsy and ineffectual little priest.

I stumbled onto the dock, jumped on the *Regina*, and pushed against the cabin door.

Locked! And they'd probably taken the key with them.

"Let me, Father Blackie." The teenager pushed me aside and rammed her power forward's shoulder against the door. It burst open.

In the fading light we saw her mother's body, bound and still. Lifeless.

CHAPTER 30

EXCEPT FOR GLOWING gray eyes.

"Mom!" our door-smasher screamed. *"Mom! Boda-cious!"*

Gently she eased the bandage off Julia's mouth.

"Mom! It's all right. We're here!"

Julia smiled weakly through cracked lips and tried to speak.

"We're *here*!"

"I know, dear," Julia croaked with great effort. "I heard you come in."

That was enough for me. I passed to Beth my Swiss Army knife, which, by some miracle of grace, I had remembered to bring along with the phone.

"Father Blackie has the coolest 1955 blue-and-white Chevy Impala," she announced with great enthusiasm and complete irrelevance as she hacked away at the ropes blinding her mother. "Totally bitchin'. Wait till you see it."

I flipped open my phone and punched in Mike the Cop's number.

It didn't work the first time. Naturally.

I tried again.

"Casey."

"Blackie. We found her. She's all right. You two get the hell out of there and get back to the apartment."

"Gotcha."

Family loyalty came next. I pushed the button which my siblings had programmed to ring the direct line to the office of my brother Packy Ryan, corporation counsel for the City of Chicago.

"Your brother, Packy. Wait ten minutes and then tell himself that Area Six Detectives have found Ms. Cain alive and reasonably well. He'll want to know how you found out and you'll smile."

"He'll know it was you."

"Fine. But deny it."

"Gotcha."

Then I dialed a third number.

"Area Six, Culhane."

"Father Ryan, John. Congratulations on having found Ms. Cain—alive, at that."

John Culhane is one smart cop. He only missed one beat.

"Thanks, Bishop. You're the first one to call me with congratulations and I appreciate that very much. Where did you say we found her?"

"You remember. Right around the corner in a rickety old boat named *Regina*. It is docked where Riverview used to be."

"Of course."

"You might tell the media that there will be an important press statement in a half hour, and then come over here in a detective car with a woman officer and someone to leave in charge."

"Gotcha."

Candibeth had freed her mother and the two were now hugging and laughing and crying. Julia was gaunt, pale, and weak. But grimly determined that she was *all right*.

"I never gave up," Julia choked. "I knew you'd get my

message. They jabbed a needle into me and shot me full of drugs but they didn't blindfold me. Figured they didn't need to. But I saw the sign on the mall. That's why I talked about riding a roller coaster and about not having a view. I knew you'd understand . . ." Julia's body twisted in spasm and then arched up in a cramp. Then she began to choke for breath.

"Mommy!" Beth screamed.

"I'm OK. I really am, just help me to walk a little. Get out in the fresh air, breathe some of that lovely rain into my lungs . . . help me out of here, Beth."

The kid looked at me and I nodded.

Maybe we hadn't arrived a moment too soon.

When John Culhane pulled into the lot, however, Julia Ross Cain had regained a little of her color and was walking a little more confidently.

"They grow them tough down there near Centralia," I said, faking her prairie drawl.

She laughed, still painfully. "Thanks for coming, Father Blackie."

"I should have come sooner."

"Soon enough."

"You like really knew it was Riverview, Father Blackie?" Beth asked.

"Naturally."

"Awesome! Totally awesome . . . But how did you know it was a boat?"

"About that I must talk to Commander Culhane in private for just a few minutes. Why don't you and Detective . . ."

"Leonard," the young black woman said, "Caroline Leonard."

"Help your mother get a few more kinks out while the commander and I have our chat."

"How long did it take you to get here from the cathedral?" John Culhane began.

"Thirteen minutes; you must not tell any of your colleagues from Traffic."

He glanced at his watch. "It took us fifteen to get our act together so we could come over here. I see your point."

"Indeed."

Culhane pulled out a notebook and pen. Rain clouds so low that they seemed almost at rooftop level were rushing towards us. I told him how I knew about the boat, who the criminal was, how the crime was done, and the kind of evidence and potential sources for it he might investigate. Finding Julia Cain, the needle in the haystack which was Chicago, had been the easy part, more her doing than mine. The tough police work remained to be done.

His pen remained poised over the book.

"Holy shit!"

"Quite possibly."

"That's the wildest story I have ever heard."

"So it would seem."

"If I didn't see this woman here I wouldn't be able to believe any of the rest of it."

"Doubtless . . . now if you don't mind, Commander, I am going to report to Milord Cronin. I take it as given that there will be no mention of me in any of your statements and reports."

"Remarkable," he said as he began to scribble in his notebook.

I would have said that my response to the kidnapping and near murder of Julia Cain Ross had been almost criminally slow.

CHAPTER 31

"WE HAVE VERY good news." John Culhane was smiling broadly, as well he might. "Ms. Julia Cain is with us here in Area Six headquarters and will make a brief statement for the media in a couple of moments. She has had a very hard time of it in the last few days, and I hope you'll be content with her statement and not ask her any questions so that she can go home immediately with her daughter. I'm sure she'll provide more details of her kidnapping in a day or two.

"For the present all I can say about her release is that it was effected through the efforts of Area Six detectives. We too will be able to provide more details shortly."

"Huh!" murmured Sean Cronin, who was watching the press conference with me in his study.

"Substantially true," I replied.

"I do want to state firmly that Ms. Cain is under no suspicion of having cooperated in her own kidnapping. The terrorists were lying when they made that allegation. We will be able to demonstrate that in the near future."

"A lot of unanswered questions, John," Rod Stone protested.

"Possibly," Culhane sniffed. "Now, Ms. Cain . . ."

Wearing Beth's trench coat and walking slowly but under her own power, Julia entered the room. The cops who were watching cheered and applauded. For that matter, so did some of the media types.

"Thank you," she said in a low but steady voice, her shyness now giving way to an emerging self-possession. "I am grateful to Commander Culhane and his colleagues for taking care of me, I am grateful to my daughter Beth for her constant support and to my husband"—she smiled— "to whom I have just spoken on the phone, for his astonishing love, and to God, who has set me free and given me two fresh starts in my life this year. She has been very good to me."

Sean Cronin sniggered.

"And I'm glad to have my mom back." Beth hugged her mother fiercely.

Somewhere she had dispensed with her bubble gum.

"What kind of people were the terrorists, Julia?" A reporter jammed a mike at her.

Apparently he expected the usual response of a captive who had come to identify with the captor.

"Monsters," Julia replied bluntly.

Then the ineffable Rod Stone pushed his way through the escort of cops who were taking the Cain women to a car and shoved aside Detective Caroline Leonard.

"Julia, do you believe that your husband killed Mary Haggerty?"

"Bastard!" Sean Cronin screamed as I turned off the TV.

"Tell me the whole story, Blackwood," he demanded. "It looks like you've outdone yourself this time."

"On the contrary." I sighed. "In the expressive words of one we must now call by her adult name of Beth, I fear that I've lost it. The evidence was all there for both mysteries. Because my mental processes are clearly deteriorating, a woman's life was needlessly endangered."

I told him the story. He listened quietly.

"Remarkable," he said.

"I think not."

"What will become of the Mary Haggerty mystery?"

"That remains to be seen. The determined Rod Stone requires containment."

I turned the TV back on. We were back in McHenry County.

Negotiations between the terrorists and the FBI broke down as soon as both sides had seen Julia on TV — which had been my intent. The Feds were demanding capitulation and were offering only "medical assistance." The terrorists were demanding "prisoner of war" status and were threatening to come out shooting.

"We'll take a lot of you with us," Ed MacSweeny shouted into the phone line, despair turning his voice raw.

There was considerable discussion subsequently as to who began the shooting. Some reporters insisted that the police had fired first, "gunning down" the terrorists. Others said that a single shot was fired from inside the house, perhaps an accidental discharge. My firm conviction is that a nervous cop actually was responsible for the "accidental discharge." In any event, the cops who had surround the farmhouse all day with tense fingers did not wait for further orders after the shooting began. Sounding like long strings of firecrackers on the Fourth of July, thousand of rounds of bullets tore at the house. Fire erupted inside. Two figures came rushing out, their automatic weapons blazing. They were cut to pieces as soon as they appeared. Then the house exploded in a fireball of flame — a propane gas tank in the basement had gone up.

No one outside had been warned about the tank. Nine cops and three FBI agents were wounded by flying debris, two seriously. All the cops, as well as the two wounded at the roadblock, subsequently recovered.

Only bits and pieces of the bodies of the terrorists were ever found.

When challenged later about the Bureau's failure to recover Bart Cain's two million dollars, the Director of the FBI chuckled. "Mr. Cain didn't lose any real money. We gave them counterfeit money printed in Iran and confiscated in a recent shipment by our colleagues in the Secret Service. There's a lot more where that came from."

The press was outraged. Was this not somehow dishonorable?

"From now on," the Director said genially, "terrorists will never be sure whether they're getting real American dollars or Iranian American dollars. That should substantially diminish their motivation for kidnapping."

"How will they know they got nothing for their troubles?"

"Well, they could bring someone from the Secret Service along to examine it for them. Otherwise we'll reveal it afterwards."

He didn't say that should the Iranians fail to keep up the supply, the United States could print its own phony dollars for similar purposes.

I'm afraid the logic of that ploy escaped many Americans. Not, however, Milord Cronin.

"Blackwood, you're a sneaky bastard."

"Unarguably."

The next morning I said Mass for the repose of the souls of the five terrorists. We humans dare put no limits on God's mercy and love.

CHAPTER 32

"IT IS TIME," I began solemnly, "and past time to bring this affair to an end."

The Cain family was gathered together early in the evening in my counseling room on the first floor of the cathedral rectory, a week after the shootout in Harvard. They came with greater or lesser degrees of reluctance.

Julia's color had returned, as had Bart's youthful vigor. They no longer pretended that their passion should be discreet. When their arms were not around one another, they held hands like two young lovers. Which, in a sense, they were. The steamy haze which seemed to float around them was neither offensive nor tasteless. Quite the contrary, to be near them was to be absorbed in pleasant warmth. Their marriage had survived a couple of terrible crises and their passion had only been reinforced by those crises.

God knew what She was doing with these two.

Dave sat on one side of Bart and Aunt Lea on the other side of Jennifer. It was very difficult in that picture of family reconciliation to face the reality that they had strong motives for the crime.

"While the terrorist threat has been removed, we are still faced with the problem of the attempts on the life of Julia Ross Cain. I believe that the falling bucket was purely an accident, though it gave the criminal an idea. So too for the car, though Beth surely prevented serious injury by her quick response to the danger. But the concatenation of those accidents was a challenge to the criminal. The falling chandelier was almost certainly that person's work, though I do not know at the moment how it was accomplished. I presume that somehow the person has acquired a key to the penthouse and enters it on occasion for various purposes."

"I don't have to listen to this fucking shit," Jenny exploded. "Get to the fucking point."

"Young woman," I said forcefully, "shut up. Do not interrupt me again."

"Of all the fucking nerve . . ."

"Be quiet, Jenny," her father ordered. "I'm fed up with you and your language and your anger."

She was quiet thereafter. Moral blackmail ended.

"I continue . . . The matter of the trip wire was more complicated and much more ingenious as a scheme. It was not difficult to see how it was done. Early in my investigations I developed suspicions about who did it. The problem has remained as to why it was done."

"How was it done, Father Blackie?" Bart Cain demanded. "I can't figure it out."

"There were, you believed, three of you in the apartment, yourself and your wife, who provide alibis for each other, and Beth, who was sleeping. Moreover, it did not seem likely that any one of you had sufficient motive for working mayhem after the party. Finally, if any of you wanted to kill one another, there were other and more effective ways of doing so. Thus I concluded that the wire was strung by someone else who was also in the apartment."

"Someone else!" Beth's eyes widened. "Awesome!"

"Our very clever criminal slipped away in the vestibule

of the apartment during the confusion while raincoats and umbrellas were being distributed. It was easy enough to do. If he were noticed, it might have been thought that he had gone to the bathroom. Since no one was paying any special attention to him, there was no one waiting for his return."

"Damn risky," Junior murmured.

"That merely heightened the challenge for him . . . I believe that he hid here"—I pointed at a large map of the layout of the first floor—"in this closet beneath the staircase. By peeking out the door he could see what was happening in the vestibule. I note that I use the male pronoun without any intention to suggest at this point the criminal was male.

"When everyone was in bed and the penthouse was quiet, he slipped out of the closet, quickly rigged his trap, ducked into the vestibule, summoned the elevator, opened the door, pushed the bell, sent the elevator back to the first floor, and scurried back to his cover. All this probably took less time to do than to describe. My assumption is that he came with a plan and a trip wire with intent to implement the plan if the opportunity arose. It did and he did.

"He was doubtless shocked when Bart Cain fell down the stairs instead of Julia Cain, but the criminal knew that the whole matter was problematic and that had not deterred him."

"So he was there when I came rushing down the stairs," Julia said in horror, "watching my terror?"

"And doubtless enjoying it. Perceive then what he did. He remained in the closet until after you three had left for the hospital, waited till he was sure a new doorman was on duty, left his hiding place, donned a simple disguise he'd brought along and stuffed in his raincoat—a wig and dark glasses perhaps—and rode down in the elevator. He peered out the window to see if the doorman was in the elevator alcove and could tell that he had come down on the penthouse elevator. Since that presumably was not the case, he strolled into the lobby, told the doorman who had not been on duty earlier in the evening when guests had arrived for the various residents that he had been at someone else's apartment, and walked unsuspected into the street, where he hailed a cab and sped off."

"I don't see what's so great about figuring that out," Lourdes Cain snapped.

"Indeed . . . in any event, there were two major reasons why I was inexcusably tardy in resolving this problem. First, I could not understand why so clever a person would utilize techniques of mayhem which were so problematic in their outcome. The criminal was willing to take not only great risks that he might be caught, but also great risks that his actions might harm no one or anyone. The second problem was my assumption that money was the motive. I was blinded by the fact that when a rich man marries a second and much younger wife, those who have expectations of inheritance will likely be angry at the prospect of seeing these expectations diminished. This seemed to be a classic case of such a marriage and such diminished expectations and resultant anger—homicidal anger, it would have seemed."

The Cains were motionless, their faces unreadable.

"I did not attend to the fact that Cain fortune had been amassed by taking risks and that part of the cultural inheritance of the family might be a propensity to addiction to risk-taking. It did not occur to me that the crimes might be an exercise in risk-taking on the part of a man who did not want or need money but reveled in playing Russian roulette with other people's lives. An incorrigible gambler, Doctor Bill Cain had told me that he had never played Russian roulette. Why bother telling me unless the hint that he had thought of it might turn me down a path that was risky? For him."

Doctor Bill smiled faintly, as if my monologue amused him.

"It would later emerge that he had developed a fascination with his father's wife, whom he wanted for himself. He had sent preliminary signals of this fascination and been summarily rebuffed. Dr. Bill does not like being rebuffed, though in his career as predator that has doubtless happened often before. He especially did not like being rebuffed by a woman who belonged, as he saw it, to his father but ought to belong to him, a woman whose emerging sexual appeal he found ever more demanding. His fascination turned into an obsession. If he could not have the woman, then it might be amusing to punish her by repeated attempts on her life and to punish his father by frightening him with such attempts."

"This is really very foolish, Bishop." Bill Cain laughed. "You can't prove any of it."

"The episode he witnessed at the bottom of the stairs gave him immense pleasure, better, he found, than mere sexual congress. A naked woman kneeling over the body of the prostrate husband and the husband his father. That they both survived did not bother him. It was almost irrelevant. The power to control their destiny, the joy of the game of Russian roulette he had played with their lives and happiness—those were his rewards. Now he was at a turning point. Either he would contain this addiction and return to safer forms of gambling or try for one last game of Russian roulette, the biggest game of all. He would put his stepmother's life in the gravest of dangers, but give her a chance to escape; a thin chance, indeed, but a chance nonetheless. Both she and his father would suffer terrible agonies but death, while probable, was not certain. On the whole he rather hoped she would survive. But to turn even survival into a risk he instructed his terrorists collaborators to claim that she had been a coconspirator. Again there was a chance that they might not be believed, but the outcome was problematic. I am sure he was not at all disappointed that she did survive. Perhaps he could play his game with her again. In the meantime she was apparently suspected, at least by some in the media, of having cooperated and that too was delightful."

Bart and Julia Cain were clinging to one another as if they were lost in a chamber of horrors.

Doctor Bill rose from his chair. "I don't have to sit still for this shit," he snarled.

"You will, however, because you want to know whether I have any proof for my scenario. When I finally and belatedly understood Julia's message about Riverview, I also understood the whole story. Obviously she was in a boat somewhere near the site of the former amusement park. Obviously only William Cain of all the family knew anything about the river. Indeed, he had told me about the small moorings along the riverbanks and in the under-brush, perhaps because he thought I would never see the connection between his words and the Russian roulette he was contemplating at that time, or perhaps to enhance the thrill of the game. I had, however tardily and however ineptly, solved the mystery."

"You have no proof, none at all." Bill Cain laughed nervously. "You can't prove a thing."

"I can build a compelling case against you.

"Item: Beth has told the police that it was you who called her the night before the crime and cleverly elicited from her the details of her morning trip to school the next day, no guards but her mother with her. This fact alone is enough to make the police suspicious. You gambled again, this time that a presumably empty-headed teen would not remember."

"Totally gross, Uncle Bill. Totally."

"Item: You admitted to me that you had seen the exchange of pictures at the end of the vestibule conversation with your sister-in-law, but you were also supposed to have left the apartment. That was not risk, that was folly.

"Item: You told me that you were fascinated by the violence in Ireland. In fact, the Irish are not a violent people, especially given their history. The violence that exists is the work of a tiny minority. I assumed you had been in touch with that minority, perhaps because their recklessness appealed to you. The special branch of the Guard Siochanna, the Irish police, reports that you were in Ennis in County Clare last spring at the same time as these terrorists are now known to have been there.

"Item: You were seen by a number of persons at the Henry Grebe Yard poking around at the old boat near the Riverview site across the river. It was a nice touch to choose a hideout within a stone's throw of Area Six Headquarters. And no one ever notices the river once it leaves the Loop.

"Item: A rubber dinghy very much like yours was used by the terrorists to claim the ransom money. They failed to sink the dinghy after they came ashore with it at the Michigan Avenue bridge. But the police recovered it, although they have not announced the fact that your dinghy is missing from your yacht."

"None of that will hold up in court," he sneered.

"Perhaps, perhaps not. But what will hold up in court is that, as I predicted they would, Area Six Detectives have found your fingerprints in the terrorist boat. You came to view your victim and delight in her plight. She was powerless, bound and drugged, but not doomed, not quite, and that was the thrill of it, even more delightful than the thrill of seeing her bent over your father's broken body. Perhaps you wanted to molest her and the terrorists, rigorous moralists that they were in their own way, would not permit it. If she should escape they did not want their public image to suffer. But your joy arose rather more from abusing her soul than from abusing her body. By the way, there had always been an agreement between you and the terrorists that they were to have all the money. From beginning to end, you could not have cared less for the money. Your fresh fingerprints on the inside door of the boat, a door which barely survived demolition when your sister broke it down to liberate Julia, are conclusive proof that you are at least a coconspirator in the kidnapping of your mother-in-law. Doubtless you wore surgical gloves in the penthouse, but not when you came to the *Regina*. That was not gambling. That was stupidity.''

Dr. Bill strolled out of the room, casual and self-possessed as ever. "Lots of luck in trying to prove all that shit."

"He's crazy," Lourdes Cain snorted.

"Totally," Beth agreed.

"Not legally. He is, however, in his own twisted way dangerous."

"Will he escape?" Julia shivered in her husband's arms.

"Commander Culhane is waiting for him outside."

"Will Bill go to jail, Bishop?" his father asked sadly.

"I suspect there will be a plea bargain which will put him in a rather benign psychiatric institution for some time."

There was dead silence in the room.

"*Well*," Beth said at last, "we don't have to worry about

that anymore. He was the one who pretended to be Mary Haggerty, wasn't he, Father Blackie?"

"I'm sure the police will find the recording in his apartment."

"I'll dance at your wedding," Bart Cain, said, his solid, handsome face filled with pain. "So many memories, so many, many memories."

"So that's the end of the ghost of Mary Haggerty," Junior said happily. "Thank God that we're at last freed from her!"

"Not necessarily, Junior," I warned him. "Until that mystery is resolved, the Cain family will always be under its shadow. The Rod Stones of our city will never forget it."

"It will never be solved," Bart Cain said firmly.

"On the contrary," I informed him. "It is about to be solved."

CHAPTER 33

"MARY!" BART CAIN exclaimed. "I told you last week that you didn't have to come to Chicago."

"It was time, Bart." The tall, handsome woman smiled. "As Father Blackie said, long past time."

"Aren't you going to introduce us?" her companion asked, a silver-haired giant who had the look of the Cain clan about him.

"This is my Cousin Jim Cain," Bart Cain said, his face alive with joy, "and his wife Mary Anne Cain."

"Mary Anne Haggerty Cain." The woman smiled at all of us.

"I gather you have already met Bishop Ryan?"

"Oh, yes," she said, "we had the nicest visit when he came to see us. He knows a lot about wine-making."

Naturally. One can read a book or two on the flight to the city of St. Francis.

"He persuaded us"—Jim Cain nodded agreement—"that there was no longer a disgrace in admitting that you'd been molested by your father a half century ago."

"And we ought to tell the whole world," his wife added, "that a very brave group of young people long ago devised a remarkable plan to free a frightened kid from such terror."

"Turn her into a runaway," Jim continued, "and send her to live with your cousins in California."

"They adopted me—I think maybe forging some documents."

"The Irish are traditionally skilled at such arrangements," I put in, "when they seem necessary for some good purpose."

"So I became one of the wine-making Cains and eventually fell in love with one of their sons . . ."

"And he with you."

"And that's the story. Bart brought some clothes for me and gave me five hundred dollars from his own bank account—that was a lot of money in those days. He packed a bag for me and slipped it into the trunk of Timmy's Packard. He told the rest of the group about our plot only before I left. They swore a solemn oath to protect me and my reputation, from which I now release them."

"Excellent!" Beth was the only one who had found her voice. "Cousin Mary Anne." She embraced the woman. "I like totally knew you weren't dead . . . do you have any kids?"

"Five of them, dear." Mary Cain was weeping now. "Older than you by a few years, but one of my daughters looks just like you."

"I mean you just totally walked away that morning?"

"Yes, dear. I kissed them all good-bye, picked up my little bag, and walked into Dowagic to take a bus to Chicago and then on to Los Angeles. I was terrified, but I made it all right."

"And you've never been back?" Julia asked.

I wondered if she realized how much she looked like Julia, not so much in her facial features as in her height, her posture, and her emerging self-possession. Probably not.

"Oh, my dear Julia, I've been back many times in the last ten years or so. And I talk to Bart every couple of

months. Our whole group, except Roger, God be good to
him, has had a reunion here every year on the anniversary
of my disappearance. Last year Bart showed us your
wedding picture and you seemed so wonderful. I was so
pleased that he had at last found someone who would give
him the happiness he deserved. I hope we can be good
friends."

"Fersure," Beth said, sealing the alliance.

There was a general exchange of tears and embraces.
Even the Juniors smiled a little.

"He gave her up to save her?" Julia whispered to me in
awe.

"Precisely."

"Incredible."

"Despite his faults, that's your husband."

"It sure is."

"Father Blackie," Bart Cain asked, "how did you
know?"

"Simplicity itself. Both your wife and your daughter
said to me that sometimes you seemed to act like Mary
Anne Haggerty were still alive. I wondered if that might be
the truth of the matter. Just as it was necessary to abandon
the assumption that the reason for murder when a young
second wife enters a rich family is money, it was also
necessary to abandon the assumption that when a girl
vanished after a prom she had probably been raped and
murdered by her date. What if she quite literally vanished
from the face of the earth, the Michigan earth, that is, and
reappeared somewhere else. Like in California, where her
date had trusted relatives." I shrugged my shoulders. "I
formed a hypothesis about how that could have happened.
I learned the addresses of the wine Cains and made a
discrete call to their parish priest, who, suspecting nothing,
especially not from a bishop, assured me that there was

indeed a Mary Anne Cain and that she was an adopted daughter who had married into the family seven or eight years after her adoption."

"It was time to end the mystery," Jim Cain agreed. "We'll tell the story to the Chicago media tomorrow, fudge a little about papers."

And they did. However, because of an intolerable lack of foresight on my part, Mary Anne Haggerty Cain hailed a certain obscure auxiliary bishop as the hero of the story. I became inordinately famous as a solver of puzzles. I had to accept congratulations from many ecclesiastics, including Milord Josef Ratzinger, heaven save us all.

His brother bishop, the Angel to the Church of Chicago, as the Book of Revelation dubs bishops, smiles smugly and takes full credit for me.

CHAPTER 34

WILLIAM CAIN WAS indicted for violation of the Lindbergh Law; a plea bargain is currently under discussion. Vin Roberts is now a senior writer for *Business Week*. The Bart Juniors remain unchanged. Bart Cain has resigned as CEO of B.T. Cain and Sons so he can travel with his wife and spend more time with his family. He continues to keep a computer at his bedside, however. The David Cains and the Bart Cains spent two weeks together before Christmas in Barbados, and seem to have become fast friends. Julia Cain is pregnant and both she and her husband are radiant. Beth Cain is as delighted as the parents. Totally. St. Ignatius did in fact beat Mother McAuley, the Chicago Bears did not go to the Super Bowl. The Bulls won their third championship. Notre Dame did not win the national championship.

But Bill Clinton was elected President of the United States.

NOTE

WHILE THERE ARE many small piers along the banks of the Chicago River, there is none across from the Henry Grebe Ship Yard on Washtenaw. Nor is there a hole in the fence protecting the river behind the shopping plaza which has replaced Riverview Park. Moreover, the City of Chicago, Richard M. Daley, Mayor, had replaced with brand-new concrete the old boat landing at the foot of Grant Park just before the time in which this story is set.

You have been reading a novel published by Piatkus Books. We hope you have enjoyed it and that you would like to read more of our titles. Please ask for them in your local library or bookshop.

If you would like to be put on our mailing list to receive details of new publications, please send a large stamped addressed envelope (UK only) to:

Piatkus Books: 5 Windmill Street
London W1P 1HF

PIATKUS
The sign of a good book